HALFLINGS, HOBBITS, WARROWS & WEEFOLK

Halflings, Hobbits, Warrows & Weefolk

A COLLECTION OF TALES OF HEROES SHORT IN STATURE

Edited by
Baird Searles and Brian Thomsen

WARNER BOOKS

A Time Warner Company

Warner Books, Inc., 666 Fifth Avenue, New York, NY 10103

ⓦ A Time Warner Company

Printed in the United States of America
First printing: December 1991
10 9 8 7 6 5 4 3 2 1
Library of Congress Cataloging-in-Publication Data

Halflings, hobbits, warrows & weefolk / edited by Baird Searles and
Brian Thomsen.
    p.   cm.
    Contents: Introduction: "Small wonders" / by Baird Searles—
The eranis pipe / by Mickey Zucker Reichert—Moon shadows /
by Jody Lynn Nye—The twice-born bard / by Michael Williams—
A sparkle for Homer / by R.A. Salvatore—A fumbling of fairies /
by Craig Shaw Gardner—The graceless child / by Charles
DeLint—Hobbits / by Maya Kaathryn Bohnhoff—The stoor's
map / by John Dalmas—The origin of the hob / by Judith
Moffett.
    ISBN 0-446-39281-2 :
    1. Fantastic fiction, American. 2. Fantastic fiction, English.
I. Searles, Baird. II. Thomsen, Brian. III. Title: Halflings,
hobbits, warrows, and weefolk.
PS648.F3H35   1991
813'.0876608—dc20   91-26016
                                                     CIP

Book design by H. Roberts
Cover illustration by Tim and Greg Hildebrandt
Cover hand lettering by Dave Gatti
Cover design by Don Puckey

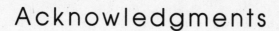

Acknowledgments

"The Stoor's Map," copyright © John Dalmas, 1991.

"The Origin of the Hob," excerpted from "Ti Whinny Moor Thoo Cums at Last" ("The Hob"), copyright © Judith Moffett, 1988, published previously in *Isaac Asimov Science Fiction*, and published here by arrangement with the author's agent Virginia Kidd.

Dedication

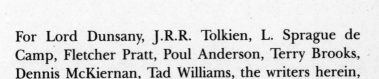

For Lord Dunsany, J.R.R. Tolkien, L. Sprague de Camp, Fletcher Pratt, Poul Anderson, Terry Brooks, Dennis McKiernan, Tad Williams, the writers herein, and all other fanciers of the wee folk.

Contents

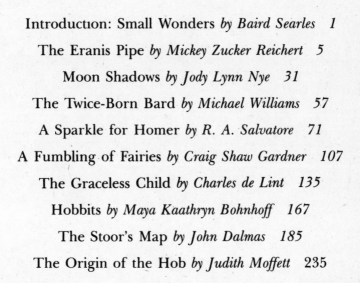

Small Wonders

Baird Searles

There are two kinds of heroes for humanity, and the dichotomy probably goes as far back as the time that Cro-Magnon and Neanderthal shared Europe. (A time that might have resulted in the first halflings— think about it.) And today it is still a major duality for the genre that has become almost the last refuge of the true storyteller—fantasy.

Obviously type one is that which immediately comes to mind when the word "hero" is said. Siegfried! Achilles! Rama! Born to be heroes, their stories are of vicissitudes overcome by their natural physical talents and, usually, their downfall brought on by a certain lack of cerebral talents. (In the immortal words of Anna Russell *re* Siegfried, "He was very strong, and he was very brave, and he was very stupid.") One might consider this an unfair judgment, but the big guys, even if endowed with large gray cells, are generally undone by trickery perpetrated by someone smarter, if not better or more heroic, than they.

But then there are the little guys. Their stories are usually concerned with coming out on top through cleverness or, let's face it, just plain luck. And here the reader of the story takes a part. Very few of them are Siegfrieds; statistically, readers are more likely to be the little man (or woman—not many female readers are Wonder Women). Small wonder that while we may be excited, awed, or moved by the story of an Achilles, a brave little tailor strikes a greater chord in more readers.

As fewer and fewer authors became concerned with telling us stories, we were given fewer and fewer hero(in)es to cheer for of either kind. But one genre persisted in giving us stories. Our fantasists kept telling tales (out of school, mostly—academia still admits few fantasies to its hallowed halls). And it's most doubtful that it's coincidence that the two major streams of modern fantasy, stemming from the two greatest fantasists of this century, have to do with big heroes and little heroes.

Robert Howard's prolific pen turned out many heroes, but the one who would immortalize his name was Conan, the barbarian. A direct descendant of Siegfried et al., Conan was the American equivalent. In a practical businesslike America with no mythology of its own, Conan eschewed culture as effete and was the mythic equivalent of the Western gunslinger, using sword for six-shooter and mowing down sorcerers and demons instead of black hats and Indians.

But from the other side of the Atlantic came a gentler tradition, resonating with centuries of myth and folklore. J.R.R. Tolkien drew together the skeins of English, Norse, and Celtic legend and created a world with sorcerers and demons, certainly, but whose central values lay with not a single character, but a whole race of small folk of pastoral lives and rustic pleasures, inhabiting their own self-sufficient country untouched by the great and mighty of their world.

Nor were these "hobbits" to be confused with the fairies of Shakespeare or Kipling, or the elves that Tolkien himself was to use as a contrasting race. They had no powers of any sort; they were, as it happened, highly suspicious of anything that smacked of the magical, while those other species of beings were specialists at magical trickery of all sorts. In fact, Tolkien's small people had no use for anarchy of any sort, whether it be the supernatural or a simple yearning for travel or adventure. They were depicted as having been so determinedly insular that they had been forgotten even by their own world, known primarily in its legends as "halflings." But in tales that have become among the few modern novels to achieve true immortality, Tolkien tells us of how several of his gentle, unadventurous folk have become heroes, by pluck, wit, and—there's no avoiding it—luck.

In a sense, here was something fresh in the annals of fantasy, a nonhuman race that was not magical. But the antecedents were there, in the gentler, unspectacular folktales of small folk who helped out on the farm in return for leavings of milk or food, and who never did anything more magical than restoring a scattered hay rick. Nonurban were these; there was no equivalent in the towns, much less the cities.

And perhaps, if one must descend to reality, these gentle halflings were a return to the true origins of the tales themselves. Those boring academics who insist on tracking down the reality of fantasy and telling us who and what were the basis of the magical and the glamorous inform us that the original elves and fairies were simply the first folk of the land (what land? take your pick) who survived the taller conquerors, hiding in the back woods and surviving as best they could. Who can say that they did not, eventually, form a sort of secretive symbiosis with their taller neighbors, trading nightly tasks for such things as precious milk from cows that they themselves were not able to keep?

But all that is science and speculation, and truth may be stranger than fiction, but fiction is but the transmutation of truth into different forms, and our small, pastoral people have taken many forms over the years. Not all of them are heroes, necessarily, but we still tend to be on their side because they are us. And though they might not come in a great range of sizes, they come in many shapes and from many sources— some, as you'll see, are even spurious. But welcome to the small worlds of the small wonders: halflings, hobbits, warrows, and weefolk...

The Eranis Pipe

Mickey Zucker Reichert

Mickey Zucker Reichert has made a name for herself in fantasy with her bestselling *Bifrost Guardians* series. Her story is very much in the Tolkien vein and shows that even a homebody can rise to heroism.

Sancho Eranis perched on a hillock overlooking the lush, green meadow that had served as home to his halfling people for as long as the eldest among them could remember. The morning sun sloped shadows of the surrounding forest across tilled gardens and wooden tunnel doors. Fresh earth perfumed the air, mingled with the sweet odor of sap and the plant smell of spring greenery as well as an unfamiliar reek that pinched Sancho's nostrils. But the latter was distant; it wafted from the direction of the human cities. As Sancho became more accustomed to it, his mind sifted and discarded it from the more pleasant mixture of aromas.

Sancho ran a hand through his dark, sun-warmed curls and dragged his bare toes toward him until they became lost beneath the bulge of his belly. Reverently, he drew the family pipe from his pocket. Sancho's great-great-grandfather had fashioned the piece from a block of lightweight, red stone with the pride of the finest artisan. The bowl was carved into the shape of a hearth, each brick intricately detailed, its center a perfect pit now stuffed full of Sancho's favorite smoking weed. Nearest the bowl, the stem jutted straight as a chimney pipe. Toward the mouthpiece, it became thinner and more tortuous, simulating smoke. There, too, the stone faded to pink, then to gray, completing the image.

Sancho clamped the stem between his teeth, lit the contents, and sucked in a lungful of smoke. Rounding his lips, he exhaled tiny, lopsided rings in short puffs. *Need practice.* Sancho laughed at his efforts, aware he would have decades to perfect the technique. The pipe had become a symbol of Eranis stability, passed from father to eldest son or grandfather to grandson as a new family elder took his place. The smoke curled around Sancho, comforting him with generations of security. He had only recently acquired the pipe himself, and under more peculiar and less morose circumstances than the usual death of the family patriarch.

Sancho shifted to a more comfortable position, one leg stretched before him, the other tucked to his buttocks, watching smoke blur the image of his village to winking glimmers of sunlight off brass doorknobs, hinges, and plowed-up chips of quartz. A group of children in their twenties and thirties raced through a patch of wildflowers, a girlish giggle ringing like lute song.

By right, the Eranis pipe had passed to Sancho's only brother, Ewar, their parents' first born. But, two years ago, Ewar had left the village for the human cities, obsessed by an inexplicable need to deliver innocents from injustice and lend aid where it was needed. The pipe had lain, respectfully wrapped, in the china cabinet. Then, yesterday, a courier had arrived, bearing a letter and a pouch holding four gold coins. Absently, Sancho's fingers strayed to his pocket. Paper crinkled beneath his touch, muffled by the fabric of his tunic. Again, he pulled the note free, reading for the seventh time:

Dearest Family:

Just writing to let you know I'm well. I'm in Kirwana, a human city not far from the Village. I'm hoping to visit, but I can't make any promises. We're on a quest, in the service of an elven king! The adventuring life agrees with me, and I expect to be away for some time. I miss you all.

Sancho, the Eranis pipe is yours. I'm sure you'll make a fine leader for the family.

—All my love,
Ewar

Sancho stuffed the page back into his pocket, wondering what sort of evil magic must have overtaken his brother to sacrifice love and security for an absurd sense of duty to strangers, to give up home, family, and ultimate safety to run around the World with an elf, three humans, and a grumpy dwarf.

The odor Sancho had noticed earlier thickened, demanding attention. Whatever produced the smell had moved much closer, now surely only a few strides from him. Alarmed, Sancho rose, listening. The crash and rattle of brush wafted to him, warning of a pack of large creatures tramping through the forest.

What? Confused and nervous, Sancho tapped the smoldering weed from the Eranis pipe, smothering it beneath the toughened sole of his foot. He replaced the pipe in his vest pocket.

The sounds whipped closer.

Sancho measured the distance to his village, then backed behind a tree instead.

Suddenly, a creature twice his height brushed through a stand of pine. It looked vaguely human; it sported the requisite number of arms, legs, and a single head. But there all resemblance ended. Red-rimmed, yellow eyes glared from a bulbous head that scanned the hillock. Long, curved canine teeth jutted from between wide lips outlining a broad mouth, and its torso hunched over so far that its hairy hands brushed the ground.

Fear paralyzed Sancho. He stood behind the tree, fingers clutching so tightly his nails buried into the bark. He wanted to hide himself more completely, wanted to warn his friends and family, but found himself incapable of any action at all.

Another troll appeared behind the first. Then another and another, until eight monsters surveyed the halfling town from the same perch Sancho had used only a moment before. They exchanged a series of guttural noises that he, at first, took for growls. One pointed to the Village.

Vertigo blurred the scene to whirling spots. Sancho willed himself to breathe and blink, unable to muster the energy for anything more complicated.

Oblivious, the children continued their game of chase. Terror loosened its hold enough for Sancho to realize that the troll's grunts were apparently an ugly form of speech, a language he did not want to recognize.

The first of the trolls started down the embankment, the others dogging him.

Panic exploded through Sancho, scattering his wits. Instinctively, he bolted for the only security he had ever known, the warm, soft safety of his hole. Logic chipped at his mind, trying to warn him of the idiocy of running toward the enemy. But rationality could not break through the wild fog of terror. He raced down the hill behind the trolls.

A root hooked Sancho Eranis's bare foot, bruising the surface. His leg twisted. He collapsed, rolling down the grassy knoll, bushes tearing at his limbs, stones slamming his ribs. His head struck a boulder, sending his consciousness spinning. He skidded into a copse of blackberries, the brambles shredding his breeches and stabbing his flesh. He struck his head again. And this time, all awareness fled him.

Sancho awakened in darkness, snuggled in the warmth of a needled cocoon of branches. His ankle ached, his ribs felt battered, and agony throbbed through his head. *Where am I?* The answer returned with maddening clarity. Panic descended on him again, but depleted of adrenaline, he found himself unable to run. Instead, he gingerly extracted his person from the tangle of berries and thorns.

A crescent moon hovered over the Village, casting an eerie glow over the meadow. Halfway down the slope, Sancho stared at the city of his friends and family, afraid for what he might see. Two trolls stood outside the burrow of the village chieftain, both armed with copper swords and one clutching a whip. Three halflings enlarged the opening with picks and shovels, earth flying as they worked with a speed Sancho could not have matched. The whip slashed air, coming down on one's back. The halfling collapsed, his sobs reaching Sancho's ears, betraying a pain that tore at his heart. He looked away, only then noticing the bones and torn cloth scattered across the meadow, halflings' bones picked clean amid the shredded remnants of their clothing.

No! Sancho vomited, repeatedly, until his stomach was empty, and he could only retch dryly. Tears burned his eyes with a pain as intense as the one in his gut. On hands and knees, he crept back up the slope. *Can't do anything for them.* He felt as if a lead weight were hammering him between the eyes, and he was hopeless to stop it. *Can't do anything but die, too.* He let the sickness crawl through him, focusing on it to avoid thinking of his people as individuals, to keep himself from remembering the look of those clothes and guessing who might have worn them.

Something ground into Sancho's chest with every movement. He reached up to remove the object, and the Eranis pipe fell into his fist. Moonlight drew a glittering line along its stem. *Ewar! Ewar and his strange friends. They may be able to do something!*

Buoyed by the thought, Sancho staggered to his feet. Replacing the pipe in his pocket, he grasped a tree for support and removed Ewar's letter once more, skimming it for the name of the human town. *Kirwana.* Sancho replaced the letter. Instantly, fear stole the name of the city from his mind, and he had to look again. Then, grimly, floundering from trunk to trunk, Sancho set out for the lands of men.

Three days later, in the evening, a sore and aching Sancho Eranis staggered into Kirwana's inn. His brown curls swarmed his head in crazed disarray, his clothes lay in rags, and his protruding gut felt pinched with hunger. Still, the crowd of humans, sprinkled with dwarves and elves, paid him little notice. Smoke churned through the confines, blurring the interior to a hazy blur of movement. Mingled with the aroma of stale beer and sweat, the exotic mixture of burning weeds choked Sancho. Sprawling into the nearest chair at the bar, he flicked one of Ewar's gold coins to the table.

As if by magic, a lanky human appeared behind the counter. "What can I get for you, little sir?"

"Food and drink. Anything I can buy with this." He poured the remaining three coins to the bar, not wanting to delay service for details. He had missed five of his meals for the day and had every intention of making up for all of them at the last one.

The bartender gawked, along with the ratty-looking human patron at Sancho's right. Snatching up the gold, the man rushed to fill the order.

A moment later cold, sharp steel poked Sancho's spine. A gruff voice and warm breath filled his ear. "Don't move, halfling."

Fear stiffened Sancho into a rigid seizure. Just as suddenly, his body went limp. Wanting to obey, he fought unconsciousness.

Abruptly, alarm filled the other's voice, and it became familiar enough to haul Sancho back to dizzy awareness. "Whoa, Sancho, steady." Strong arms enfolded him, bracing him back onto the chair. "It's all right, little brother. I was only kidding."

Ewar! Sancho spun, throwing himself into Ewar's arms, crushing his brother into a hug. "Ewar! The gods' mercy, it's you. The Village! The family! You have to help. I need..."

"Whoa! Whoa! Slow down." Ewar gave Sancho a brief squeeze, then extracted himself from his brother's exuberant embrace. Bright, brown eyes met Sancho's muddier gaze. Sweat dampened Ewar's curly, blond mane, he looked as slender as an elf, and a pale scar marred his left cheek. A matched pair of swords and a jeweled dagger jutted from sheaths on his belt. Otherwise, he looked the same as Sancho remembered. "Whatever it is, it can wait until after you've had some food and ale. Oh, and by the way, you overpaid that bartender, even if he brings you a feast. I'm going to have to get three of those coins back, you know." He disappeared into the smoke, returning a moment later with a chair. Scooting it to Sancho's side, he sat.

Sancho gawked.

"Now, what were you saying about the family?" Ewar waved at a passing barmaid.

"Trolls," Sancho started. "At least I think they were trolls... I've never seen a troll... or not before this... if they are trolls..."

"Stop!" Ewar commanded.

Sancho obeyed.

"Take the deepest breath you can, and let it out."

Sancho inhaled and exhaled.

"And again."

Sancho repeated the action.

"All right. Now, tell me the facts. One by one. In order."

Sancho launched into his tale, beginning with the appearance of the first troll and ending with his journey to Kirwana. The food appeared halfway through his discourse, a bowl of stew flanked by a myriad of vegetables and a cold mug of ale. He spoke around mouthfuls of stew while Ewar plucked boiled carrots from his plate, chewing thoughtfully. By the conclusion, tears filled both sets of eyes. And Sancho finished with a plea. "You and your friends? You can save the Village." He added painfully, "Can't you?"

Ewar sighed. "I'm afraid my friends have an urgent responsibility." He clamped a hand to Sancho's shoulder blades.

Sancho dropped his spoon, not daring to believe what he had heard. "What do you mean? Your friends can't help? What kind of friends are they? What could be more important than this?"

"The life of an elven queen and her tribe has to take precedence over one halfling village." Gracefully, Ewar clambered down from his seat. "My friends are already pledged to her cause. Afterward..."

Frustration ripped through Sancho. "Afterward will be too late." He clenched at the pipe through the fabric of his tunic, needing its reassuring presence to keep him from breaking into desperate, hopeless sobs. "We have to do something! We have to do something *now!*"

"I know." Ewar's voice sounded calm beyond all reason. "And we will. Brother, you and I are going to have to handle this alone."

The words struck Sancho like a physical blow. It required concentration to keep from falling from the chair. "You and me? Me? What can I possibly do?"

"Anything but nothing. Here." Ewar passed him one of the short swords.

Sancho shuddered from the weapon. "What do you want me to do with that?"

Ewar popped one last carrot into his mouth. He

stuffed the sheathed weapon into Sancho's fist, then shouldered through the crowd. "I figure you've got about three days of travel to learn to use it. Sancho Eranis, you and I are the only hope our people have. And we're not going to disappoint them."

Chilled to the marrow, clutching the sword like a lifeline, Sancho stumbled after his brother.

Three days later, Sancho Eranis sat on the woody hillock, staring numbly over the wreckage of the halfling village. The stench of the pair of troll sentries had become familiar during his daylong vigil. They crouched at the mouth of the chieftain's enlarged tunnel, presumably guarding it from intruders or preventing halfling escapes. Clouds obscured the sun, giving the trolls' skin a sickly green-gray cast.

Long ago, Sancho's tear ducts had emptied. His eyes burned, striped scarlet and swollen, and the remnants of the salty droplets had crusted on his cheeks. Ewar had instructed Sancho to study the pattern of the guard, and his wiser brother's insistence that he remain alert and in place was the only thing that kept Sancho from abandoning his post. He kept his gaze locked on the trolls with a fanatical intensity that further pained and blurred his vision, aware that a glimpse of his murdered friends would snap the fragile walls he had built to contain panic.

At midday, another pair of trolls emerged from the tunnel, exchanged a few guttural syllables with the previous group, then took their positions as sentries.

The original guards disappeared into the vandalized halfling burrow.

A cold rain drizzled from the heavens. Sancho huddled into the clothes he had worn for nearly a week without a chance to change. He had always enjoyed rain before, in the days when he reclined in a warm burrow with his parents, sisters, and brother. Then, he could hear the rain drumming on the wooden doors, its knock unanswered, and the world dry, close, and secure around him.

Sancho fondled the Eranis pipe through the fabric of his tunic pocket, a half smile forming on his features at the memory. Then, the rain quickened, pounding him with cold hailstones, and reality intruded on his reverie. His fingers cinched around the pipe until the stonework gouged his palm. *The Village is dead. All the people I love are eaten or enslaved.* The tears started again, erratic from eyes that had already become agonizingly dry. The urge to flee seized him with a suddenness that sent him surging to his feet. *There's nothing I can do, no chance that two halflings could fight eight trolls.* Sorrow thickened within Sancho, and he mourned his people, one by one, though he knew most still lived. *I'm sorry. There's nothing I can do for you but die with you.*

The idea sent a shiver of dread through Sancho. *I don't want to die.* The words tore through his mind, as if from another source. But they were his own, a primal terror that came from his core. The rain's coldness seemed to treble as realization struck. *I'm a coward. Sancho Eranis is a coward who would rather save himself than try to rescue his family.* The understanding hurt. Yet, a peace accompanied it, too, a self-actualization accompanied by self-loathing, a rationalization of the driving need to sneak away and never return, to find a new start elsewhere and become a part of another halfling village leagues distant.

Still, Sancho remained, frozen in place by his brother's orders. Courage did not hold him, nor, he believed, did loyalty. It was simply a matter of inertia.

Sancho awakened to a hissing sound in his ear. His eyes flew open, and he leapt backward, his own sudden movement making it twice as hard to get his bearings. A firm hand steadied him, and he glanced through night's darkness into Ewar's dirt-streaked face. The elder halfling made a curt silencing gesture, then pulled his brother deeper into the foliage. "I thought you were supposed to be spying."

"I am," Sancho whispered back defensively. Then, realizing he must have drifted into sleep, he amended, "I mean, I was. I'm sorry."

"Never mind." Ewar's thin frame looked frail in the sliver of moonlight. "What did you find out?" He stooped to recover some object from the ground that was obscured in blackness.

What did I find out? That I'm a coward. Sancho blinked, silent, not daring to believe his brother knew about his shameful revelation.

Ewar rose holding Sancho's short sword and offered it back. "Did you get a feel for the sentry patterns?"

"Oh." Sancho felt flushed. *Of course that's what he*

meant. "They stayed in twos. And they changed at midday and nightfall." He accepted the hilt from Ewar's filthy, callused hand, the weight of the sword awkward in his own grip.

"And sunrise," Ewar supplied from earlier observation. "And presumably midnight. Which confirms your belief that there's probably eight of them." He clapped a hand to Sancho's shoulder. "Nice work."

Sancho withered under the praise. Though only entering his sixth decade, barely mature, he felt ancient and tired. The night breeze chilled through his sodden clothing, adding cold to his distress. *At least it's not raining any longer.* He drew scant comfort from the thought. "Listen, Ewar. There's four times as many of them as us. They're twice our height, probably five times my weight."

Ewar nodded somberly. "And they've got the strategic defense of the burrows. Lucky thing, too. Otherwise, there'd be no challenge in it at all."

Sancho gawked in silence. He held the blade low, so that its tip touched the ground. "You don't understand. I think we should run."

A strange grin broke across Ewar's face. "Run. Run, indeed." He leapt to a boulder, scanning the Village through a huddle of maples. "That's exactly what I had in mind."

Hope spiraled through Sancho. "Really?"

"Yes, really." Ewar clambered down from his perch. Catching Sancho's sword hand, he absently hefted it, rearranging the hilt into a more appropriate grip. "With the trolls chasing, of course."

Sancho's face lapsed into horrified wrinkles. His breaths quickened.

"While you've been watching, I've been digging and carving..." Ewar looked up. Apparently noticing his brother's expression, he broke off. "Just come with me. I'll take care of it." He brushed into the woods, following the edge of the meadow, just beyond the tree line.

Sancho's body went clammy with relief, and his breathing slowed. It felt so right to let someone he trusted take the responsibility from him. Quietly, he followed in Ewar's wake.

"Here." Ewar stopped and indicated a position beneath a stately oak. "You wait here and watch, in case I need backup. Just don't step there." He gestured to an area of spread leaves. Without awaiting confirmation, he skirted the area and headed toward the Village.

Sancho slumped to the ground at the base of the oak, the sword cradled in his lap, his fingers caressing the pocketed pipe in continuous, jerky motions he could not have stopped had he wanted to do so.

Shortly, he heard the snap of breaking brush as Ewar sped toward him, the troll sentries crashing at his heels. *He's leading them to me!* Sancho staggered to his feet, willing his legs to carry him deeper into the forest. But all he managed to do was rise and cling to the bark before Ewar came into sight. The elder brother whipped lightly over the spread of leaves.

A moment later the trolls galloped into view. They hit the leaf pile just as Ewar gained the far side.

But the thin framework of twigs that had formed a bridge for the halfling could not support the weight of trolls. Twigs cracked with the vicious finality of bone. The trolls plummeted into a freshly dug pit. Their screams wafted to Sancho, mournful as wolf howls, the sound muffled nearly to obscurity by the sides of the pit.

Briskly, Ewar raised his fist in a silent sign of victory. He grabbed Sancho's hand, pumping it to indicate teamwork, though the younger Eranis felt more comfortable giving all the credit to his brother.

"They'll climb out." Sancho stepped nervously toward the pit, but could not gather enough nerve to glance into it. "The others will hear and come after us."

Ewar grinned. "I put enough sharpened stakes down there to stop a dragon. They're not coming up." Craning his neck, he looked into the pit, his grimace convincing Sancho not to take a peek. Already, the trolls' cries had died to shallow whimpers. "And, as to the others, you know as well as I that sound doesn't carry underground."

"I don't like this," Sancho said.

The words seemed ludicrously understated. "Sorry." Ewar continued his vigil at the edge of the pit. "Which part don't you like? The trolls cannibalizing and trapping our family, or us killing evil intruders to save them?"

"Either," Sancho said, unable to keep a quiver from his voice. "Both." Hope rose guardedly. "Do you think we can get all the beasts this way?"

The trolls fell silent. Ewar kicked the ground, sending a shower of leaves, twigs, and dirt into the grave. "I'm not cleaning this hole out. It took me a day to make this trap. We don't have three more to spare, not when they're eating our people."

Sancho winced.

Undaunted, Ewar continued, "Besides, when the first sentries show up missing, the others are going to get cautious."

"So what do we do?" Sancho put complete faith in his brother.

Ewar considered. "I'm going down there." He inclined his head toward the halfling village. "At sunrise, when the new sentries come, I want you to draw their attention."

"Me?" Sancho's voice rose an octave. "Draw their attention?" The thought of trolls rushing him made Sancho queasy. He gripped his stomach.

"Just make some noise so they look your way. I'll take care of them. They shouldn't get anywhere near you." Ewar started down the slope, his form soon lost to darkness, but his voice reached Sancho in a hoarse whisper. "If they do, run."

Sancho nodded to no one in particular, only slightly comforted. He found it difficult to argue with a plan that gave him time and freedom to flee. *Good luck, brother. I love you.* The tears began to course again.

Sunrise smeared pink and blue amid the hovering grayness of a cloudy sky. The morning glow resolved nameless shapes into piled bones, earth, and burrow doors. A stillness lay over the Village. Even Ewar was nowhere in sight.

Sancho paced a track so worn that the sticks had been crushed to powder, and even the collage of needles and leaves made no sound beneath his step. Since Ewar's departure, tension had risen to a taut crescendo. At any moment, Sancho feared he might burst or collapse, and only the certainty that Ewar would not abandon him kept him walking the same course, watching and waiting.

At length, two huge, hunched forms emerged from the chieftain's tunnel. Through a fear that nearly paralyzed him, Sancho forced himself to move. Wedging his fingers beneath a boulder, he heaved with all his might. The stone shifted, rolling a short distance. A sudden kick sent it careening down the hillside.

Both trolls turned toward the movement. One made a sound of alarm, quickly stanched by a short sword thrust into his kidney, the blade wielded by a tiny figure that emerged, abruptly, from behind him. *Ewar.* Sancho held his breath as the first troll crumpled and the second spun. The blood-wet sword whirled between them, then ran through the second one's abdomen into his spine. That one collapsed, too.

Tearing his sword free of the body, Ewar waved in the direction from which the boulder had toppled. He followed the gesture with a dragging motion that could only mean he wanted Sancho to approach.

Timidly, Sancho picked his route down the hill-ock, his feet feeling weighted. Though he moved as slowly as possible, he arrived at his brother's side far too soon.

Ewar whispered, "I don't know whether they heard that scream or not. We have to move fast."

"Move? What do you mean move?" Though he spoke as softly, Sancho could not hide his hysteria.

"We know the tunnels better than they do. We have to go in."

"In?" Sancho repeated. "In there? Where the other four are?"

"Right."

Sancho tried logic. "But then we're just as bad off as the others."

"No. Look here." Ewar turned and trotted toward the entry to the Eranis burrow. A stone covered it, apparently to keep those inside from pushing it open and escaping. "They're enlarging the holes to their size. But they haven't gotten to them all yet. So long as we stay with the ones that aren't troll-sized, they can't get us."

"In there?" Sancho became mired in contemplating the danger.

"Come on. I need some help." Ewar slipped his fingers beneath the stone.

Reluctantly, Sancho came forward and placed his hands beside his brother's.

"On three." Ewar crouched in a position for best leverage. "One...two...three...."

Sancho hefted, feeling the weight of the boulder shift through his back. Then, the stone skidded aside, leaving the door uncovered. Seizing the handle, Ewar jerked it open.

Dirt sprinkled to the ground. The panel opened to reveal the familiar dry darkness that had served as Sancho's dwelling all his life. Troll odor and halfling sweat obscured the familiar smells he had learned to identify with home. Other thoughts came to him, too, the coarse weave of the rug on which he and his cousins had wrestled as children, the bright yellow-orange dance of the hearth fire, its warmth finding every edge and corner of the burrow, a quiet evening of cocoa and talk on a snowy night.

Ewar leapt through the opening, disappearing into the darkness. With trepidation, Sancho followed.

Apparently, the trolls had not penetrated here. The room appeared precisely as Sancho had left it, down to the dirty dishes from second supper. But Ewar did not take the time to study furnishings. Without a glance, he slipped from the main room into the connecting tunnels to the remainder of the halfling village.

Quivering, half crawling though the ceiling allowed free access, Sancho entered, too.

Shortly, the passage ended at a stone, wedged like a cork from the opposite side. Lying flat on his back, Ewar braced his feet against the boulder and strained. Gradually, the granite shifted, then popped free amid a shower of loose dirt. Now, the corridor opened onto a familiar, perpendicular tunnel running left and right. Sancho knew both directions ultimately led to the same place, the high-roofed community meeting chamber that seemed the best place to set up a troll stronghold. Grit powdered the floor, indicating recent digging, and huge, clawed footprints flattened it in patches. The tunnel had been dug out to nearly twice its normal height. Ewar stepped out onto the dislodged boulder, looking tiny and helpless in the giant passageway. Turning right, he trotted down the walk, soon disappearing around a bend.

Sancho hesitated at the joining of the larger and smaller tunnels. The wider space admitted a breeze, making him feel naked and vulnerable. The trolls could maneuver there, so it only made sense to remain in the smaller, communicating tunnel. Clutching the short sword's sheath to keep it from banging against his leg, he took a cautious, awkward step into the widened tunnel.

The sound of approaching footsteps sent him scurrying back to safety.

Ewar returned. Glancing from Sancho to the gap between them, he frowned and gestured his brother to him.

Sancho approached in a timid hunch. As they slipped around the corner, he saw neatly carved branches standing, at intervals, in a central row, running from floor to ceiling.

"Support beams." Ewar whispered a quick explanation. "The heightened ceilings require them to prevent a collapse. I've examined these first two." He indicated an oaken pole and a willow limb. "And I think removing them both at once could bring down a large section of the roof."

The significance of Ewar's words would not penetrate. Sancho just nodded as the elder halfling removed a coil of rope from his travel-battered backpack and wound it around the poles using unfamiliar knots. His nimble fingers flew. "There." He handed the free end to Sancho.

Sancho took it from habit, then studied the frayed hemp with overzealous fascination for detail.

"I'm going to get their attention. When I run by here, let me through. Then brace yourself and pull."

Sancho blinked, putting the plan together slowly. "The roof will fall."

Ewar nodded patiently. "On them, right. We'll be on this side of the cave-in."

"All right." Sancho found a position in the middle of the corridor. Despite the additional size of the tunnel, he felt hemmed in, trapped from all sides and squeezed.

"If things go badly, run down the home tunnel. They can't reach you there. They won't know we moved the stones, and that ought to gain you time." A moment later Ewar seemed to disappear.

Shivering, Sancho Eranis waited.

Time passed, each moment multiplying into an eternity. Sancho remained in position, both hands wrapped around the rope until his fingers went numb and the coarse strands left indentations on his hands. His toes had ground a steady purchase in the packed earth floor. Sweat twined down his forehead, tickling. Still, though his limbs cramped and his skin felt clammy, he appreciated the seemingly endless peace that accompanied his vigil.

Then guttural voices echoed through the cavern. Accustomed to localizing sound underground, Sancho guessed without need to concentrate that they came from the direction Ewar had taken. He tensed with a twitch that nearly caused him to pull too soon. But Ewar's life hung in the balance, and Sancho would rather let the trolls run free than imprison his brother with them.

A myriad of footfalls sent dull thuds shuddering through the tunnel. Ewar appeared suddenly around the turn, his expression more grim than Sancho had seen it since their reunion. A split second later, the reason became obvious. All four trolls chased him. But the first two had come so close their clawed fingers could touch if not quite close on him.

Sancho's wits exploded like a frightened flock of birds. The abrupt rigidity of every muscle was the only thing that kept him from fleeing in panic.

"Run!" Ewar hollered. "Run!"

The shout mobilized Sancho. He whirled, still clutching the rope, meeting instant resistance from the branches. He threw all his weight forward. Nothing happened. The limbs were too heavy and too well wedged in place. Sancho tugged harder, driving his shoulders forward.

A slapping noise echoed through the tunnel, followed by Ewar's agonized scream. Something slammed into Sancho's back with enough force to send him crashing to the floor. Breath blasted from his lungs. An object slit the skin over his breastbone, and the short sword bruised his hip. The support beams' resistance disappeared. A sound rumbled through the cavern. A block of ceiling collapsed, dropping mounds of earth and stone onto the two trailing trolls.

"No." Sobbing, Sancho twisted free of the weight that pinned him to the floor. Spurred by panic, he fled, only then registering that the thing that had held him was Ewar's limp body. "E-war!" he screamed. "Eeee-war!" Without pausing to see if his brother followed, he dove into the narrower tunnel. Only then, he regained enough presence of mind to turn.

The two remaining trolls had finished gawking at the tons of rubble that buried their companions. They turned toward Ewar.

The elder halfling opened one eye. Though scarcely above a whisper and gruff with pain, his words emerged clearly. "Carry on, Sancho. You're the only hope now." The lid slid shut, and Ewar went flaccid. Not even the subtle signs of breathing disturbed his stillness.

Sancho collapsed to the dirt, his tears so thick he felt as if he were watching the scene from the bottom of a lake. The trolls converged on Ewar, battering the corpse beyond all possibility of life. *Ewar.* Helpless and alone, he surrendered to the inner voices that told him he did not have the strength or skill to act. He tried to stand and run. But his muscles felt liquid; as before, they would not obey him. *I can't carry on, Ewar. It's over.*

Rolling prone, Sancho managed to draw his limbs

to his heaving belly. He rose to his hands and knees. Vertigo swam down on him, all but obscuring thought and vision. Something shifted, stabbing the gash in his chest. Absently, he reached for the object. His fingers delved into his pocket, emerging with two jagged halves of the Eranis pipe.

Sancho stared. And gradually his mind settled, his grief and sorrow crushed beneath a sudden tornado of rage. No longer obscured by a curtain of cowardice and disbelief, reality became a stark lash. Home and hearth existed no longer. His people were enslaved. His brother's corpse lay mangled near the burrow that had spawned him. Sancho's hand clinched violently. A sharp edge sliced his palm, and blood wound between his fingers.

Sancho hurled down the Eranis pipe. The bowl half bounced. The stem landed flat, snapping a second time. And Sancho Eranis emerged from the halfling tunnel like a whirling blur of vengeance. His short sword sliced a quarter way through a troll's waist and tore free before the second managed to spin in his direction. The injured troll fell without a sound. Howling like a rabid hound, Sancho sprang for the second.

The troll ripped his copper sword free in time to meet Sancho's steel one. The weapons rang together, the impact quivering through the halfling's fist. Driven backward a step, Sancho launched for the troll again. This time his blade cleaved air, hurling a spray of blood across earthen walls. The troll riposted with a competent stab. The homely face registered confusion.

Sancho ducked, driving in low, beneath the troll's guard. Inexperience and lack of training made his attack wild and wholly unpredictable. Missing his target, he threw his arms up defensively, unaware that he had bullied in too close for the troll's longer weapon.

The troll leapt backward to regain his advantage. His foot came down on his dying companion's leg. Overbalanced backward, he fell. He crashed onto Ewar's body, tensing to roll.

Further enraged by the defiling, Sancho bore in, burying his short blade in the creature's throat.

The troll's eyes bulged. Its sword whipped toward the halfling. Then, death glazed the red-rimmed, yellow eyes, the copper sword toppled, and the hand sank back to the floor.

Abandoning his own weapon, Sancho caught the troll's body by an arm, heaving the filthy, stinking corpse from his brother's body. He hefted Ewar into his arms, heedless of the crowd his noise had drawn.

From the opposite corridor, dozens of frightened halfling eyes watched the Eranis patriarch sit amid the rubble and trollish bodies. They watched him cradle his brother's corpse, watched the muddy eyes trail tears and the damaged hand smear blood across Ewar's scalp.

Like shadows, the halflings glided into the widened corridor. And, like a family, shared his sorrow.

Moon Shadows

Jody Lynn Nye

Jody Lynn Nye has collaborated with Anne McCaffrey
on several projects but saves her weefolk stories
for solo efforts in her *Mythology* novels and
stories such as this.

The full moon floated above the thick forest and
touched with her light the slanting roofs of the tiny
village that lay in a clearing at the foot of the hill. The
Great Mirror was the name the Folk gave to the shape
she made once a month when she was roundest,
reflecting back to Earth, so it was said, all of the
things that they would otherwise not be able to see. It
would be a night for true dreams and visions.

From the breast of the hill, Medlun looked down
on the village, already slumbering within the four arcs
of its walls. The stream that ran beside it, cradling it
within a gentle curve, glittered in the moonlight,
throwing back in diamond-bright points the reflection

of the huge round shape that hovered over the horizon. From this distance he couldn't hear the stream's busy chuckle.

He knew every house, and every person inside it. The oldest dwellings, which occupied the center of the circle, had been there since before living memory. Those were the houses with reed roofs and woven walls slathered with hardened mud, stubbornly inhabited by his aunts and grandparents and great-grandparents. Newer, more comfortable homes like his own had been built in a ring around the original settlement, and chiefly of wood. They belonged to the old ones' descendants, on average a hundred years younger than they. The single house still fully lit, on the border between the old and the new, was that of Tarktee the Archivist. That old one was probably transcribing some of his notes. He must be too preoccupied to drape the skins over his windows and prevent his midnight wakefulness from annoying his neighbors.

There was one more light still aglow in the small compound, at the door of Medlun's own home. His wife Galjinna had left a crystal of soft blue light to guide him and their daughter safely home when they were ready to return. Medlun sighed, and turned away. She was a good wife and mother, but far too protective, in his opinion. She was not interested in visions.

"Where are we going, Father?" Darli asked, hurrying behind him to catch up. She was five years old. Her short legs covered only a third of the distance each of his strides ate up. He stopped to wait for her, and she shoved her hand into his. Reflexively, he closed his fingers about hers.

"Up to the top of the hill," he said absently, guiding her carefully over a slippery patch of mud. It was late spring, and rain had saturated the ground. He breathed in, smelling the rich earth spiced with the scent of wet bark and the more delicate aroma of young leaves.

"Why? What's there?" Darli demanded, holding tight to his thumb.

Medlun stopped and looked down at her. "Don't you know? Haven't you been up here in daylight by yourself?"

"No. Mama never lets me go up the hill. She says the wolves would get me. I always stay in the village."

Far too protective. He would have to talk to Galjinna about that. "Do you mean that you've never set foot outside the enclosure in all your life?"

"No, Father."

Surprised, he studied her. He hadn't paid that much attention to her until recently, and for that he chided himself. In his own defense, he pleaded that there wasn't much you could say about a five year old. It was only in the last year that she had begun to develop a personality and notice things outside herself. Before that, he'd had to define her by what she looked like. Her hair was the pleasing shade of walnut shells, and it framed a face shaped like a kernel of corn. The child's mild, blue eyes were like his, the other Folk said, though he didn't see the resemblance himself, and her ears, too, in the way they swept back and up from her high, rounded cheekbones, then curved slightly before coming to a point.

In her complacency never to find anything out on her own, she resembled her mother's kin and, for that, most of the village as well. They had little interest in finding out about anything that lay beyond their own fields. The far side of the hill they climbed sheered off straight down into a steep cliff overlooking a vast river. The stream that ran beside the village fed into it. Medlun had heard in the old ones' stories that not very far beyond the sunset lay a body of water that dwarfed the river and its lake the way a single drop vanished into the stream, but he knew no one living who had ever seen this "sea." In fact, there were some who had never so much as seen the river. They believed the faint roaring sound that could be heard on still days was the voices of wild beasts in the forest. That his Folk cared to know nothing new bothered him. They had philosophy and legends and science to study, skills and crafts to perfect, but they might as well have been floating on a leaf in the stream as set where they were, for all the attention they paid to their surroundings. If he left Darli's education to Galjinna, she'd be as ignorant of her world as the rest of them.

Medlun had married at sixty, to a timid girl ten years his junior. Darli had been born only a year later. It was a sufficiently mature age for marriage among his Folk; even a little too old, some had opined. Sixty was considered a respectable age for parenthood, too, but Medlun was beginning to wonder if waiting so long was wise. The truth was, he'd been so long an adult that he remembered little of what it was like to be that small. Surely he wasn't so uninquisitive as this offspring of his. At least, he recalled several moonlight excursions of his own in his early youth.

It had been just such a thought that had prompted him to take Darli with him on the very first Mirror Night that followed his decision.

"What, have you never wandered out by yourself before dawn to watch the sun rise? Not even out of the house?" he asked, feeling incredulous that he even had to ask such a question.

"No, sir."

"What an incurious child you are. You don't even seem to feel the lack."

"I'm sorry, Father."

Medlun found he was being irritable, and it wasn't Darli's fault. Something was aggravating his ears, a terrible sound in a frequency he didn't normally hear. It got louder the closer he was to Darli. Puzzled, he bent to look at her clothing. The embroidered coat was one she'd been wearing for years, made huge and with adjustable fastenings so she would have plenty of room to grow into it. Medlun was surprised to see that Darli had nearly done so. She would need another before the next winter.

Galjinna had packed the child into two pairs of woven woolen hose to keep warm over a chilly spring night. Medlun shook his head. Under a warm tunic,

one would have been more than enough. That's what
he was wearing. Her socklike leather shoes were nothing out of the ordinary. He'd carved the wooden soles
himself. Medlun took another, closer glance at the
coat. It was closely sewn with small objects. They
weren't meant to be decorative, now that he examined
them, for not one matched another or the fancy
stitchery they were affixed to.

Medlun frowned. Since she needed to stay home
and look after their infant son, Galjinna must have
loaded Darli down with every charm, amulet, and
protective object she could lay hands on to ensure the
child's safety while out of her sight. Medlun recognized a shiny silver charm against burning oneself
that belonged to his own great-grandmother; no doubt
the old woman had been persuaded to lend that at
one of the weekly sewing sessions after Medlun had
announced the proposed outing. No doubt that some
of the other baubles came from those meetings as
well. He thought he knew the white medallion, carved
with clusters of grapes. It was a charm against drunk-
enness. Medlun shook his head. Galjinna must have
taken every single amulet offered, with no regard for
its purpose.

"A child is fortunate if only one of its parents is
foolish," Medlun observed dryly.

Some of the charms sewn to her little coat were
feeding back against one another. It should have been
obvious to Galjinna that the nature of the enchantments might not be compatible. The sound was making the points of his ears twitch, and it was getting

worse. Fighting the discomfort, he stooped beside the child and found the offenders: a serpentine and garnet charm against snakes, and an amulet carved from shell that was meant to protect against bellyache. With a quick jerk, he ripped the bellyache medallion off her coat and threw it away. With the two elements separated by distance, the noise died away. He sighed deeply, and his muscles relaxed.

"Tell your mother it got torn off in the brush," he told the child, whose shocked face was upturned to him. "You won't need it."

Galjinna had been against this outing from the beginning. She protested that it was mad to expose a small child to the wilderness outside the wood and stone enclosure. Medlun had insisted that Darli couldn't be coddled forever. The younger she was when she began to find out about the world, the more self-sufficient she would be when she grew up. He promised to look after Darli, but a visit to the forest on Mirror Night was an important part of her education.

"Nothing will happen to her," Medlun promised, quashing his exasperation. "There is nothing up there but insubstantial visions and shadows. Besides, I will be there to protect her."

Reluctantly, Galjinna had agreed. She seldom disagreed openly with him, rather taking refuge in hurt silence when he did something she didn't like. Medlun loved her. He didn't like to go against her wishes and seldom did, but there were some needs that had to be met, no matter whose toes got stepped on.

Darli had had a nap so she could stay up all night with him. She was so excited about the mysterious excursion to come that Galjinna had been forced to resort to a gentle suggestion to make the child sleep. The enchantment, laid by loving fingers on Darli's pillow with a feather and a bit of spider silk, had drawn her down into a calm, restful state. Even over her mother's objections, Darli had been intrigued by the hints her father dropped of the wonders to be seen under the moon.

It was on one of these nights, when he was a child who sneaked out over the sill after his parents had gone to bed, he had noticed the shadows for the first time. Each time he came out, he was filled with amazement and wonder that they were still there. That such a phenomenon returned each Mirror Night without fail, even as the full moon herself did, was miraculous. He wanted Darli to see them, but more than that, he wanted her to be as intrigued by them as he was.

"Now, keep your steps and your voice as quiet as you can," Medlun cautioned Darli, at the top of the hill. "It isn't kind to frighten the animals who live here. We're only visitors."

Darli nodded, her eyes wide. "Are there any deer?"

"Perhaps." Medlun smiled at her. She loved all animals, but she had a special fondness for deer. Once, the summer before, a doe and her fawn had wandered into the enclosure, and were nibbling on Galjinna's garden when the family woke up that morning. Darli saw them through the window. The two young creatures, fawn and Folk, had locked eyes and remained motionless for a long time. Galjinna had always said that Darli had formed an instant rapport with the fawn. Medlun had scoffed at the idea of forming relationships with deer, but perhaps it was because he had always been intimidated by the size of the creatures. He was tall for one of the Folk, but he stood only as high as a buck's shoulders. Still, they were gentle animals, easily frightened away. He wished some of the other wild creatures were as manageable.

He sent his sense forward to see if there was anything dangerous waiting for them in the deep forest. Until they fought their way through the brush, they were vulnerable. Once, Medlun had seen a boar snorting angrily among the trees, but it had not seen him. There was nothing there tonight. The way was clear. Medlun held branches and switches back to allow the little girl unimpeded passage through.

The crown of the hill was ringed with thicket, surrounding the great trees, oak and beech, that commanded the heights above small clearings and copses. Darli glanced up at them timidly as she followed her father's silent steps toward the heart of the hilltop. These forest giants were hundreds of years old, some even exceeding living memory.

The shadows always began at moonrise, no matter what time of day that occurred. Under the blazing eye of the sun they were invisible, though they could be seen wherever there was a mix of shade and light, telling the story of the world from the beginning of time to the end. The very first visions were incomprehensible to him. Medlun had studied them with fascination, wondering what the images he beheld meant, when the land appeared to rise and fall around him, heaving itself into fantastic shapes and then receding again. No one in the village who would even acknowledge the shadows could tell him. The moon kept her mysteries to herself.

With Darli in tow, the climb up the hill had taken longer than usual, so the shadows of the land had already settled down. Medlun didn't mind. He was more interested in what followed immediately thereafter. Lizards popped into being, giant cousins to the tiny salamanders and other snake-brothers that frequented the forest he knew. One fiercely toothed specimen was so huge that it took him five successive Mirror Nights, standing in four different places and climbing a tree once, to see its whole form. The picture of it he had put together seemed more than unlikely, but Tarktee assured him that he, too, had seen that great beast, chewing on the tops of trees as one of the Folk would chew on a strand of grass.

There were smaller beasts that could be seen all at once. One, only three times as tall as Medlun, was perching on its oversize haunches and delicately eating a piece of greenery that it held between slender paws. Medlun was gratified to see that Darli had noticed the creature, and was watching it with her eyes and mouth wide open. It vanished in a heartbeat; none of the images ever lasted long. Darli blinked.

As the moon rose farther, the creatures grew smaller and furrier, until he recognized them without difficulty. Then, people shaped like himself came and went. He recognized the tall ears with elegant, back-swept points protruding through their rich hair, smooth skins, and hairless hands. They were different, though. They were twice as tall as the Folk, towering above the deer, and seemed not to be made of flesh, for the light didn't so much shine off them as it was part of them. He glimpsed their luminous eyes before he saw their faces, and drew Darli's attention in their direction.

"Be very quiet, but look!" he whispered, pointing to the first ones as they stepped out of the shadows.

She gasped with wonder, as well she might. These people were very beautiful. Their flesh ranged all the colors of the rainbow, any shade that light might prick from a prism, but did not remain the same from one breath to the next. The eye rested comfortably on the texture of the gowns and cloaks they wore. He knew somehow that the fabric would feel good under his fingers, and be at once warm and light. The men and women laughed, danced, played musical instruments, and sang silently as they walked. Loving pairs leaned together, and light flashed between their eyes as they walked hand in hand. After years of watching them, Medlun thought he could tell the difference between the ones who were really in love and those who were merely friends touching. The beings walked through trees and vanished in midstep. He wondered who these people were and where they had gone to when they left these woods. The Folk did not travel farther than they needed, so they knew little of the lands beyond the forest. One day, he might follow, to find these people if he could.

His daughter saw the last of them leave, and waited eagerly for more to appear. He understood her disappointment, and shared the same heartfelt lack. No more would come. He knew that from long years of waiting. "Where did they go, Father?" Darli asked sadly. "Why don't they come back?"

He shook his head. "I don't know. That was a very long time ago."

"Do you know any stories about them?"

Darli was showing curiosity now, and she was taking full advantage of having all his attention to herself. He chuckled. "I don't think even my grandfather's grandmother knew anything certain about the Tall Folk, but there are always legends." He looked around and nodded toward an oak root that humped out of the grass just at the edge of the small clearing. "Let's sit down here, and I'll tell you what I know. It's a good place to watch from."

Darli settled down beside him, her elbow on Medlun's knee. He took off his belt pouch and put it behind her for a pillow. Animals, both living and shadow, passed silently through. A shadow bear appeared within feet of them and lumbered by, so near that Medlun could reach out and stroke it. Its little eyes were fixed on a point far ahead. It walked directly through an oak tree and disappeared.

A couple of young martens emerged from the undergrowth, squealing and twisting their long bodies as they ran, sometimes side by side, sometimes one nearly on top of the other. Their dark fur picked up a shimmer from the moonlight.

"What are those?" Darli asked, surprised to see something real.

"Martens," Medlun said, and told her a little story he knew about them, and the way they were made so they could fit through small, winding tunnels. He picked up a fallen stick from the ground and began to whittle at it with his belt knife. The bronze edge glistened with the same dark patina as the martens' fur. Medlun was proud of his knife. He'd made it himself under Argeir the Metalsmith's eye, more than forty years ago.

"Anyone can bespell a piece of bronze to be strong and sharp," the smith had said, "but good metalwork has its own, better magic. You'll do well if your knife has both."

Darli stopped watching the animals and watched him carve instead.

"A youth's first knife makes her independent," he told Darli. "With it, you'd never lack for food, or shelter, or protection."

Darli sat in silence for a while, picking up and playing with chips of wood that flew away from his blade. The stick took a more defined shape under his fingers. It was going to be a spoon. "Father, can I have a knife?" she asked suddenly.

Medlun dug out a tiny knothole and shaved the place smooth where it had been. "What would you do with it?" he asked casually.

"I'd defend our house from wild animals..." she

began, but under her father's incredulous glance, veracity won out. "Mostly I'd cut up my own food. Mama does that for me now, but I would do it myself if I had a knife."

Medlun chuckled and patted her hand. He put the spoon aside. "All right. I suppose you're never too young to learn how to use one properly."

Wood would do for a beginner's knife. There was no lack of raw materials from which to choose. He selected a piece of root that dangled from a storm-felled tree, sending his sense throughout its fabric to feel it inside and out for weak places. There were none. "I'll use this," he said.

They sat under the tree, and he watched shadows as he whittled. Roots were tough to carve, but made the most durable goods. He trusted his fingers to shape the hilt and blade well. Darli curled up beside him and rested her head on his knee. He thought she went to sleep, but her breathing and occasional gasps of interest proved she was watching the shapes, too.

The moon was passing her halfway point, the present. Shades of the Folk who frequented the hilltop on Mirror Nights appeared and disappeared. This was their time. Medlun recognized the image of Irina the Poet, seated at the foot of an old beech tree, plucking at the strings of a silent harp. Irina's poems were still sung in the village, though she had been dead two hundred years. His ancestors and neighbors, and no doubt descendants, sat among the trees at various moments, contemplating the moon or the shadows, or one another, for a good hour and more.

Medlun knew that if he turned his head slightly, he might see the brief flicker of an image of himself and Darli.

At last, the wooden knife was completed. "There you are," Medlun said, nudging Darli. "Wake, little one."

She raised her head and planted her chin on her palm. Her long, walnut-colored hair was tousled, and one of her cheeks was pink. "I wasn't asleep," the child said accusingly. "Oh, you finished it!"

Medlun handed her the root, which he'd carved into a small semblance of his own knife. Cooing with pleasure, the child turned it over in her hands. Even in the dappled light, she could read the symbols that meant "Darli" that he had engraved on the hilt. "It's beautiful, Father," she said, and tested the edge against her palm. "But it won't cut anything."

Medlun took it back. "Yes, it will." He held the blade between his thumbs and concentrated on it, enhancing the strength of the edge, but to a particular purpose. "It will cut food, and only food. If I catch you attempting to torture the cat with it or threatening your baby brother, I will take it away. And do not put it into the fire. It is a tool. Treat it with respect." He handed it to her, hilt first.

Delighted, Darli swiped at the grass beside her, and then frowned her disappointment. "It didn't cut."

"Do you eat grass, like a deer?" her father asked, amused. He gave her a pat on the back to make her sit forward, and took an apple from his pack. "Try this instead."

True to its imbued charm, the wooden blade parted the apple in two. Delighted, Darli wanted to cut the fruit again and again to see the knife slice.

"No, no," her father admonished her, taking a piece of fruit out of the bag for himself. "You'll have apple sauce. Let's peel our apples and plant the seeds here in the clearing."

He turned his own apple in a circle, and the peel, meeting the glinting bronze blade, spiraled down over his hands in an unbroken ribbon of red and green. Darli copied his movements more clumsily, hewing off chips of fruit and rind in all directions, but she seemed pleased anyhow and concentrated on the task herself instead of asking for help. A knife truly made her more independent.

The visions changed again. The second half of the evening always made him very sad. After a while, a short while, he no longer saw images of the Folk in the woods. What concerned him most was that there was no suggestion of what made them leave or where they went. He tried to content himself by saying that the time must have come for the Folk to move on and look for others of their kind. It would not do for the village to become inbred. Yet, he would have been more content knowing that his home would remain where it was for all the rest of time, and that his descendants would live in it. An interval followed when the only visions he saw were animals, and then more Tall Folk came.

These were not the shining ones who were there before Medlun's Folk. These were curious beings.

Their ears were abnormal, rounded and small like those of newborn kittens. They were clumsy and bearlike. Though their stature was no greater than the shining ones, they moved as if they were so big they couldn't control their bodies. The deer fled before them; trees fell, leaving gaps of empty sky above; and they carried a disquieting air about them, banishing peace.

Even in their strangeness, there was beauty and symmetry to these Tall Folk whose time was yet to come. When they felt joy, it showed in every move, in every lineament. Most fittingly, they seemed to be in awe of the great forest, regarding the trees with heartfelt respect. He liked these Folk.

The clothing they wore interested him. Some of the future Big One's garments he saw fitted very tightly, and it took care and the right angle to see how they went on. It was a great relief to him to know that magic would still exist in the far future. There assuredly must have been charms of some kind, or the blue trousers that predominated, once on, wouldn't be able to come off. He was also puzzled when these Folk danced, as they frequently did, because they had no instruments with which to make music, only flat black boxes with handles.

The Tall Folks' faces were fascinating. Unlike the first Big Ones, their colors ranged only through the shades of wood, from birch bark to oak gall, and never changed. Some were varying shades of bronze. Some of them had skins the color of the beaver's fur, and others like the birch's leaf in autumn. He had never seen people like these in solid flesh, and guessed, by the length of the moon's progress across the sky, that he never would. These were too far in the future.

He wished he could speak with them. They were not mere shades, but the reflections of real people, whenever it was they lived. A slender young man with hair the color of the fox's fur and eyes the color of wonder met his glance, and stopped, startled. He had seen Medlun and Darli, and must have wondered who, or what, they were. Equally surprised, Medlun bowed to the man. With only a brief hesitation, the figure returned his respectful gesture, then passed on, vanishing among the trees. Medlun admitted he was taken aback. Only once before had one of the figures noticed him in the woods, a man with black hair and eyes as black and bright as flint, though his face was kind.

And soon, these too would go. As the moon neared her setting point, the last of the Tall Folk would appear to be walking several feet above the ground. None would return.

When they had finished eating and the seeds and cores buried, Medlun stood up. Watching history pass always made him feel profound and sad. He needed to break the spell.

"Would you like to see the Great River?" he asked, holding his hand out to Darli. "The moon is far enough west now to show us both banks."

"Oh, yes!" she exclaimed, jumping up and taking his hand. She still brandished her new knife in the other hand, but Medlun wasn't worried. The way the blade was spelled, she couldn't have an accident with it. He sheathed his own knife and buckled on his belt pouch.

The cliff face that looked out over the river was tricky. He and the others who came out here had to test it constantly for erosion. Thanks to Uncle Brudlan's ability to listen to the earth and translate what he heard, no one had ever been caught in a landslide, but missteps were always possible. The tumbled, shattered boulders at the cliff's foot were a warning that even the earth's bones could be broken by such a long fall as that.

"Let me go first," Medlun said, leaving Darli at the edge of the cliff path. He felt his way carefully nearly to the edge.

The bluff had been cut away by wind and weather into promontories like fingers. Earth and stone seemed to be solid enough, and there was plenty of tough creeper vine for Darli to hold on to.

"Come on, little one," he beckoned her, speaking loudly to drown out the amplified rush of the river. "You have to climb under the brush. Not too far to your right, now. Good." He edged off the promontory as she came forward. No sense in daring the cliff edge to support all of their weight at once. He'd already proved it could hold him. "Take hold of these vines, and don't lean out too far."

Darli nodded, winding her fingers into the mass of creepers. She sat down, and turned her face toward the moonlit river. "Oooh," she breathed.

Medlun moved a few yards away, onto another

tooth of land, and lay on his belly to have a look for himself. Sighing, he gazed at the strip of silver that bisected the river at a right angle, and looked up and down the long water's length. Willow trees brushed the water's surface with their long hair, and armies of reeds marched in the shallows where a strand of the river looped away from the main flow. He wondered how he could ever have thought the village stream was big. The river was nearly as wide as the hill, and the fish that swam in it could grow as large as one of the Folk.

"Father?" Darli asked. He glanced over, but she was hidden behind the thick undergrowth.

"Yes, little one?"

"What's on the other side of the river?"

The question took him pleasantly by surprise. Medlun laughed long and loudly, and heard his voice echo on the river's surface. "You *are* a child of mine, after all, aren't you?"

There was a pause, and the little voice said rather uncertainly, "I think so."

He laughed again, filled with a joy that embraced the moon, and the river, and the whole earth. "I don't know, child. Perhaps one day you and I will go and find out."

The moon was sinking rapidly now through the last quarter of the sky. Medlun noticed it and got hastily to his feet. He wanted to use her last light to find his way back to the crown of the hill. It was a short night, and the sun would be rising soon, but false dawn would light the wrong side of the hill. He bent to edge under the tangled creepers, brushing the leaves out of his face with both hands, and called out to Darli as soon as he was back on the path.

"Come on, little one. It's time to go home."

He heard rustling as she scrambled to her feet, and then saw her silhouette through the lacework of greenery. "This way, Darli," he beckoned.

"I can't, Father," she said in a low, strained voice. It sounded like she was about to cry.

It was then Medlun heard another sort of rustling, low in the grass. A shadow reared, looking like a fist clenched at the end of an arm, but a sinuous, almost boneless arm that swayed from side to side. A snake! They must have walked right over its sleeping place and awakened it. Darli's subsequent movements toward it would have seemed like an advance or an attack. The creature was preparing to defend itself.

Medlun's heart pounded in panic. The forest snakes had a poisonous bite from which few adults ever recovered. That much toxin could kill a little girl in moments.

"Don't move, Darli," he cautioned her. He had to have time to think of what to do.

"All right, Father," the tiny voice said. She was being very brave in the face of a hitherto unknown danger, and he was proud of her.

Concentrating, Medlun willed the grass around his feet to be more pliant, enhancing the fibers' softness until the blades wilted like silk. When he was satisfied he wouldn't make any noise, he slid forward to get a better look.

It was a kingsnake, and a granddaddy at that. It was probably three or four ells long. Darli was standing only an arm's length from it, and she was trembling. Any motion helped keep the kingsnake's attention. Medlun felt for his belt knife. He was close enough that he couldn't possibly miss the snake, then realized with his heart in his throat that the terrain was against him. He could see every detail, through an impeding curtain of creepers and brush. There wasn't a hope that he could get a clear throw, and he wouldn't be able to get to her before the snake struck. He couldn't get closer, and he had to stand like a statue to keep from rattling the branches and scaring the snake into attacking.

He almost ordered Darli to stab at it with the little wooden blade she still held in her left hand, but charmed as it was only to cut up food, it wouldn't so much as bruise a serpent of that size. He wasn't close enough to enhance its nature to include defense. He felt helpless, and he hated it. The moon, huge and red, was sinking swiftly beneath the horizon.

Medlun resolved to make a throw anyway, to distract the snake while Darli escaped. There was just room for her to edge around it, if she went slowly.

"Darli," he instructed her in a calm, low voice, "move back away from the snake. Tiptoe as if you are trying not to wake anyone up. You know how to do that? Pretend it's early in the morning."

"Yes, Father," Darli said. He could see that there were tears on her face, and cursed himself. This was supposed to be a pleasant evening out for the two of them, and she was in danger of her life. He should have checked again for wild creatures. It was his fault. He kept talking, hoping his voice would soothe her, trying to project calm he did not feel.

"Do not move toward the snake. Back away, but to your left, the hand your knife is in, or you'll fall over the edge. Do you understand me?"

"Uh-huh." Her voice cracked. Medlun hoped she wouldn't panic and try to run. He willed her to be calm.

"All right, move, starting now. Move one foot, then the other...."

The child, eyes pinned on the coiled snake, began slowly to edge backward, but she was moving too far back. In a moment, she would be over the precipice.

"Darli!" Medlun shouted. "Toward your knife hand!"

Remembering, the child turned to look at her hand. The sudden movement enraged the snake. It uncoiled and struck at her knee. Darli screamed, a shrill tone that tore the air.

Freed from immobility, Medlun flung aside the creepers and dashed to save her. He prayed that he would have a chance to stop the poison's progress and drain the wound. The process was tricky and didn't always work. What would he do if she died? The snake hung thrashing on the girl's leg, dyed red by the moon, and Darli continued to scream.

Medlun seized the serpent behind the neck and squeezed to force the jaws open and away from Darli's body. Then he noticed that its fangs weren't piercing flesh at all. The snake's head was held a span's worth of thin air away from the child. One of the charms on her sleeve was glowing with energy in the chilly air. The snake was angry, but it couldn't get free.

Relieved, Medlun began to laugh weakly.

"A child is fortunate if she has two wise parents," he said. He put his arm around Darli. "It didn't touch you, little one. Look. The charm your mother sewed here saved you. Do you see?" He passed his hand between her leg and the trapped snake. "Now, be calm."

His laughter was beginning to have the taste of hysteria, so he forced himself to stop. He felt around the edge of the protection spell, and broke it loose as he took the snake by the back of the neck. Impassionately, he turned away from Darli's line of sight and slashed off its head. The body jerked and struggled. Medlun hated to kill a natural creature, but once it struck at one of the Folk, it might do it again, and at one who was not as well protected as Darli. When the carcass stopped moving, he coiled it up and tucked it into his pouch with a wad of grass to absorb the blood.

"Come here, my little one," Medlun said, kneeling next to Darli. She flung herself into his arms, and he gathered her up, holding her close to his heart, grateful that she hadn't been hurt. He hadn't known until then how precious she was to him. They'd both learned some lessons this night.

Darli sobbed for a few moments out of pure reaction, and Medlun rocked her. Gradually, her breath-

ing calmed, and the taut little body relaxed. He relaxed, too, but the scare he had had would remain
with him always. Wryly, he realized he owed Galjinna
a humble apology.

"It's nearly morning," he said, standing up with
his arms still tight around Darli. "We ought to go
home now. Your mother will be making us a good
breakfast."

"I am hungry," the child said hopefully, sniffing
the air as if she could smell cooking all the way up
here from the village.

Medlun kissed her on the temple and shifted her
so she'd be easier to carry. "So am I."

He retraced their path to the top of the hill and
over it toward the village side. As the sun sent tentative fingers of light over the distant hills, the last wisps
of vision evaporated and vanished, leaving behind
only the solid world. Or did it? Medlun wasn't sure.
Perhaps other shadows remained to be seen, only he
didn't know where to look for them. He'd have to
discuss the idea with Tarktee.

Darli rode silently with her arms around his neck
until they reached the edge of the hilltop and were
beginning their descent to the well-worn path. "Father,
will you take me up here again?" she asked suddenly.
"Next Mirror Night?"

Medlun tweaked her ear playfully. "Are you sure
you would feel safe? What happened tonight could
happen again."

"Oh, yes. You took care of me, and I have my
own knife now, and Mama put the protections on my

coat." She helped him push away the hazel switches so they could get through the ring. Medlun stumped down the path as color began to creep upward in the eastern sky. "Besides, you promised we could go across the river someday. I wonder if there are shadows there? I would like to see them."

Medlun chuckled. The child's eyes were already full of dreams. "That's my girl," he said.

The Twice-Born Bard

Michael Williams

Michael Williams, in addition to his solo fantasy novels for TSR and Questar, has earned himself the title of poet laureate/bard for the Dragonlance world. His contribution to this anthology continues with a poem in the style of *Sir Gawain and the Green Knight*.

In the long past, lost in the dream of the land,
where the heart's song is hostage to rumor,
and memory summons a map of stars,
before the naming of things and the language to
    name,
there once was a king, as always there is in a story,
King Cronos he was, king of the old Philokalians,
the dwellers in visions and dreams and minarets.
His queen was Amelia, dark among marvels,
famous for grace, for the green of her fabulous eyes,
and their daughter was dear to her doting father—
both women melodious, lovely as larks.
Had this been the story, we would not have heard it,
for history rides on the baffled heart,

on the failings of sons, not the fairness of daughters:
therefore the lad, the lumpish Leofric,
a prince half-borrowed from pride and boding,
a cramped boy, cruel as ravens,
suckled in violence, weaned on the scorpion's venom,
                     and unfair
               the habit and the face
               of Cronos' son and heir:
               Leofric lacked for grace,
            for conscience, for clean hair.

A hideous boy this was, a haven for adders,
his skin as pocked as a skimming of whey,
the face of an ettin, an eater of children,
a brow that stunned birds in the rafters,
that masked the wax and wane of the moon
in a single, thickheaded stare.
The bane of his mother Amelia, he was,
her fathomless sorrow, her sea of troubles,
the thing whose presence promised the end of the
    world.
But the end never came, and the cruel boy flourished,
pillaging larders, imperiling servants and animals,
until Amelia vowed that out of the greed and venom
surely a wisdom must rise, and so
she went from chymist to wizard, from wizard to sage,
                     to find out
               how herb or chemistry
            might turn the heart about,
               distilling subtlety
               from an obvious lout.

*   *   *

Magicians and conjurers counseled Amelia,
reading her future in leaves, in the flight of rooks,
in the facets of gems, in the faint agenda of stars:
all prophecy sunk to a simmering cauldron,
to an old convergence of water and herb
and slow time, for a sorcerer's year and a day.
Into the kettle the queen poured camphor,
nettles for wisdom, wormwood for knowledge,
a phoenix feather, smelling of ash and forgiveness,
eye of a basilisk, breath of a panther,
a faerie's glove, a philosopher's stone,
a dozen ingredients, grim and unnameable,
known to Amelia only. Masked by night,
by guard and command, she minded the potion,
                    and no one,
            nor king nor servant, heard
                in moonlight or in sun
            the hushed and magical word
                cast over the cauldron.

But the nights were deep and the watch undying
and the golden ladle large in her hand.
Amelia yawned, then mulled, then nodded
and stirred and wrestled back sleep.
Weary, disquieted, the queen imagined
Leofric lost to mayhem and larceny,
wine-lulled, useless, illiterate,
more poet than prince, impious and dissolute,
all for her nap in the possible night:
so was her nightmare, so her vision.

Rising and shaking off sleep, Amelia
rode to the land of the coblyn, the little folk,
where an orphaned lad named Orfeo lived
in alleys and stables, in amphitheaters,
gathering alms and dust in the garrulous alleys,
paying for dinner with plea and deception.
Amelia carried him off to the castle,
and set him on sentry, knee-high and scared,
a cowering coblyn at the cauldron's lip.
"Tend the elixir, ladle the broth
until the appointed time," she said.
"And great the riches born of my gratitude—
a sack of coins, a suit of linen,
a pair of fine shoes and a pewter ring,
                    and more,
              unless a small drop spills:
              then you will beg me for
              a thousand plagues and ills
              instead of those in store."

He lost track of time as he ladled the cauldron,
standing on tiptoe, lost in the thinking.
Lulled and drowsy, the coblyn dreamed
of palaces in the pools and reflections,
of fabulous beasts in the bubbles and eddies:
of gryphons and drakes and dragons and ogres,
and as each emerged, Orfeo mastered and named it,
by wit and words, and over its wings or scales
sang a ballad to grace it and bless it,
and named and familiar, each found its place in the
    story.

But the watch was long and weary the labor.
For the space of an hour, the queen would spell him,
and Orfeo slept on the kitchen straw,
but he carried the cauldron with him in sleep,
he stirred exhausted in unsettled dreams
                    and it seemed
            waking spilled into slumber:
                over the pot he dreamed,
        and the dreams were unencumbered
          as the cauldron roiled and steamed.

Hard in the twelfth month, hard in impossible times,
when the rain swelled the surging triad of rivers
far to the north, as a new map settled
over dark and emerging oceans,
at the lip of the kettle the coblyn listened
hearing nothing at first, the airy nothing
that lulled and muddled him over eleven months,
but then, faint harmonies rose from the fire,
rising with sleep unexpected and subtle.
Below him, about him, a choir of birds
alighted and sang an old lullaby
of night and fatigue and remembered dreaming
as slowly the coblyn traveled the country of sleep
and the moon passed over the murmuring room.
Orfeo awoke with the evening over,
the ladle dropped in the cauldron, the potion in
        chaos.
All of the citadels Orfeo dreamt
had collapsed in the swirl of steam and elixir,
one by one winked out the animals,

and suddenly out of the storming brew
three splashes of potion spilled from the kettle
onto his careless hand. The coblyn cried out,
then looked about him, then licked up the evidence.
He stirred the brew, he skimmed the froth,
his thoughts were stirring and skimming and hoping
          desperately
      that Queen Amelia's fabled eyes
        were fabled for beauty,
        and could not recognize
     the loss of a drop, or two, or three.

As he worried and reckoned, the chamber erupted
    with voices:
from the window they came, where the willow leaned
    in
and whispered a story dark and disturbing,
they arose from the branches, from the rustle of
    leaves,
for the trees were talking, the oaks and the tamarack,
the elder, the blackthorn, the boxwood and elm,
all speaking a lazy, surprising language.
Beyond them ascended the bright persuasions of birds,
the squirrel's loud scuffle and whir,
and the slow incandescent hymn of sunlight.
Below them the steady measures of stone
tilted and hummed at the heart of the world.
And Orfeo knew at the heart of his knowing
that the thing he had stirred in Amelia's cellars
was a treasure of secrecy, sweet and eternal
kept for the rich and the royal sons,

kept from the commoner, kept from the coblyn,
kept from the usual, kept from all of us,
so that the world seems somber and senseless,
the trees are mute and the memory falters,
and the harsh and scrutinous sun takes from us
all darkness, and with it all depth and direction,
leaving us lost and lorn and hopeless.
Orfeo saw it all in the simmering potion,
                    and he swore,
            the ladle raised like a wand,
            that all the wisdom, all the lore
            splashed on his spattered hand
        belonged to the humble and poor.

He knew she approached by the sound of her thoughts,
loud on the stairwell as the shadows lifted:
Amelia considered irreparable sons,
the power of brews and potions, the strange
adventure of hope and invented wisdom,
and as she approached, the appointed year
turned for them famously there in phantasms of light.
As Amelia looked into Orfeo's eyes,
the coblyn saw truly that the queen had counted
each coal-black drop from the bubbling kettle,
and missing three, her thoughts were murderous:
instead of the sack of coins, or the clothing,
she would mire him in deep and immutable silence.
They would find him if they found him at all
                    transmuted
                into a weasel or plover,
            a boot or a crust of bread

or a lost wind coursing over
the gray land of the dead.

So then and there the tale might have ended,
the coblyn transmogrified into lint, into embers,
the story an oddity left from the earliest time,
Leofric remembered as wise past imagining,
a talker with trees and the trilling birds,
Amelia an icon of mothering ardor,
once again history harboring lies.
Above us the years would descend in yearning,
Amelia and Leofric always above us,
their story as faint and deceptive as onyx,
forbidding and heirless as fashioned gold.
But Orfeo sank to unruffled stillness,
his mind tilted into the calm of new terror,
in the slowed country where he caught himself thinking
idly and foolishly, *If I were a hare*
I would run I would race and be out of this,
and before his mind had recovered, before Amelia
raised her hand in a ruinous spell,
the coblyn was out through the mountainous kitchen,
out through the corridors, over the courtyard,
long ears and whiskers bowed in the wind.
Through the courtyards of Cronos, through the king's
    bailey
he galloped and leapt like a ghost of light
into the undergrowth there by the edge of the moat.
Behind him the queen pursued her quarry:
green-eyed Amelia murmured and chanted,
as muzzle and flews emerged from her face,

from her graceful neck a gray dewlap,
and she became a greyhound, coursing
out through the corridors, over the courtyard
straight to the moat and into the stagnant waters,
up to the opposite bank and the undergrowth,
    and once there
   through mud and reed she nosed
    growling and sniffing the air
    as the frightened rabbit froze
    in her dark, embracing stare.

Out from the undergrowth Orfeo sprang,
into the still, encircling waters,
down to the bed of the moat, where the darkness
was clean and complete and cold and enfolding.
He imagined a colder current beneath him,
water a million years in the making,
the first and primal time in its flowing,
and deep in his dream he entered the current,
the witch forgotten, the flight from the cauldron,
as the lost light danced on his dwindling back.
The light danced its last on his dorsal fin
and out of the water came breathing, and Orfeo
surged through the eddies, silver and scaled,
a salmon sustained on the cradling stream.
Above him, the queen abandoned the sunlight.
Into the twilight of waters she tumbled
and she dreamt coldly, and the current dreamt,
a sleek new form arising from nightmare
as oiled and webbed, an otter emerged
out of the witching dark of water.

Oiled and webbed, Amelia descended
and Orfeo fled the otter behind him,
the otter whose green eyes were fabled and ominous,
as the shadowy water whispered, *Surrender,*
surrender I bring you the endless slumber
of needles, the hot deliverance of knives,
and Orfeo listened in the lower waters,
there at the barren edge of believing,
as the song of the otter descended upon him.
Again and again the tale would have ended,
the salmon torn in the teeth of the otter
and Orfeo lost past lore and memory,
scarcely recalled in a season's turning,
but then light engulfed him, a gift of grace
or of instinct, or infinite luck,
and the salmon turned in eternal water,
and soared and fled toward the fathomless light.
Approaching the surface, the pendulous sun,
the theaters of air and high wind and thermals,
Orfeo rose on wings from the watery regions
and sang as he folded the sky in flight.
Awash in light, in wind and feathers,
he passed like a crow over castles and nations
and the blue world rolled in the black of his wings,
and below him the country recovered its meaning.
Orfeo turned in the innocent air,
the sky incandescent and strange about him,
and the dream of his wings was the dream of the rain.
Slowly the coblyn climbed through the clouds,
in the back of his mind the memory of waters,
his thoughts fixed on light and freedom,

on freedom and light, until like a phantom
a shadow passed over him, distant and shapeless,
and poisonous, like a play of wind
across an expected country, surprising you
out of freedom and light, forecasting
transition of years and the several deaths
you await as the vanishing world devours
your dear friends, your light and freedom.
The bladed wings of a hawk wheeled over,
above him, its back to the pitiless sun,
and wiser this time for the wind and water,
Orfeo swooped toward the swell of the ground,
toward the safety of farms and fathomless shires,
the hawk far above him, following, scouring
the country with cruel and fabled green eyes.
The witch queen searched for the vanished quarry,
her eye descending past poplar and cedar,
knifing through leaf and the leaf's anatomy,
bisecting river and road and rick,
to alight on a barn, on a sleepy loft,
             on a grain
        of wheat on a hay-strewn floor,
          lost in the sun, the rain
      of dust motes through the granary door,
          changed past changing again.

Never would mortal eye have noticed
the coblyn transformed on the floor of the loft.
There in the uncertain core of himself,
most easily lost, collapsed to a kernel,
prey to the rodent, to the ravenous swallow,

to a scattering draft in the drowsy loft,
Orfeo rested, awaiting miraculous change.
Under the calm of ancient philosophers,
Orfeo waited past music and alchemy,
as all mathematics matured to a cipher
and logic disjoined in the heart of geometry.
Calm he remained on the outskirts of miracle.
The time came soon, as the coblyn reckoned:
after the scuffling of mice subsided,
when the daylight drifted toward the dark,
he heard the scratching, the scrape and cackle
as a hen drew near in the hush of the loft,
her green eyes like corposants, cruel and shifting.
Unceremoniously, Queen Amelia
scratched up and swallowed the waiting seed,
and there in the tilting loft returned
to her flesh and form and her first demeanor.
Vicious in victory, the dark queen vaunted,
Amelia danced and the dust motes scattered,
the fragmented sunlight slipped to the edge of the
      sky
and the trees lost their names in the language of dusk
as the rising night unraveled the country
expectant and quiet at the queen's revels.
Amelia danced and the day declined
and suddenly something stirred and kicked
hard and obscure in her secretive depths,
as it had when Leofric leapt in her belly
in the long months nine and maternal,
                  and the gloom
            of the loft descended on her,

baffled and beaten and doomed,
and her words dried in the river
as the child stirred in her womb.

The story concludes with the coblyn child
born to the queen, a green-eyed baby:
a lad so lovely the queen relented,
staying her murderous hand, though her mercy,
the mercy of villains, was cruel and venomous:
in the night she sent the infant upriver,
borne in hazard and a basket of reeds:
she watched as the child, who was her child only
and yet never hers, rode on the horizon.
To her castle she came, to her ruined cauldron:
the kettle basin was black and crusted,
the potion dried up in her ominous pursuits.
Slowly and angrily Amelia watched
the long years ahead, as Leofric left
all princely resources, all prospect and charm,
past cure or enchantment the child evolving.
But Leofric's story we leave untold,
fuel for another night by the fireside
when talk is of misrule and monstrous things.
Another story there is, how far to the north,
where the rivers forked and the darkness faded
Orfeo found care in a king's house,
up where the days have different names
and the stars bow down at immeasurable distance.
There he was renamed, renewed in the Umbrian
    courts,
Felix the child, then Felix the coblyn,

warm by the hearthside, winsome and happy,
for *happy* his name means, *happy* and *blessed.*
Eventually he grew in vision and voice
into the bard, the twice-born poet,
prince of all song and preposterous story,
and singer of deep inexpressible wisdom,
who animal, fish, and fowl renamed
in a language of water and light....
But that tale also we leave untold
for midsummer night and the shadowy nexus
of wind and star and wine and story,
when talk is of miracle, myth, and marvel.
No, those are the stories for other occasions:
tonight we end in the eddying waters
the basket and Felix afloat on the river,
mired in the vast and mothering night.
We end with the readying dreams of an infant
who sails with history loud in his newborn heart,
already gathering stories, taking stock,
                    as the names arise
          from the reeds, from the crossing bars,
                    as deep infinities
              cascade from the expectant stars,
              fall from the singing skies.

A Sparkle for Homer

R. A. Salvatore

R. A. Salvatore's *Forgotton Realms* books have been one of TSR's bestselling series. "A Sparkle for Homer," however, is set in a world all his own.

Horatio Hairfoot was a most respectable halfling. In fact, his friends and neighbors in Inspirit Downs, a village in the easy land most centered in The World, called him Homer, which is a fair compliment, I might tell you, implying all the lovely homely things associated with respectable halflings: plentiful meals (Horatio preferred eight a day, thank you, Breakfast, Brunch, Lunch, Late-afternoon-snack, Dinner, Supper, Before-bed-to-quiet-the-belly, and, of course, the inevitable Midnight-raid-the-larders); sitting by the hearth, toasting his toes; and sitting on the side of a hill, blowing smoke rings at the lazily passing clouds. Yes, most respectable villagers spent most days off their feet. They could watch their toes wiggle that way—that is, when their bellies hadn't gotten too round for such enjoyable sights as wiggling toes!

Horatio rolled and stretched in his slumber, twisted about and worked his diminutive frame every which way in search of elusive comfort. Finally, he caught something sharp in the small of his back and that woke him with a start. He remembered at once where he was, and that awful thought sent him burrowing back under the shelter of his blanket, which simply could not cover both his head and toes at the same time.

"Let's go, lazy one!" barked the too-awake voice of Bagsnatcher Bracegirdle, a not-too-respectable at all sort of halfling. "Bags" had a bit o' the dwarf in him, so it was said, and a fondness for adventure that kept him out of Inspirit Downs more than in. Indeed, he was a burly one, nearly as muscled as a dwarf, though of course he had no beard, and he bragged openly about dragon fights and goblin wars and other sorts of things that others loved hearing about, but generally scorned. On those occasions when Bags was in town, and always in the Floating Cloud Tavern, few went too near to him, but many remained within earshot of his continual spoutings. So it had come as quite the surprise, you can imagine, when Mayor Faltzo Furstockings announced that his tender and most respectable, if not overly cute, daughter Tippin and Bagsnatcher Bracegirdle would be wed on midsummer's morning.

Oh, the rumors flew wide and thick that day, I tell you! Some said that Bags had come into a fortune along in his adventuring and had promised Mayor Faltzo that he would settle down. There was talk of a dowry—they called it a bribe—paid by Bags to the mayor. Others, looking for a bit more fun out of the unexpected announcement, claimed that Mayor Faltzo had an inkering for adventuring himself, and that Bags and he would start off soon after the honeymoon on a most extraordinary journey. Whatever the intent, the news came unexpectedly, as I have told you, and so too, especially to Horatio, did Bags's proclamation that Horatio Homer Hairfoot would stand beside him as his Best Halfling.

Horatio hardly knew Bags, had never even talked to the adventuresome fellow as far as he could remember, and being named as that one's Best Halfling set off a whole new round of whispers, these speaking of most unpleasant things, like "yearning for a dragon fight," concerning Horatio. None of them were true, of course; Homer had earned his nickname in heart as well as in reputation. To this day, no one knows exactly why Bags chose Homer, not even Bags probably, but most tavern-philosophers have come to agree that the wayward adventurer just wanted a most respectable fellow by his side to add the right flavor to the extraordinary wedding.

All in all, being named as Best Halfling had been an unwelcomed declaration to Homer, and sitting on the rocky, sloping ground, sore in a dozen places and his belly rumbling in protest of the bland and not-so-plentiful food, Homer's glare at Bagsnatcher's back was not a pleasant one! He had accepted the invitation to stand beside Bags, of course, not much choice is given in these matters (not if one intends to remain respectable). Homer figured that if he could afterward stay low-key enough, the damage to his reputation would heal in a year or so, though he knew that he would hear a whispered laugh at his back every now and again whenever he chanced a visit to the Floating Cloud. If, however, Homer could have imagined the trouble his acceptance would land him in, he would have become ill, or broken his foot, or done anything else that would have allowed him to bow out gracefully, so to speak.

For now Homer had his own adventure, it seemed, and he did not like it, not one bit. A chill and moist wind blew in with the dawnslight, making the creaks all the more prominent in Homer's backbone. The night had been crystal clear—far in the west and far below, the traveling companions had spotted the lights of Inspirit Downs—but now the mist hung thick as dwarven ale.

"A fine day to be climbing over hard rocks," grumbled Homer before he even got all the way out of his tangled blankets. The sarcasm in his voice was even more evident now than it had been on the previous three days of this trek, though it was quite lost on Bags, thoroughly pleased by the morning, foggy or not, and by the adventure in general.

"We'll be picking our paths careful, is all," Bags snorted in reply. "There's just the one way to go, ye know—up!" He chuckled and swatted Homer playfully on the back. Homer took it with a grunt and did well to hide his cringing at Bags's dwarven-flavored accent, an accent that only reminded Homer of his predicament.

"Up," Homer echoed grimly. Now he cast a scornful look at his companion, barely more than a dark silhouette in the thick fog. "You do not have to enjoy this so much!"

Bags chuckled in reply, understanding, but hardly accepting, the respectable fellow's gloom. "'Ere, go on yerself," said Bags. "I'm the one what's injured here, bein' a newlywed and all! Should be back with me best girl, not up here leading yerself into a fine and, if we're lucky, dangerous journey! Ye get a bargain, by me seeing! Ye get an adventure easily bought 'n handed right to ye!"

Homer did not reply, realizing that he and Bags saw things simply too differently for him to explain his point of view. Homer did want to throttle Bags for his claims of being the "injured one," though, for it was Bags, and Bags alone, who had landed them here. The wedding had gone splendidly, but the reception was quite another matter. The unusual circumstances had provided a good deal of mirth to the whole town, and the gathering had howled even louder when Bags, tipping his twelfth mug of black dwarven mead (another testament that he had a "bit o' the dwarf in him," for none but a dwarf or dwarf-kin could put down even an eight pack of that stuff without being put down himself!), made a somewhat crass and undeniably stupid remark about his soon-coming adventures with his new wife. Always the protective father, Mayor Faltzo had promptly invented a "vital" mission, and Bags, without ever remembering it, had promptly volunteered, and had volunteered, too, to take his Best Halfling and best buddy Homer along with him.

So here they were, Homer miserable and Bags three days married and with his waiting wife miles away. Back in the town they were all laughing, Homer knew, for even Tippin Furstockings-Bracegirdle, always ready to join in on the fun, had thought the whole thing hilarious.

"We'll be reaching the summit this day, by me guess," Bags remarked after they had silently, and sullenly for Homer, eaten their breakfast.

"To find a stone," Homer grumbled.

"*The* stone," the adventuresome fellow corrected with a gleam in his pale gray eyes. "If the rumors hold to true, the heart stone o' the One Mountain's sitting at the top for our plucking! Such a gem'd be worth many thousands o' gold coins, I don't mind telling ye!" Bags rubbed his hands eagerly together, and if he missed his new wife in the least, Homer could not see it. "Heart stone!" he declared.

"Hearth stone would be better," Homer muttered under his breath. His family was well off, and Homer saw no need for any adventures, however they might add to the treasury. Besides, Homer knew it, even if Bags was too blinded by the thought of excitement to see it, that Mayor Faltzo's sudden proclamation that the heart stone was just sitting out in the open atop the One Mountain was only just a ruse. Rumors of that fabled stone had been tossed about for years, centuries even, and if anyone had ever actually seen it, then no one had seen him see it, if you understand my meaning.

"Ofttimes the greatest treasures be sittin, for the grabbing right in front of us, lad," Bags replied to Homer's obvious disbelief. "Just waiting for to be plucked!"

Homer narrowed his eyes and firmed up his hairless jaw at Bags's choice of words, a similar phrase to the one Bags had used at the wedding reception, the one that had landed them in this lousy adventure in the first place.

Bags gave up against that unrelenting stare, a vile grimace that only an underfed and uncomfortable halfling could properly produce. "Might be we'll catch sight of a dragon," Bags growled, stealing every bit of Homer's bluster, and pulled his weapon off his backpack to heighten the other's terror. It was a curious thing, unlike any weapon Homer had ever seen (not that he had seen many), with a hammer head on one side, an ax head on the other, and a cruel barbed spear tip topping the whole of it off. Bags just called it his banger-chopper-thruster and left it for his enemies to see what it could do. Whatever it might have been, it looked unwieldingly heavy to Homer, and even he— though not inclined to magic—could sense the powerful enchantments on the thing. Homer should have been comforted to have one who could wield the weapon well standing beside him, but the mere sight of the thing unnerved him and turned his stomach so that it made him think that eating might not be a very fine thing.

Homer stood up then and looked all about, a futile attempt in the wall of fog. Before he could begin to grumble about the weather, though, Bags scooped up his pack and started off at a quick pace. Homer swallowed his complaints, and then, when he realized that he was alone, swallowed his fear and ran off to follow.

They made good headway, despite the mist, but even though the dawn soon moved fully into day, the gloom only increased. Soon the companions couldn't see each other, couldn't even see their own furry feet.

"We shall tumble down to our deaths," Homer moaned at Bags's back.

Bags, ever alert, was too engaged to respond to the comment. The ground had become soft under his feet, springy as a thick bed of moss, a curious fact since they had left the trees and most other vegetation far behind. Also, the ground had leveled off, though Bags had noted no upcoming flat regions along the chosen trail when they had set camp the night before. Instinctively, his experienced hands went to his banger-chopper-thruster. With a word to the magical weapon, "Foe-faces," he enacted a blue faerie light along the weapon's multiple heads. But the glow only reflected off the pressing fog back in his face, and though he was not a tall creature, and though he stooped to get even lower, Bags could not even discern the nature of the ground beneath him.

Homer came rushing up then, having lost sight of Bags when Bags dipped low, and bounced off his sturdy companion and tumbled down in a heap.

"You should warn me when you plan to stop!" the respectable halfling cried. Poor Homer was quite unnerved, and you would be too, I should guess, if you were half a head more than three feet tall, with a belly wider than your shoulders, and caught in a strange fog on a strange mountain, expecting a dragon to swoop down at you, or a ghoul to jump in your face, or a wolf to snap at your behind, or a million other things, terrible things, that were said to happen on adventures. Even a low-flying bird could pose a threat to one of Homer's stature!

Again Bags let the comment pass. They were in the Wilds, after all, and should take every step with measured caution. Bags could not believe that Homer, however inexperienced, would be so reckless as to run up all of a sudden, with not a hint of a warning. Shaking his head, he hoisted Homer to his feet, placed one of Homer's hands squarely on his hip, and told him to stay quiet and not let go for any reason.

A short time later, the wind kicked up and the fog thinned for just a moment. Bags was indeed relieved to see that the summit of the mountain, above them on the left, had grown much closer, though the sight only reminded Homer of his aversion to places higher than his top cupboard. Bags slapped his banger-chopper-thruster across his open palm and proclaimed, "This day'll see the end of our road!"

Homer glanced around nervously at the echoing blasts of the adventuresome halfling's cry. The ground was still soft, something quite out of the ordinary, or a bigger and thicker patch of moss than Homer had ever heard of. And Homer, most respectable, as I have said, understood well enough that "out of the ordinary" inevitably signaled trouble. But Bags, undaunted, pounded on, no longer giving his unusual surroundings a second thought. He wanted to get to the summit, find the stone, and get back to Tippin (and to thousands of gold pieces!).

When another wind gust thinned the mist again a few moments later, though, even determined Bags began to understand clearly that something was not as it should be and took pause. The mountaintop was still on their left, and still not high above them, but it was much farther away.

"How is this?" Homer cried, letting go of his companion and nearly swooning. He wandered right by Bags, eyes fixed on the curious sight, then caught himself after a moment and turned back, seeing the blue faerie light of Bags's enchanted weapon and, behind it, the shadow of the burly halfling.

"Take ye not another step," Bags whispered. Before Homer could begin to ask why, the end of a rope slapped into his chest and fell at his feet. "Tie it about yer waist," Bags instructed.

"Where are we?" Homer demanded in a high-pitched squeal, much like a pig that sees the farmer's cleaver and knows that a holiday meal is not far off. Homer was thinking that Bags knew something that he did not, and trying to catch up with the reasoning, he looked helplessly back in the direction of the mountaintop. The opaque veil had returned.

Bags walked by him then, again taking up the lead and starting out at a slow and cautious pace. He did indeed have his suspicions, but they seemed too outlandish to be taken seriously or to be shared at that time. "Keep yer steps right behind me own," he explained to his flustered companion.

"Steps?" Homer replied defiantly. "Confusticate your own steps!" Then he sat down, "Plop!" and crossed his soft arms over his chest, taking care to look dangerous and not to let his arms rest casually on his belly.

"Ye mean to sit there?" Bags asked, curious and somewhat amused.

"And if I do?"

"Then keep the rope," Bags said, beginning to loosen his end. "I'll come back for ye if I can, and if I cannot, well..."

Homer was up and moving, though grumbling with every step.

They went on slowly for a few minutes, and then Bags had his answers. He heard Homer shriek out and then the rope went taut so suddenly that it nearly pulled him from his feet. Bags stumbled forward and knew by the dropping angle of the line that he would soon join his companion in the fall. His dwarflike, corded muscles pulled hard, and luckily, he caught his balance in the nick of time. Then Bags scrambled along cautiously, following the lead to a hole in the spongy ground, or more particularly to a hole in the cloud island. Peering through the inconstant fog, he made out Homer's frantically flailing form, dangling free, a mile or two above the flat farmlands.

"Ahah!" Bags called at the confirmation that they were indeed on a cloud. "Now we're getting somewhere!"

"Getting?" Homer stuttered, barely able to breathe, let alone speak. Homer had thought adventures most unpleasant things before they had ever started out, if you remember. He had liked a soft hearth chair, or a hard kitchen chair, or the soft grass of a gentle hill beneath his bum. Now, hanging free, except for the pinching tight rope about his waist, he...well, you can imagine his face accurately enough, I should guess—eyes popping wide, mouth opening and closing weirdly to catch gulps of air, and a general expression that would make a respectable fellow shudder just to hear described about on another, much less wear himself.

For all of his complaining about Bagsnatcher Bracegirdle (and Homer would complain about that one till the end of his long days!), Homer was glad to have one so capable and strong beside him at that time. Bags pulled and hauled with all his strength, then caught hold of helpless Homer, who had come up upside down, by the toes and pulled him back onto the soft, but tangible ground.

"Where are we?" Homer finally demanded again

after several unsuccessful attempts to spit out any words.

"On a cloud," Bags replied calmly. "Haven't ye learned that yerself?"

Homer's reply came out once again as an undecipherable gurgle and he toppled, and would have gone through the hole again had Bags not caught him.

"A cloud," Bags explained when Homer awoke many minutes later, "with holes in it." He helped his reluctant companion, mostly by the threat of leaving him once again, unsteadily to his feet. "And drifting afar o' the mountain."

"Then where are we to go?" Homer demanded in a broken, squeaky voice.

Bags shrugged and started off. "Any way's as good as another," he muttered. "Just keep a firm hold on that rope!" Homer hardly needed to be reminded.

They had just started off across the bouncy surface when the fog cleared again briefly.

"Another mountain!" Homer cried hopefully, seeing a gigantic form rising before them. "Quickly, before the cloud drifts beyond it."

Bags wasn't in so much of a hurry. He, too, had seen the mound, but he wasn't so certain of Homer's identification. The One Mountain was so named because it was the only thing larger than a hillock for many, many miles. Homer trotted past him and continued on, though, and for all his strength, the burly fellow could hardly hope to slow his excited, and terrified, companion. He put his banger-chopper-thruster over one shoulder, just in case, and checked the knot of the rope around his waist. With Homer rushing along blindly, building so much momentum, Bags had to wonder what useful purpose the rope might serve if his companion flew headlong into a hole.

"Loyalties," the adventuresome Bags muttered and secured the knot.

The next time the wind thinned the mist, Homer skidded to an abrupt stop. Looming before him was no mountain, though certainly it was mountain-sized, but a castle, carved of smooth marble. Unable to tear his eyes from the spectacle, the stunned halfling lumbered on, coming to a stop before a door that stood fully twenty feet high.

"Not a dwarf's home," Bags remarked, coming up behind Homer.

Homer's glare showed that he did not enjoy the sarcasm. He reached up as high as he could and jumped, but came nowhere close to the crystal doorknob. Even so, Bags slapped him on the arm for the attempt.

"Once did a wise man note that often there be a better way to enter a giant's home than by the front door," Bags remarked. His simple logic reminded Homer of many things, most notably, the danger, and the timid fellow promptly slapped himself on the arm, just for good measure.

Bags started off then, around the base of the castle, pointedly giving a sharp tug on the rope as soon as the slack tightened. Halfway around the immense building, the companions found a high window.

"A better way in," Bags remarked with a wink and a smirk. When Homer realized his companion's intent, he cast a doubtful gaze and started quickly away, only to be dragged back, cursing ropes with every passing foot.

Short of stature and with plump hands, halflings are not the best of climbers. But though the blocks of the wall were well fitted by a giant's estimation, cracks that seemed tiny to the hands of a giant proved to be ample holds, even perches, for Bags. Just a few short minutes later, though Homer was still far below, Bags peeked in the great window. He had come to a bedroom, huge but nearly filled by a gigantic canopied bed, a desk that he could have used as a lean-to, and a wardrobe large enough to serve as a gathering hall for half of Inspirit Downs. A mural-sized painting hung on the wall opposite Bags, a marvelous work depicting handsome, blue-skinned giants dancing through the mist swirls of their cloud world.

When he was convinced that the room was empty, Bags swung in and secured the rope to a leg of the huge desk. Too amazed by the quality of the furnishings, he didn't wait for poor Homer to catch up. He crept up to the room's wooden door and cracked it open, looking out on a high and wide corridor of red-veined marble, lined by statues and paintings and lighted by a crystalline chandelier that glittered with a thousand candles. A second door stood across the way, a third twenty feet down the wall from that, and a fourth marked the end of the corridor, where it took a sharp bend.

Still seeing no signs of the castle's inhabitants, Bags crept back to the window. Homer sat frozen, twenty feet below, staring down into the mist and shaking his head in disbelief.

"Are ye coming then?" Bags called down to him.

"No," Homer replied evenly.

"Yes!" Bags corrected and he heaved and tugged on the rope until his reluctant companion was pulled to the windowsill. Still Homer did not move, not, that is, until Bags pointedly untied the knot about the desk leg and dropped the rope loosely to the floor.

"Have yerself a fine drop," the burly fellow said, and before he finished the statement, Homer was long past him, peering out the bedroom door. Bags promptly resecured the knot on the desk, just to keep their escape route open.

"Lots to check in here," Bags said, but Homer, suddenly entranced (now that he had solid footing again under him), was too busy staring at the hallway's magnificent chandelier to even hear him. Before he realized what he was doing, Homer had dropped the rope off his waist, slipped across the hallway, and put his ear to the closest door.

Footsteps—big footsteps.

But not from beyond the door, Homer realized, coming out of his enchantment. He looked down the corridor just as a tremendous boot appeared around the bend. Homer looked desperately back to the bedroom, but realized he couldn't make it without being seen, and realized that Bags wasn't close enough to help him this time. He pushed through the unknown door, hoping that no other giants waited within.

"Homer?" Bags called softly when he looked up from the desk drawer and realized that his companion had moved away. Too curious to worry, Bags scaled the huge desk, wondering why in the Nine Hells giants would need a desk. The size of the quill pen he found made him earnestly hope he never encountered the bird from which it had been plucked! Likewise, the ink well could have held enough ale to keep even Bags content for a month!

Other giant-sized artifacts littered the desktop and filled the central, topmost drawer, including a leather bag that seemed more suited to the hands of a man, or a halfling, than to a giant.

"Ho, ho, thee dost indeed speaketh simply theeee most marvelous things!" squealed a high-pitched, but undeniably giant voice from the hallway. That the giant could speak was enough of a surprise to Bags, but the dignified, almost haughty tone of the statement nearly floored the halfling. Remembering his immediate predicament, though, he snatched up the bag, swung down from the desk, and rushed to the wardrobe, diving inside.

"Wit is indeed a blessing of the gods," a deeper voice replied. Bags held his breath when he heard the two giants enter the room and close the wooden door behind them. A single, unnerving thought came into focus then: the rope.

He heard the bedsprings creak, and hoped that the giants would retire without noticing. He clutched his banger-chopper-thruster tightly, though, suspecting that he would soon have to put it to use. "Homer?" he asked quietly, suddenly remembering his companion.

The thought was stolen a second later though, in the boom of a giant's voice. "What ho!" called the deeper-voiced colossus. "Intruder!"

"Oh, dear," piped the higher voice—from the bed, Bags guessed. "Not now, I pray thee! Alert someone else and be done with it."

"That chicken-stealing . . ."

"Goose-stealing," the higher voice corrected.

"That goose-stealing peasant boy!" the deeper voice boomed. Bags followed the resounding thumps of the giant's footsteps to the desk and then to the window.

"Didst he retrieve the beans?" the higher voice squealed, almost in desperation. Bags looked down curiously at the beans in the bag and scratched his hairless face, wondering what marvelous artifact he might have stumbled upon. You or I in Bags's situation would have stayed put right then, and wisely so, and let the giants go off on their wild goose chase, or wild goose-stealer chase, as the case may be. But Bags was of a different mind-set than you or I, and most people and every halfling, too. Always was that rascal thinking of bards' songs and cunningly trapped treasure chests and other sorts of dangerous things, and at that moment, Bags was thinking too that he owed some loyalty to fragile Homer, wherever that one might be. The last thing on Bags's mind sitting in that dark wardrobe was sitting tight and letting events pass him by.

Now was the time for action.

At first, Homer thought he had jumped into a bear cave and it took his best effort not to rip out a revealing scream. As soon as he realized that the furs pressing in all about him were no longer attached to their original owners, Homer relaxed and pushed his way blindly through the long and narrow closet, and soon came to the other door on this side of the hallway. He cracked it open and looked back to the bedroom. The wooden door was closed, but Homer could still hear the giants speaking within. Should he go back and check things out? he wondered, remembering his companion. Homer realized then that he admired Bags, even if he did not particularly like him, and he boldly strengthened his resolve to go and see if he might help out. He straightened his belt, tucking his belly back under it, and almost took the first step.

But then, singing down the far end of the corridor caught Homer's attention, a song as sweet as a morning dove's, though obviously much louder. Also, a sweet fragrance wafted down to titter, tantalizingly, under Homer's nose, an aroma of springtime and newly blossomed flowers.

"Bags can handle them," the enchanted (and relieved) Homer told himself, and before his loyalty could argue back, his curiosity had his ear pressed against the far door in the hallway. The volume told him that the singer was probably a giant, but Homer had never heard of a lark, much less a giant, that could carry a tune so very well.

There was a keyhole high above him and, fortunately, a stately, high-backed chair against the wall beside the door. Homer glanced all about, then scrambled up the chair. Drawing one deep breath to steady himself, he peered in through the keyhole and saw . . . nothing.

"Confusticate it," Homer mumbled under his breath, for apparently the key was set into the lock on the other side.

He reached up cautiously and grasped the doorknob, meaning to use it for support as he slipped his hand inside the lock and fumbled about. Unknown to him, though, the door was not locked, and as soon as he leaned forward, the knob turned under his weight and the door swung in.

You can imagine the look on the giantess's face, sitting in her claw-footed bathtub with bubbles all about her a dozen feet from the door and staring back at the helpless halfling, dangling, kicking, from her doorknob. But you cannot, I assure you, fully appreciate the expression on Homer's face when the blue-skinned giantess, all spectacular, fresh-smelling, and abundantly curvy, eighteen feet of her, jumped up, twisting and moving her arms about in a futile attempt to cover her bigger-than-life, bigger-than-Homer's-wildest-dreams, naked body.

*   *   *

Bags took a deep breath and slapped his banger-chopper-thruster across his open palm. "The gods of battle be with me," he growled and burst through the door, hoping that his estimation of the giants' whereabouts would prove accurate.

The giantess, wearing a satiny, lace-trimmed peignoir, sprawled languidly across the bed; her companion stood at the window, leaning out and looking out for some clue as to the identity of the intruder.

Though he had spent many seasons in the Wilds, battling all sorts of nasty things, Bags had never before seen humanoids of this size. Fearlessly, the rugged halfling ignored the shock and followed through with his original battle plan. He charged the bed first, swatting out one, and then a second, canopy support with his banger. The heavy canopy dropped down on the reclining female like some giant net before she even had time to scream.

Bags paid her no more heed at that moment. He charged the other giant, arriving just as the towering humanoid spun about in surprise.

Bags barely knew where to hit the thing; it was simply too tall for him to hope of getting in a critical strike. Always ready to improvise, he slammed, again with the banger section, down on the giant's toes.

"YEEEEOWW!" the giant howled, and grasped at his foot and hopped up into the air. "You chicken-stealing..."

"Goose-stealing," came a muffled correction from under the canopy.

Bags wasn't hearing any of it. Now using his thruster, he charged ahead, driving the stooping giant backward. Unbalanced and too startled to respond, the giant recoiled, and tumbled out of the window. More agile than his size would indicate, the giant did manage to grab the rope as he fell, but his momentum was simply too great and the act only snapped off the desk leg securing the rope's other end, and it followed him in his drop.

Bags watched the giant plummet down into the misty shroud, then reappear above the fog for an instant on his first bounce. Thinking himself quite clever, the hobbit spun back toward the bed, spinning his weapon about to bring the chopper ominously to bear.

The giantess had risen and had managed to rip one of her arms through the canopy's cloth. But her thrashing had only tightened the cloth's hold on her and she stumbled and fell, hopelessly entangled.

Bags's warrior instincts told him to rush up and finish her. He might have done it, though the idea of killing a female, even a female giant, did not please him. Bags was no slaughtering warrior, no matter how he blustered about his adventures in the Floating Cloud in Inspirit Downs. He had always preferred the thieving style of adventuring; that way, no one really got hurt, least of all himself! Now he found himself in a dilemma, though. Could he dare to leave a giantess unharmed behind him? Before he could work things out, a shriek from down the hall caught his attention.

* * *

"Eeek! A mouse!" the naked giantess in the bathtub squealed. "Somebody step on it! Kill it! Kill it! Hit it with a broom!" She squirmed and twisted, kicking up bubbles every which way.

Homer had not lived an adventurous life, but in The World, so full of spice and variety, he had witnessed (or thought he had witnessed) many wondrous spectacles. But the flummoxed fellow had never seen anything to match the magnificence of the sight before him now. He tried to babble out an apology for his intrusion, or a warning for the giantess to be silent, or anything at all.

Whatever he was trying to say, the giantess could only guess, for his words came out as simply, "Hummina hummina."

While Homer hung transfixed from the crystal doorknob, the giantess leapt into action. She scrambled out the back side of the tub and grasped it in her huge hands. Giant muscles corded and flexed (and poor Homer verily swooned at the sight, dropping down to the floor and barely holding his balance) as the great lady hoisted the side of the tub.

Hundreds of gallons of soapy water poured out under Homer, knocking him from his feet.

The snarling giantess came on, flipping the tub right over the prone Homer. Then, though he couldn't have hoped to lift the tub anyway, the giantess sat down atop it and started calling for her husband.

Hopelessly trapped, Homer just rolled to a sitting position in the soapy puddle and put his back to the side of the tub. He should have been thinking of a plan of action, but he could not shake the image of the giantess, of the suds rolling wide and long around her curves.

"Coming, Homer!" Bags roared, charging down the corridor, his banger-chopper-thruster waving high above his head, readied to throw.

"Oh, dear," the giantess replied to the yell, and she rolled off the far side of the tub just as the wild-eyed halfling loosed his weapon.

Bag's aim was almost always perfect, but he, too, became a bit distracted at the sight of the naked and soapy giantess, and the throw came in just a tad low. The heavy weapon slammed into the side of the metal bathtub with a resounding "BOOOOING!" A stunning, deafening peal that shook even the incredible image of the giantess from the mind of poor Horatio Hairfoot.

Unable to slow on the slick floor, Bags slid in heavily against the tub. His weapon lay on the ground beside him and he quickly scooped it up. Seeing the frantic, and embarrassed, giantess making no move toward him, and guessing the fate of his reluctant companion, Bags slipped the thruster part under the edge of the tub. With a great heave, Bags brought the side up and Homer, recognizing the scruffy, fur-lined boots of his rescuer, quickly scrambled out.

"Are you unharmed?" Bags asked, truly concerned.

"Huh?" was Homer's reply. He wiggled a slender finger into his still-vibrating ear.

Alarms rang out all through the castle. In the doorway down the other end of the first corridor appeared the tangled giantess, dragging the bed behind, and the thunder of a dozen giant boots resounded down the corridor to the side of the bathroom.

"Run away!" Homer cried. He looked around, confused, at how distant his own words sounded.

"But we're heroes, lad!" Bags protested. "Run? From mere giants? Whate'er might the bards write?"

Though Homer, again wiggling a finger in his ear, could hardly hear his companion, he read Bags's lips well enough to understand the protest. "Our epitaphs," he remarked, then he was off. He stopped at the bathroom door, though, and turned back to the huddled giantess. Again wanting only to apologize, Homer managed to utter, "Thank you."

The giantess crinkled her surprisingly delicate features, covered herself as best she could, and looked around for a broom.

Bags came into the corridor casting a scornful glare at the back of his retreating companion. "Heroes!" he muttered grimly, and he set his feet firmly and stared down the side passage, his banger-chopper-thruster waving menacingly.

Then a half-dozen eighteen-foot-tall (and nearly as wide), blue-skinned giants, wielding the biggest swords and clubs that Bags had ever seen, appeared from around another bend.

"To Hell with the bards!" Bags gasped and he set off after Homer, whose respectability so suddenly seemed an admirable trait.

"Oh, no, you don't!" the bed-dragging giantess sneered at Homer. The deafened fellow barely heard her, but words didn't seem necessary at that moment. The giantess rushed out from the bedroom and Homer recoiled.

The bed caught sideways in the door, abruptly ending the giantess's charge. The remaining canopy supports snapped off after the initial jolt, and the giantess tumbled headlong. Homer took off at once. He leapt atop the back of the giantess and ran right over her, scrambling and diving over and around the blocking bed.

Bags came next, leaping the prone giant in a single bound, then dipping a shoulder and bowling right into the bed. He promptly bounced off and landed on his butt in the middle of the hallway. Growling in defiance, the halfling took up his weapon and charged headlong, tearing and chopping wildly.

"Finesse," Homer remarked sarcastically when his companion crashed through amid a snowstorm of feathery mattress filling.

"Finesse, Bagsnatcher style!" Bags promptly and proudly replied without missing a beat.

"The rope?" Homer asked, noticing the broken desk and the missing leg.

Bags shrugged helplessly and charged to the window, scrambling up to the sill, the thunder of giant boots fast approaching the doorway behind him.

"Climb?" asked Homer, terrified, but moving up to join his companion.

"Sort of," Bags tried to explain. Thinking an action worth a thousand words (and not having the time for a thousand words), he grabbed Homer by the collar and heaved him over and out. Then Bags leapt after his dropping companion, hoping the cloud to be as pillowy as he remembered.

"I will pay you back for that one day!" Homer, puffing angrily, promised fiercely when he and Bags had finally stopped bouncing. Bags let the threat go without reply, not having the time to pause and debate the issue just then.

Great horns sounded all throughout the giant castle.

"Where do we go?" Homer, suddenly timid again, cried.

Bags threw his hands out wide and ran off into the mist. "Any way," he answered as the castle disappeared into the fog behind them. "Just beware of..."

"Holes!" Homer cried, and Bags spun about just as Homer dropped from sight. The adventurous fellow dove to his belly, thinking his companion doomed.

But fat little fingers, grasping wildly at the edge of cloud stuff, showed Bags differently. "Holes," he agreed, hoisting Homer back up to the cloud.

"Long way down," Homer remarked weakly, trying futilely to smile.

"But sure it be a beautiful day!" Bags replied, trying to brighten things up.

Homer was glad to realize that his hearing had returned, but he really didn't appreciate Bags's lame attempt at levity, not with a horde of angry giants chasing them! "But how are we to escape?" he asked.

"There must be some way," Bags replied, turning serious. "Might that the cloud'll find the top of another mountain." He looked back toward the castle. "Or might it be that the giants possess something...

"Beans!" Bags cried suddenly.

"Beans?"

Bags produced the leather bag and waved it at Homer's uncomprehending stare. Then, as Bags revealed the small sack's contents and handed one bean to Homer, Homer's expression turned curious. Legends of the properties of magical beans were not so uncommon.

"Surely, it cannot..." Homer began, but now the giants had apparently come out of the castle and the cry of "Release the beast!" took away any logical protests he might have had.

"Plant it!" Bags yelled at Homer.

Homer dropped a bean onto the cloud and stood back, seeming confused.

"Not on the cloud!" Bags cried.

"Over here!" yelled a giant, homing in.

"Then where?" Homer pleaded, positively flummoxed.

Bags dropped to his knees and blew with all his breath, waving his hands as he did to try to clear away the fog. "Down here," he explained, pointing into the hole.

Homer dropped down and peered through the hole, nearly swooning from the dizzying height. Far, far below, the farmlands of Windydale, a human settlement on the back side of the One Mountain, east of Inspirit Downs, loomed lush and green.

"Down there?" Homer asked, unbelieving.

Bags nodded frantically.

"But the prevailing winds," Homer protested. "And the drift of the cloud, combined with the time-lapse of the falling bean..."

Bags shot Homer his most incredulous look, and the helpless halfling shrugged and dropped the bean. It plummeted from sight, lost in the wide view of the wide world.

"Sneaking rats!" boomed a giant. The companions jumped up and spun around to find themselves helplessly surrounded by a dozen armed and armored giant warriors.

A long moment of uneasy silence passed as the two sides took a measure of each other.

"So what d'ye think the bards'll put in our epitaphs?" Bags asked Homer offhandedly.

The giants started to circle, gradually closing in. Suddenly, though, the cloud began to shake violently. Barely able to keep their footing, the giants and the companions watched in amazement as a huge green stalk burst up through the hole and rolled up lazily into the air.

"Beans!" Bags and Homer shouted together, and not waiting to hold a lengthy discussion over their good fortunes, they sprang onto the beanstalk and slipped down under the cloudy fog.

Their descent was rapid, but their troubles were far from over. A brave giant started down after them, and even more disturbing, "the beast" soon appeared under the far rim of the cloud.

"Now I'm knowing where they get their writing utensils," Bags muttered grimly when the gigantic, eaglelike bird, with talons suitable for snatching full-grown cattle, swooped into view, bearing the largest giant of all, and still another giant warrior besides that, on its black-feathered back.

The monstrous bird rushed past the friends, the wind of its great wings nearly pulling them from their tentative perch.

Farmer Griswald Son-o'-Jack was not very happy when the magical beanstalk roared up and overturned his chicken coop, sending his prized hens fluttering in every direction. Nor was Griswald overly surprised, certainly not as surprised as you or I might have been, for he had heard of such trouble-bringing plants in his day—from his father, repeatedly, when he was a young boy. Indeed, there was a saying among Griswald's family, founded on solid experience, so it's said:

> *Cows for beans is folly;*
> *Sow's ear, no purse of silk.*
> *Better off to keep the cow*
> *and barter with the milk.*

That was a pretty common saying among the farmers in those lands in those days, and a pretty respectable one as well (since trading a valuable cow for beans usually will lead one to woe).

Griswald looked up at the sky, where the stalk disappeared into a cloud and where the outline of a huge bird could be seen rushing back and forth past it.

Griswald's farmhands appeared then, bearing axes and knowing what must be done. On a nod from their boss, they set to chopping.

The largest giant, driving the huge eagle, swooped the bird in low beneath the companions, and his lesser giant companion sprang out into the beanstalk.

"The way is blocked!" Homer cried, looking down at the formidable obstacle, and then up again to the descending giant above.

"Not for long," Bags promised. He put his back to the stem and found a secure foothold. Then he took aim with his banger-chopper-thruster, putting it in line with the blocking giant's head.

Looking up at the wild fires burning in the halfling's blue eyes, the giant realized the potential for some serious pain. "Please, good gentlesir, do not do that," he begged.

"Hold yer words, foul giant!" Bags roared, acting the hero once again. "Brave are ye in advantage, but ye've not reckoned with the likes of Bagsnatcher Bracegirdle, son o' Brunhilda Bracegirdle! Know that yer evil heart'll beat no more!"

"Evil!" cried the largest giant as the eagle swooped by yet another time. "Why, I take that as a most uncalled-for insult!"

"Give it to them good, King Cumulonimbus!" yelled the giant on the stalk high above.

"But you, diminutive one," the eagle-rider continued. "I see well enough what demeanor your most harsh actions bespeak! Whilst I admit curiosity as to how two halflings (for that is what you are, I believe) might"—his voice faded and then came again a moment later as the eagle banked through a wide and distant turn—"I'll not wait to hear your lies!" The great bird came in again, and now the king leveled a barbed lance at poor, shivering Homer.

"Ye're a giant!" Bags huffed, unafraid—of course, the lance wasn't aimed at him. "Thus are ye marked as evil!"

"Er, Bagsnatcher," interjected Homer, looking pointedly at the point. "Perhaps this is not the time for name-calling." Homer thought his suggestion an excellent one, and indeed it was, but his whisper was lost in the continuing banter between the blustery halfling and the giant king.

"We most certainly are not!" the giant roared. "But thou hast come to us as thieves! Thus I proclaim you to be evil!"

"I am not!" Bags shouted back, stamping his foot against the beanstalk, which nearly dislodged him. With a mighty heave—for a halfling—of his free arm, Bags sent his banger-chopper-thruster head over handle at the approaching menaces. The weapon caught the eagle square in the head, and the bird squawked out a piercing cry and spiraled out of control.

The giant king, suddenly losing all interest in

spearing the halfling, dropped his lance and leapt out, catching the beanstalk in a tentative hold just above his lowest companion, between the giant and poor Homer.

If big King Cumulonimbus had any intention of parlaying, or of attacking, at that point, his words were lost in the first shudders of the blows from the farmer's axes.

The giant looked around pleadingly at the trail of black feathers, but the great eagle was not to be found.

"Not evil?" Homer asked the king.

"Nor are you?" Cumulonimbus, clutching more desperately now, replied hopefully.

"Pray, might I suggest that we carry on this conversation back up at the cloud?" called the highest giant, who had already begun his ascent. The stalk creaked in protest as the farmer's axes continued their work.

Homer abruptly shifted his posture and looked for handholds above him. Hearing a growl to the side, he turned to see Bags, now with a knife between his teeth, working his way down toward the giant king.

"Lef the bards seft their phens to pharchmenth!" the wild-eyed fellow lisped. "Vhat gwories we'll be findin' dis day!"

"Shut up, Bags!" Homer snapped. "And put the knife away!"

Bags cast a wounded glance at his companion. "Dey're giants," he argued around the knife blade.

"An' giants er ephil thins. We must vanquisht dem—rule oft heroes!"

As if in response, the stalk suddenly rolled out wide.

"Polly!" screamed the giant king. The eagle swooped out of a nearby cloud, meaning to come to the call of its master. But the bird hesitated when it saw the warrior, now secure in his footing and holding the tip of a readied throwing knife.

"Come on, birdie!" he roared.

"Shut up, Bags!" both Homer and King Cumulonimbus yelled together. "And put the knife away!"

Bags looked doubtfully at Homer and at the giant king. On his adventures in the Wilds, Bags had learned a simple rule concerning monsters from which he could not flee: kill them before they kill you. But with the beanstalk obviously heading down, that rule somehow simply didn't seem to apply. With an embarrassed shrug, Bags stuffed the knife back between his teeth.

The eagle glided in.

"Might I offer thee the hospitality of my table?" King Cumulonimbus said to the companions as he and the other giant sprang out onto the great bird's back. The third giant had already disappeared back up through the mist of the cloud. "Please. Thou must come and meet my beautiful wife, Queen Cirrostratus."

Homer, a sudden sparkle in his eyes, looked hopefully over to Bags.

"I'll not dine wif giants!" the stubborn fellow protested around the steel-bladed knife. The beanstalk creaked and fell.

"I shall see that those words are etched on your epitaph!" Homer promised as he tumbled. King Cumulonimbus caught him by the toes and pulled him on the bird.

"Epitaph," Bags muttered, spitting out the knife as he plummeted. "Sure that I'm beginning to hate that word."

They caught him about a mile down. Out of breath, Bags offered no speech of gratitude when he climbed onto the eagle's back to take a seat between Homer and the two giants.

But neither did he waggle his little fist in protest.

"And could you later set us down back on that mountain?" Homer was asking, pointing off into the distance. "A little mission concerning a certain stone, you know."

"Oh, the heart stone," replied King Cumulonimbus. "Only a rumor, of course. We only just inquired into it ourselves."

"Of course," said the other giant, noting the incredulous stares they exchanged. "Why else would we come in so low, where any vermin might..."

The murderous look that came immediately to the sturdy fellow's eyes stuck the words right in the callous giant's throat. "Where any noble adventurers," he prudently corrected, "might wander onto our cloud?"

"Then no sense'n going back to the mountain." Bags beamed, suddenly remembering his waiting bride and willing to put aside all of his stubborn prejudices concerning the giants. What a tale he'd have to tell in the Floating Cloud that night! "Right after supper, then, ye can put us down in Inspirit Downs, thank ye, the town on th'other side of the mountain."

But Homer wasn't so certain that they would be getting back so soon. He had a hunch that he had already met King Cumulonimbus's wife and if his suspicions held true, Homer figured that he could spend a week, at least, just enjoying her company.

If your travels of The World ever bring you near to Inspirit Downs, you might consider stopping in to hear the tale of the cloud giants told one more time. Don't go to the Floating Cloud, though, to hear Bagsnatcher's nightly recounting. That fellow's as full of bluster as ever, and his tales of his heroic struggles in the castle are lengthy and boring, and ultimately untrue.

You might find Horatio, though, sitting on the side of a hill, shooting smoke rings up at passing clouds. They don't call him Homer anymore in Inspirit Downs, and hardly ever refer to him as "most respectable." Not that Horatio minds; the memories, he figures, one in particular, are well worth the dent in his reputation.

A few kind words and a block of pipeweed should get Mr. Hairfoot to tell you about his one great adventure, and he'll tell it pretty well (though he won't go into details about the giant queen and the claw-legged bathtub; he's too much the gentle fellow for that!). You should be able to imagine that part well enough for yourself, though, by the depth of the sparkle that inevitably comes to Horatio's eyes.

A Fumbling of Fairies

Craig Shaw Gardner

Craig Shaw Gardner, bestselling author of movie
tie-ins and funny fantasies, has blessed us with a
brand-new Ebenezum story, which goes to show that
in addition to heroes, sometimes the weefolk
can be a real pain as well.

1

"There are times in a magician's career when the results
of a conjuring are not exactly what that magician expected.
When this inevitably occurs, there are certain points of
etiquette that should be observed. Firstly, it is generally
considered very bad form to scream and run in terror,
especially in front of your client. Secondly, the professional
mage should act as if whatever has just occurred is exactly
what was intended in the first place, while that same mage
is hastily performing whatever additional magic is required
to reverse that which has already occurred. And, lastly,
whatever the nature of this unexplained occurrence, your
client should, of course, be charged extra for its appearance."

—from *The Teachings of Ebenezum*, Volume I

This was not going at all the way it was supposed to. Richard the giant meant well, really he did. But, as I'm afraid I had learned from far too much personal experience as a wizard's apprentice, meaning well and doing well were entirely different things.

"Oops," the giant uttered once again. This time, at least, he had only tripped over his extremely large feet and hadn't managed to crush any more of the scenery or miscellaneous stagehands.

But the giant had a greater problem than his own clumsiness. Alea, that strikingly beautiful veteran of the recently disbanded dance team of Damsel and Dragon, would not be so easily defeated. She studied her new song-and-dance partner (the team was now "A Giant and a Girl") with her cool blue gaze, a look that had caused far greater men than mere giants to fall.

"Once more, Richard." She brushed her perfect blond hair away from her face and waved wearily at the pit before the stage, where half a dozen musicians held their lutes and lyres at the ready. "From the top, maestro?"

The musicians began to play again, more or less at the same time.

"Oh," Richard mumbled after a moment's pause. "That is my cue. See? I know my cue."

Alea did not appear unduly impressed.

Richard shrugged and began to sing.

"Fo Fi Fum Fee,
Won't you come and dance with me?"

*   *   *

With that, Alea made a high-pitched noise that might be taken for a cry of fright if her voice was not so melodious. She thereupon danced so nimbly across the stage that one might barely even notice the twisted ankle she had sustained somewhat earlier in the rehearsal. She flashed her dazzling smile and sang in turn:

"Oh, good sir, you gave me a start,
But a man your size must have a giant heart."

The music plodded brightly onward until Richard realized it was once again his turn. "Oh, yeah," he murmured, and then sang the following:

"Fee Fi Fo Foo,
I've got love enough for two!"

With that, Richard attempted the most rudimentary of dance steps. Unfortunately, the most rudimentary of dance steps was far beyond his ability.

"Oops!" Richard screamed.

The musicians scattered as the giant fell forward into the pit. All seemed to escape serious injury thanks to Richard's warning shout, although a couple of the chairs they had left behind were reduced to kindling.

Alea sighed as she observed the wreckage. "I think now would be a good time to take a few minutes rest. Shall we resume the rehearsal in a quarter hour?"

There were no objections, either from the frazzled musicians or the prostrate giant.

"Very well," Alea stated with authority. "Fifteen minutes it is, then." Her cool blue eyes flitted from the giant to the orchestra. "And when we resume our number, we *aren't* going to leave here until it's perfect." She smiled sweetly at all her fellow workers. "That's what we all want, isn't it?"

The musicians grumbled agreement and obligingly disappeared as Richard struggled to arise. But Alea had put her act behind her for the nonce, for I saw that her long-(and very attractive) legged stride was directed straight at me.

"Oh, Wuntie," she cried in beautiful despair. "Never have I known anything to be this impossible!"

I decided that impossible was as good a description as any for the demonstration I had just seen. I started to form a reply about how I had never realized how much work went into the preparation of a variety act. But before I could get the first word completely from my mouth, I found Alea's hands upon my shoulders, and her face mere inches from my own.

"My dearest Wuntvor," she said softly, her words little more than a low whisper. "It is such a comfort to have you here." Her hands left my shoulders and slowly moved behind my neck. "Even though you are a wizard's apprentice, and have seen vast portions of this world and countless other realms as well, somehow you remain unspoiled, as if you had barely left your father's farm."

Unspoiled? I frowned at the thought. Even though

I now resided in Vushta, the self-proclaimed City of a Thousand Forbidden Delights, and even though dear Norei—the young witch who was my own true love— dear yet very busy Norei, was here as well, I was all too afraid that Alea was correct. It was perhaps my fate to remain unspoiled, no matter what I tried.

"My little Wuntola." Alea sighed and managed to shift her body so that even more of her weight rested against me. "This is the first moment that I have felt truly relaxed!"

I cleared my throat. My little Wuntola? I could feel her sweet breath against my cheek. And wasn't it getting awfully hot in here?

"In-indeed," I somehow managed through my difficulty.

But things were to become more difficult, still, for not only was her face close to me, but she was pouting as well. I had to admit it. Alea looked absolutely breathtaking when she pouted.

"Don't you feel sorry for me, Wuntie? Mean old Richard is *so* clumsy." She thrust her leg against mine and pointed down toward her foot. "He made me hurt my little ankle."

I glanced quickly away from where she had pointed. My mouth was too dry to swallow. Really, Alea meant nothing to me at all. She did have an awfully attractive ankle, though.

I found myself pressed against one of the backstage walls. She seemed to be leaning almost all her weight on me now. Perhaps her ankle hurt her so much she was forced into such a position. Her large blue eyes were very close to mine. "Perhaps I was too hasty embarking upon this new career." With a rustle of velvet, she somehow moved even closer to me. "You cannot stand still, you know, once you have ventured upon the stage." If her weight shifted any nearer, I would be carrying her. "Still," she sighed, "taking a giant for a partner may have been a bad career move. Hubert was so sweet, especially for a dragon, but he was off adventuring, with not a thought about how I'd put bread on the table. Could anyone blame me? I was looking for new vistas. New challenges." She glanced back down at her ankle, and my gaze was forced to follow. Her pale and delicate skin was turning a very becoming shade of blue. "Could I somehow have been mistaken?"

My mind raced, trying to think of something positive to say about the rehearsal. "Um, the band is very lively."

"You do appreciate the finer things." She nodded wearily at my compliment. "If only I were not so sore"—she paused so that I might better see the misery in her eyes—"all over." Her red lips pouted ever closer toward my own. This close, I had to admit that her pout was not only attractive, it was magnificent. She rubbed her ankle softly against my legging. "Oh, Wuntie. If you could only kiss it and make it better!"

This time, I managed a cough. "Your—your ankle?"

"Perhaps I am asking too much." Her cool eyes

looked heavenward, as if this was all too great a burden for her. "But there are far many more sore spots than my poor ankle." She pulled at the top of her dress to reveal the flesh beneath. "I think I wrenched my shoulder."

Even I, unspoiled apprentice that I was, had to admit it was an awfully enchanting shoulder. I did not trust myself, in my present state, to even examine her ankle. But the shoulder, well, perhaps that was another matter entirely. What would be the harm of a little brotherly kiss?

I leaned forward to do Alea's bidding.

"Wuntvor?"

The second woman's voice broke my concentration. I would recognize that voice anywhere.

Norei.

I lurched forward.

Norei, my true beloved, my very busy beloved, who hardly ever visited me.

I shifted my feet, desperate to maintain my balance.

Norei, who might not immediately understand the present circumstances. I had to get support immediately, or I would entirely lose my balance.

Alea was available. My arms went around her.

"Oops!" I cried.

"Let me know," Norei added, "if I'm interrupting anything!"

How did I manage to get into these positions? Such things, somehow, seemed to be the lot of my life as an apprentice, which perhaps wasn't so unspoiled after all. And once this sort of situation presented itself, well, suffice it to say that I now waited for some exclamation of even greater magnitude, from Norei or Alea or both.

But I heard nothing from either of them. In fact, I heard nothing at all except for a high trilling sound; so high was the noise, in fact, that I was barely aware that I was hearing it, until I saw *her*.

At first, I only noticed the darkness, as if a haze had surrounded every candle flame set in the embrasures around the theater's perimeter. And then, at the very rear of the theater, I saw the single point of brilliant light. In that light there stood a young woman, dressed in a gossamer gown the color of a springtime sky.

In the instant I saw her, I heard a voice, with my mind more than my ears, a lilting voice that made even Alea's speech seem common, and that voice spoke but three words.

"There you are."

Somehow I was quite certain she was talking about me.

She seemed at first to be far away, as if this theater I was in had somehow magically become three times as large as it had been before. It took me a minute to realize that she was not really that far away, for although she had the shape and proportions of a full-grown woman, she was in actuality very small.

She waved.

The whole world trilled around me, as if her movements were accompanied by a chorus of invisible bluebirds. She stepped forward, and the chairs obligingly moved out of the way, clearing an aisle for her passage.

I could not take my eyes off this tiny but perfect presence. Just as a pane of glass might shake with the intensity of a choral note, I noticed that her musical accompaniment seemed to find a sympathetic vibration within my heart. And if the breathlessness I sometimes felt around Alea was somehow like running into a doorknob with my stomach, I now felt as if a horse had kicked me full in the chest.

As she came closer I could discern her fine, symmetrical features, beneath a great crown of hair that it would be inadequate to describe as yellow or even golden, for it was more the exact shade of sunlight, with all the colors of creation hidden within the almost white.

But she was not content to merely show off her beautiful tresses. She flung out handfuls of magic dust that lit her way through the darkened amphitheater. The dust glittered blue and pink and yellow as it fell at her feet.

And as she approached, I once again heard that voice within my mind. "What is your name?" Even though she walked through a darkened theater, her hair glowed with that certain quality of light that you get reflected off a spiderweb immediately after a rainstorm.

My lips were frozen in wonder. If I could somehow remember how to open my mouth, I knew I would have forgotten the true purpose of my tongue.

"No, don't tell me," the magic voice continued

with great amusement. "Your name has been spoken recently. It still hangs about in the air. Wuntie?" I could see a frown form upon the perfect little face that still approached me. Could she read my very thoughts? Was she not only beautiful, but all-knowing as well?

"No, that's not quite it." Her beautiful smile returned. "Ah. I have it. My little Wuntola!"

Oh, I thought. Perhaps she wasn't quite as all-knowing as I imagined. But I still had to admit that her lighting was superb.

But, somehow, with that realization that she might have the slightest imperfection, I found my voice as well. "Um," I replied. "Who, or what, precisely are you?"

"I am a fairy, of course. Could anyone else be so perfect?" Her laugh was like a gentle waterfall upon a warm summer's day. "My true name is very difficult for humans."

"Ah," I replied, certain that I understood. "It is in the fairy tongue, and impossible for humans to pronounce."

Her tiny yet perfect smile took my breath away. "No, silly. It is in the fairy tongue, and is impossible for humans to remember. My true name is Lalalilly-lololoobaloobashebangshebang."

"I see what you mean," I replied, truly impressed.

"Such is the fairy's lot." She shook her head, the vision of sadness. "But you may call me La."

"La," I repeated, the syllable springing from my lips.

"See? That wasn't so hard. Now I have something else for your lips to do."

Her head bobbed, and she frowned then, and I realized that she might have stumbled ever so slightly on the uneven floor of the theater. It occurred to me how difficult it must be to walk properly in a floor-length gossamer gown.

But something else had changed. Not only was she closer, but she seemed to be much more my size than before. Was she growing? Was I shrinking? Had the theater really grown to three times its original size? None of those possibilities seemed to matter as her lips grew ever closer to mine.

This time, her mouth opened, and I knew her lips would form my name.

"My little Wuntola."

Well, almost my name. Wait a second. I was looking up at her now. Wasn't this growth or shrinking or relative size of the theater thing getting a little out of hand?

"Oh, dear," she whispered. "I seem to have misjudged. Quick, grab my hand before I get away!"

Get away? What did that mean? I reached for her hand anyway.

Somehow, her hand missed mine entirely.

"Oops!" she cried.

The world seemed to be filled with fairy dust.

And then all was darkness.

2

"Even the most knowledgeable wizard is not immune from the occasional physical attraction. Wizardry is,

after all, an occupation full of danger and stress, so that it should only make sense that the mage might need to look outside his or her occupation for the occasional dalliance or even romance, so that the wizard might experience danger and stress from another quarter entirely."
—from *Megamagic: Better Wizardry and a Better Life,* by Ebenezum, the Greatest Wizard in the Western Kingdoms, (fourth edition)

I opened my eyes. I remembered feeling like I was drowning, or lost beneath an avalanche. There, staring down at me with beautiful concern, was Norei, my own true love.

"What happened?" I whispered.

"So far as I can ascertain," my beloved replied in her usual no-nonsense manner, "you were almost smothered when a giant fairy collapsed on top of you."

"A giant—fairy?" I replied, trying to comprehend.

"She was really big," Richard agreed gleefully. "Made me look tiny. Almost took the top off the theater."

"You mean Lalalilly—" I paused in confusion. The fairy was right. I couldn't remember her name, except there was something like an explosion toward the end. "But she was tiny!"

"The correct word in that sentence is 'was,'" another extremely sarcastic voice added. I turned my head to see the sickly green form of Snarks, a demon who was compelled to tell the truth, no matter what the cost, but an ally in my recent battle with Death.

"By the time we got in here, that fairy was as big as your average castle!"

"We?" I asked, still attempting to gain my bearings.

"Doom," remarked another dour voice belonging to the immense warrior Hendrek. "Snarks and I ran in as soon as we heard the crash."

"It was a big noise!" Richard agreed cheerfully. "Made my feet sound quiet!"

"A crash? But Lala—I mean La—was petite."

"Apparently," Norei explained patiently, "when she changed her size, other things changed as well. She quite simply lost her balance."

"She was so clumsy," Richard agreed heartily, "made me look like a dancer."

"I don't know if I'd go that far," Alea interrupted. "Still, it was pretty amazing. We'll have to get a whole new set of chairs in this place." She leaned down to take a closer look at me. "It's a miracle that you escaped unharmed."

Norei cleared her throat. "Don't you think we should give Wuntvor some room? He's had a harrowing experience."

Dear Norei! It was so wonderful to hear her concern.

"You, of course," interjected Snarks in the most doleful of tones, "do realize the implications of what has so recently transpired."

"Doom?" Hendrek remarked, obviously wishing to hear more.

"A creature as clumsy as Wuntvor?" Snarks elucidated. "Even worse, a *magical* creature who is as clumsy as Wuntvor? The entire world shall tremble."

"Doom," Hendrek agreed.

It was truly a sobering thought. That lovely creature was as clumsy as I? I felt a small shiver run up my spine. Perhaps La and I were truly meant for each other.

But my thoughts were interrupted by a familiar sneeze; a sneeze I hadn't heard in weeks.

"Wuntvor!" called the voice of my master, the great wizard Ebenezum. "What is the meaning of this?"

Snarks pulled his hood back over his head while the warrior Hendrek self-consciously checked that his enchanted weapon was properly sheathed.

Some weeks before, my master had had a confrontation with the dread rhyming demon Guxx Unfufadoo. He had defeated the fiend in the end, but the fight was not without its cost. From that moment forward, whenever Ebenezum was in the presence of magic of any sort, he began to sneeze.

We had therefore come to Vushta, the City of a Thousand Forbidden Delights, in order to seek a cure. But though many cures had been attempted, none had been successful thus far. But my master did not recognize defeat. He decided, if he could not remedy his malady instantaneously, he would increase his resistance to sorcery in a gradual fashion. Thus it was that he regularly brought himself into contact with the demon Snarks, or Hendrek's doomed warclub Headbasher, so that he might withstand the presence of either of them for a full five minutes, and suffer little more than clogged nasal passages.

This procedure seemed to be having some positive result, then, until now. I said but a single word to my master, who, after repeated sneezes, now looked down upon his soaking handkerchief as if that piece of cloth had betrayed him.

"Well?" my master prompted.

"Fairies," was my response.

"A new source of magic?" the usually dynamic Ebenezum muttered. "And I am back where I began."

I told my master that I was sorry to see this setback in his therapy.

"Indeed." He answered me with a deep sigh, so different from his usual air of self-possession. "It is slow work, and many is the time that I fear I shall never be rid of it. I am afraid that my malady knows no cure; at least with whatever human magic I and indeed all of Vushta might be able to muster."

He turned away from us then, as if too depressed to even be among his fellows. And, indeed, I could appreciate his despair. For if all human magic would fail, where could he possibly find a remedy?

My master strode rapidly from the theater, and I hurried to follow, though I had no idea how I might help the wizard to escape his present state and temperament. But my thoughts were interrupted yet again, the moment I stepped from the building into the late-afternoon sun.

"Wuntvor," that very familiar, very enticing female voice said in my mind. "Then that is your name?"

I stopped short, my mind no longer upon my master. "In-indeed" was my eventual reply.

But the fairy was nowhere to be seen. Yet the very air seemed to giggle around me.

"La!" I called out. "Where are you?"

"Here, silly," came the reply as she stepped forward from what I first thought was a group of shadows, but soon realized was the mottled wall of a building. And she had changed again. Instead of being very tiny, or very large, she was almost exactly my size.

"I think I've gotten the hang of the growth spell," she confessed with the most enchanting smile imaginable. "Now I want to get the hang of you."

I babbled something about how I often found spells difficult. My hands and arms didn't seem to notice my discomfort, however, for I found that I had swung them wide to accept La in my embrace.

"Ah, yes," she whispered as my arms enclosed her. "This is where I want to be, at least for starters."

Once again, I wondered how I got myself into this position. I found my nose in her hair. It smelled wonderfully, like flowers in early spring. Then again, I have often found myself in much worse positions.

"There is something about you, Wuntvor—what an odd name that is. No doubt we can change it later." She giggled. It was a wonderful sound. "While you are largely human, there is a certain otherworldliness about you that I find interesting—an otherworldliness I should like to explore."

I blinked. What was that she was saying? The flowers were so wonderful. And she was so close, and so warm. Anything she wanted to do was fine with me.

"Together," she whispered close to my ear, "we could make magic together."

Magic? I blinked. This must be magic that made me feel this way. Not that this fairy wasn't attractive; oh, she was more than attractive. But I had a duty to my master, who still hadn't found a cure to his malady.

And then the thought came to me with the suddenness of summer thunder. If fairy magic was so new and strange that my master still reacted to it, maybe that fairy magic had some extra power to it that we had not yet explored, some power that could cure Ebenezum where human magic had failed.

"La?" I asked, managing to find my voice for so important a question. "Might you do me a favor?"

"Anything you desire," she replied, "for you will soon do something for me." Her agreement made me feel all warm and tingling, as if I never wanted to be anywhere but with the lovely La. I would tell her about Ebenezum's malady, oh, in another moment or two.

She looked me straight in the eye. Her eyes were bluer than blue, and highlighted with tiny flecks of gold. "I will do this little service for you," she said softly, and her breath was like the most caressing of spring breezes. "Then, of course, you'll have to come back to fairyland and live with me there forever, but let's not talk about that now. Let's kiss."

I decided that sounded like a good idea.

Our lips met, and I could feel that kiss not just with my mouth, but with my entire being.

I broke away to catch my breath.

"More," La commanded. What could I do but obey?

"I shall make these kisses such that you shall never forget," she added as our lips joined again. And, indeed, it was more than flesh upon flesh. It felt more like our lips intermingled, and our tongues knew each where the other one would be at every minute, and then, no matter which way I turned, it seemed as if La's lips were everywhere, and I was surrounded by her passion.

Except that I might need to find a way to breathe again. Was there no way out?

Her voice, when next it came, was enormous in my ears.

"OOPS!"

Once again, all was darkness.

"Wuntvor!" Norei's voice brought me back to my senses. "Can't I leave you alone for an instant?"

I looked about me. The young witch was joined by the others from the theater. I seemed to be sitting on the ground just beyond the entrance. My clothes also appeared to be soaking wet. Oddly enough, my damp garments also seemed to glitter slightly in the late day's sun.

I glanced up at my beloved's frown. I was certain Norei would be more understanding once I outlined what had occurred. "Oh, dear, well you see, I'm certain that I can explain everything, except—" I added somewhat less certainly, "I don't know precisely what happened."

"You were being attacked by a giant pair of lips," Snarks informed me.

"Doom," Hendrek added.

"We heard this tremendous smacking sound," Alea agreed. "Ah, Wuntie. Something like this could only happen to a kisser like you."

"Boy," Richard added gleefully, "there was saliva everywhere. I tell you, those lips drooled even more than I do!"

So that was what had happened to me? I shivered again, but this time it was no longer because of warm thoughts. Perhaps this fairy magic was more than I could handle.

I managed to stand with Hendrek's assistance, and excused myself so that I might change my clothes. The living quarters that I shared with my master were but a few doors away from the theater. They were somewhat smaller than what we had at first anticipated, as they were given to us by a grateful populace after we had saved them from certain doom at the hands of demons—but also after the populace realized those demons had come to Vushta looking for the wizard and myself. Still, for the floor immediately above a stable, it was reasonably roomy and comfortable.

I entered the front room to find my master pouring over one of those weighty tomes that I often found myself carrying in my pack.

"Ah, Wuntvor!" he called to me, his spirits

apparently much revived. "It is good to see you, except—" He paused and frowned. "Have you been swimm—" It was then he began to sneeze.

How could I explain that I had been drenched by fairy saliva?

The wizard managed to hold his nose. "Get rid of those clothes immediately! If I didn't know better, I'd swear you had been drenched in fairy saliva."

I walked quickly into the small cupboard that I called my room and changed my garments, tossing my sodden clothes out an opening to the hay below.

"Ah. Much better," my master acknowledged as I reentered the main room. "I have been doing some studying, Wunt, and I believe that I have overlooked certain things in my search for a cure to my malady."

Then did my master have much the same thoughts I had had? I quickly asked him if he was considering somehow using fairy magic?

"Indeed," he replied. "I was considering the use of alternate magics in affecting my cure. One must approach these things carefully, however. Unfortunately, when one is talking about employing fairy magic, one is talking about employing fairies."

Was that all? "But I have been talking to fairies!" I announced.

"So I have surmised," the wizard answered. "And no doubt the fairy you have been talking to is beautiful in the extreme."

It took very little thought to answer that. "Well, yes."

"And as beautiful as she was," Ebenezum said soberly, "she is also that deadly."

"Deadly?" I asked incredulously. How could anyone as delightful as La be—well, how could she be anything but delightful?

"She did mention something about a fairy bargain?" my master prompted. "Something, perhaps, about living in fairyland forever and ever."

I frowned. Now that my master mentioned it, there had been something like that. I really hadn't given it much thought.

"Could I be under some sort of spell?" I asked tentatively.

"Nonsense," an enchanting voice interrupted. I knew who it was before my master even had a chance to cover his nose. There was a burst of light, and La once again stood before me in the room.

"Forgive me, my darling Wuntvor." With a smile like that, I could forgive her anything. "I will conquer the fine points of that kissing spell soon enough, especially if I have a chance to practice with you."

My master's sneezing caused me to look away.

"You can't be here!" I called to La as Ebenezum rushed for a window at the far end of the room.

"I want to be wherever I might find you," was her reply.

"No," I replied as the mage threw back the shutters and began to sneeze prodigiously, "you don't understand. Your presence here causes my master to have great nasal distress."

"So we should go elsewhere," La replied coquettishly. "Some place private."

As much as I wanted to agree to her request, my master's sneezes held me back. When else might I have such a willing fairy about to perform her magic.

"I will go with you," I said, "if you will do something for me first."

"Ah," La replied gleefully, "then it is a bargain. What do you wish before we leave forever?"

That bargain seemed a little extreme, even for someone as enchanting as La. Still, if my master could be cured once and for all, I was sure he could extricate me from any predicament.

"Very well," I therefore said. "If you can stop my master from sneezing when he is in the presence of magic, I will go with you."

"Oh, is that all?" She danced over to my master, with such grace that I thought staying with her forever might not be such a bad arrangement after all. She lifted both her hands above her head and opened them to release fairy dust in Ebenezum's hair.

The wizard stopped sneezing.

"There," La announced. "That wasn't so hard. Now let's go off and cuddle for all eternity."

The wizard turned around.

"Oops," La remarked.

Ebenezum had stopped sneezing because he no longer had a nose.

"This wasn't exactly what I wanted," I began.

La smiled sweetly. "A bargain is a bargain," she replied.

The door to our quarters slammed open. Norei strode into the room.

"Oh, no, you don't!"

The witch had come to save me. Perhaps, I thought, La wasn't quite so enchanting after all. I ran toward my beloved.

"Oh, no, you don't!" La yelled. "I've always wanted a real man!" She dove for my running form and grabbed my leg. I found myself being dragged toward a deep green hole that had suddenly appeared in a wall, a hole that seemed to glow with the same strange light that came from La herself.

"Fairyland," she called enthusiastically, "here we come!"

"It's not that easy!" Norei declared, diving and grabbing my other leg. "Wuntvor is staying here one way or another."

Each one pulled. I felt as if I would be torn apart.

"Mayhaps," La remarked darkly, "it is time for some fairy magic."

"Magic?" Norei laughed derisively. "I'll show you magic!"

Still they tugged. Except now I noticed that we were no longer on the ground. Instead, the three of us were tumbling through the air some three feet above the floor. And we were tumbling straight for that large gap in the wall that led to fairyland!

Now that I had seen another side of La's character, I was not so sure I wanted to be in fairyland for all of eternity.

I therefore did what any strong, young, and

totally frightened apprentice would. I screamed for help.

I was answered by my master's voice chanting a complicated incantation! While he sounded as though he had a bad cold (no doubt the result of being noseless), the words came as fluently to his tongue as they had before he had been visited by his malady.

We stopped spinning toward the bright green hole, and instead reversed our direction and flew out an open window. I looked down, and saw Alea, Snarks, Hendrek, and even Richard beneath us, a Giant and a Girl busily practicing their dance routines in the relative safety of the open air, and all of them oblivious to the drama going on above their heads.

Still did La tug upon one leg, and Norei upon the other, turning us around and around and making me exceedingly dizzy and wishing, furthermore, that I had not eaten quite so heavy a lunch. Their magics seemed evenly matched, causing us to twist and turn and rise ever higher above the Vushta street, so that, should the magic suddenly cease, a certain apprentice (at the very least) would plunge to his death. I wondered if this was truly the spell that Ebenezum meant to use. Perhaps incantations had a slightly different result when you had no nose. So it was that we rose ever upward toward the sun. I had been saved from fairyland, but at what a cost?

"I'll show you what I do to disagreeable humans!" La declared.

"I will not be beaten by anyone in blue gossamer!" Norei replied every bit as vehemently.

We had stopped spinning for an instant. "Indeed," I interjected. "If I might interrupt?"

"This is between the two of us!" La cut me off, her eyes alight with fairy fire.

"Wuntvor," Norei said somewhat more kindly. "It is for the best that you stay out of this."

I looked down from our present vantage point. How, I wondered, could I stay out of something that had lifted me close to a hundred feet off the ground?

"If you were to look—" I began.

It was at that instant that a Giant and a Girl decided to rehearse their song in earnest.

The giant began:

> "Fee Fi Fo Fove,
> Now it's time to win your love!"

We stopped twisting again. La looked down below, her eyes widening as she saw the giant. "Who's that?" she whispered.

As if in response, Richard continued his song:

> "Fee Fi Fo Fug
> I'm gonna give you a great big hug."

La ran her tongue over her lower lip. "Now that's a *real* man."

Alea was singing in return.

> "We'll tell you something not so profound
> A giant's love really gets around."

"Well, Wuntvor, it's been nice," La remarked casually. "Now, how did that growth spell go?"

I was shocked. This was loving me forever; cuddling with me for all eternity? First the nauseating dizziness, and now this?

I had to admit there was, however, something worse than dizzily spinning through space. I felt myself falling through the open air.

I managed my usual scream.

"And now," La murmured as she swooped down toward Richard, "for some real fairy magic."

"I believe there has been too much fairy magic already," another, deeper voice said.

"Oops," La remarked.

I realized I had stopped falling. Norei drifted down beside me, her incantations allowing us to both drift lazily toward the ground. How, I wondered, could I ever have imagined that I loved another?

I looked above us, and saw that somehow the green hole had followed us outside, and further, there was someone standing inside it; a man, or something like a man, for he was only two feet tall and sported wings that poked out from his dark robes.

"Why do you always leave," his deep voice called to La, "when we should be making that magic together?"

"Oh, Nananinnyninnyheyheyhey! Just because we're betrothed, does that mean I can't have any fun?"

"Oh, my impetuous Lalalillylololoobaloobashebangshebang," Nananinnyninnyheyheyhey replied with a chuckle. "I love that spirit."

"So the two of you are promised to each other?" I asked with a certain relief.

"By her father," Nana etc. agreed. "King Ramal-amadingdong."

"Without even consulting me!" La pouted. Even after all we had been through, I had to admit that her pout was more magical than even Alea's. "Although I have to admit that Nanny here isn't bad—for a fairy." The short man reached forward and somehow managed to take La's hand. Suddenly, she was transformed to two feet in height and was standing beside him in the lip of the hole. Somehow, I seemed to be having a real perspective problem.

"But how did you find me?" La asked her betrothed.

"True love will always find a way." He winked at the rest of us. "Besides, she's always leaving holes behind her." He waved to the rest of us. "With that, we take our leave. And, of course, all has been set right again. You could expect no less from a future prince of the fairies."

With that the green hole disappeared in a flash of crimson light. The entire audience could not help but exclaim in admiration.

Snarks glanced over at a Giant and a Girl.

"That," the truth-telling demon declared, "was by far the best part of your act."

"Doom," Hendrek agreed.

3

"Endings are always the hardest part. So finish the story already."
—from *The Abridged Ebenezum: His Wit and Wisdom Without the Words,* by Ebenezum, the Greatest Wizard in the Western Kingdoms, (fourth edition)

So it was that all was again set right in Vushta. Ebenezum seemed to have regained his original nose. At least, it sneezed as well as the one he had before.

A Giant and a Girl finally began to perform at the Vushta Art Theater. They opened, if not to critical acclaim, at least to a large curiosity factor. I didn't appreciate that they revised their new act to incorporate fairy wings.

Alea went back to pouting, and Norei got too busy to see me again. And I took the opportunity to straighten up what had happened to the stables as a result of our spinning on the second floor.

And my master had gone back to exploring different magics as a cure for his malady. Not fairy magic, mind you. Ebenezum had decided that it was far too unpredictable. But how about those spells the elves used—

I heard my master sneeze again.

His voice called but a moment later! "Wuntvor!"

I scurried upstairs to our living quarters.

I did not ask for whom the mage sneezes. He sneezed for me.

The Graceless Child

Charles de Lint

Charles de Lint is one of the contemporary masters
of fantasy. His short stories have graced numerous
anthologies and his novels include such critically
acclaimed works as *Moonheart, Greenmantle*, and
The Little Country. This story, set among the fairy folk,
gives a new twist to the concept of a halfling.

I am not a little girl anymore.
And I am grateful and lighter
for my lessened load.
I have shouldered it.

—Ally Sheedy,
  from "A Man's World"

Tetchie met the tattooed man the night the wild
dogs came down from the hills. She was waiting in
among the roots of a tall old gnarlwood tree, waiting
and watching as she did for an hour or two every night,
nested down on the mossy ground with her pack
under her head and her mottled cloak wrapped around

her for warmth. The leaves of the gnarlwood had yet to turn, but winter seemed to be in the air that night.

She could see the tattooed man's breath cloud about him, white as pipe smoke in the moonlight. He stood just beyond the spread of the gnarlwood's twisted boughs, in the shadow of the lone standing stone that shared the hilltop with Tetchie's tree. He had a forbidding presence, tall and pale, with long fine hair the color of bone tied back from his high brow. Above his leather trousers he was bare-chested, the swirl of his tattoos crawling across his blanched skin like pictographic insects. Tetchie couldn't read, but she knew enough to recognize that the dark blue markings were runes.

She wondered if he'd come here to talk to her father.

Tetchie burrowed a little deeper into her moss and cloak nest at the base of the gnarlwood. She knew better than to call attention to herself. When people saw her it was always the same. At best she was mocked, at worst beaten. So she'd learned to hide. She became part of the night, turned to the darkness, away from the sun. The sun made her skin itch and her eyes tear. It seemed to steal the strength from her body until she could only move at a tortoise crawl.

The night was kinder and protected her as once her mother had. Between the teachings of the two, she'd long since learned a mastery over how to remain unseen, but her skills failed her tonight.

The tattooed man turned slowly until his gaze was fixed on her hiding place.

"I know you're there," he said. His voice was deep and resonant; it sounded to Tetchie like stones grinding against each other, deep underhill, the way she imagined her father's voice would sound when he finally spoke to her. "Come out where I can see you, trow."

Shivering, Tetchie obeyed. She pushed aside the thin protection of her cloak and shuffled out into the moonlight on stubby legs. The tattooed man towered over her, but then so did most folk. She stood three and a half feet high, her feet bare, the soles callused to a rocky hardness. Her skin had a grayish hue, her features were broad and square, as though chiseled from rough stone. The crudely fashioned tunic she wore as a dress hung like a sack from her stocky body.

"I'm not a trow," she said, trying to sound brave.

Trows were tall, trollish creatures, not like her at all. She didn't have the height.

The tattooed man regarded her for so long that she began to fidget under his scrutiny. In the distance, from two hills over and beyond the town, she heard a plaintive howl that was soon answered by more of the same.

"You're just a child," the tattooed man finally said.

Tetchie shook her head. "I'm almost sixteen winters."

Most girls her age already had a babe or two, hanging on to their legs as they went about their work.

"I meant in trow terms," the tattooed man replied.

"But I'm not—"

"A trow. I know. I heard you. But you've trow blood all the same. Who was your dame, your sire?"

What business is it of yours? Tetchie wanted to say, but something in the tattooed man's manner froze the words in her throat. Instead she pointed to the longstone that reared out of the dark earth of the hilltop behind him.

"The sun snared him," she said.

"And your mother?"

"Dead."

"At childbirth?"

Tetchie shook her head. "No, she... she lived long enough...."

To spare Tetchie from the worst when she was still a child, Hanna Lief protected her daughter from the townsfolk and lived long enough to tell her, one winter's night when the ice winds stormed through the town and rattled the loose plank walls of the shed behind The Cotts Inn where they lived, "Whatever they tell you, Tetchie, whatever lies you hear, remember this: I went to him willingly."

Tetchie rubbed at her eye with the thick knuckles of her hand.

"I was twelve when she died," she said.

"And you've lived"—the tattooed man waved a

hand lazily to encompass the tree, the stone, the hills—"here ever since?"

Tetchie nodded slowly, wondering where the tattooed man intended their conversation to lead.

"What do you eat?"

What she could gather in the hills and the woods below, what she could steal from the farms surrounding the town, what she could plunder from the midden behind the market square those rare nights that she dared to creep into the town. But she said none of this, merely shrugged.

"I see," the tattooed man said.

She could still hear the wild dogs howl. They were closer now.

Earlier that evening, a sour expression rode the face of the man who called himself Gaedrian as he watched three men approach his table in The Cotts Inn. By the time they had completed their passage through the inn's common room and reached him, he had schooled his features into a bland mask. They were merchants, he decided, and was half right. They were also, he learned when they introduced themselves, citizens of very high standing in the town of Burndale.

He studied them carelessly from under hooded eyes as they eased their respective bulks into seats at his table. Each was more overweight than the next. The largest was Burndale's mayor; not quite so corpulent was the elected head of the town guilds; the smallest was the town's sheriff and he carried Gaedrian's weight and half again on a much shorter frame. Silk vests, stretched taut over obesity, were perfectly matched to flounced shirts and pleated trousers. Their boots were leather, tooled with intricate designs and buffed to a high polish. Jowls hung over stiff collars; a diamond stud gleamed in the sheriff's left earlobe.

"Something lives in the hills," the mayor said.

Gaedrian had forgotten the mayor's name as soon as it was spoken. He was fascinated by the smallness of the man's eyes and how closely set they were to each other. Pigs had eyes that were much the same, though the comparison, he chided himself, was insulting to the latter.

"Something dangerous," the mayor added.

The other two nodded, the sheriff adding, "A monster."

Gaedrian sighed. There was always something living in the hills; there were always monsters. Gaedrian knew better than most how to recognize them, but he rarely found them in the hills.

"And you want me to get rid of it?" he asked.

The town council looked hopeful. Gaedrian regarded them steadily for a long time without speaking.

He knew their kind too well. They liked to pretend that the world followed their rules, that the wilderness beyond the confines of their villages and towns could be tamed, laid out in as tidy an order as the shelves of goods in their shops, of the books in their libraries. But they also knew that under the facade of their order, the wilderness came stealing on paws that echoed with the click of claw on cobblestone. It crept into their streets and their dreams and would take up lodging in their souls if they didn't eradicate it in time.

So they came to men such as himself, men who walked the border that lay between the world they knew and so desperately needed to maintain, and the world as it truly was beyond the cluster of their stone buildings, a world that cast long shadows of fear across their streets whenever the moon went behind a bank of clouds and their street lamps momentarily faltered.

They always recognized him, no matter how he appeared among them. These three surreptitiously studied the backs of his hands and what they could see of the skin at the hollow of his throat where the collar of his shirt lay open. They were looking for confirmation of what their need had already told them he was.

"You have gold, of course?" he asked.

The pouch appeared as if by magic from the inside pocket of the mayor's vest. It made a satisfying clink against the wooden tabletop. Gaedrian lifted a hand to the table, but it was only to grip the handle of his ale flagon and lift it to his lips. He took a long swallow, then set the empty flagon down beside the pouch.

"I will consider your kind offer," he said.

He rose from his seat and left them at the table, the pouch still untouched. When the landlord met him at the door, he jerked a thumb back to where the three men sat, turned in their seats to watch him leave.

"I believe our good lord mayor was buying this round," he told the landlord, then stepped out into the night.

He paused when he stood outside on the street, head cocked, listening. From far off, eastward, over more than one hill, he heard the baying of wild dogs, a distant, feral sound.

He nodded to himself and his lips shaped what might pass for a smile, though there was no humor in the expression. The townsfolk he passed gave him uneasy glances as he walked out of the town, into the hills that rose and fell like the tidal swells of a heathered ocean, stretching as far to the west as a man could ride in three days.

"What...what are you going to do to me?" Tetchie finally asked when the tattooed man's silence grew too long for her.

His pale gaze seemed to mock her, but he spoke very respectfully, "I'm going to save your wretched soul."

Tetchie blinked in confusion. "But I...I don't—"

"Want it saved?"

"Understand," Tetchie said.

"Can you hear them?" the tattooed man asked, only confusing her more. "The hounds," he added.

She nodded uncertainly.

"You've but to say the word and I'll give them the

strength to tear down the doors and shutters in the town below. Their teeth and claws will wreak the vengeance you crave."

Tetchie took a nervous step away from him.

"But I don't want anybody to be hurt," she said.

"After all they've done to you?"

"Mama said they don't know any better."

The tattooed man's eyes grew grim. "And so you should just... forgive them?"

Too much thinking made Tetchie's head hurt.

"I don't know," she said, panic edging into her voice.

The tattooed man's anger vanished as though it had never lain there, burning in his eyes.

"Then what *do* you want?" he asked.

Tetchie regarded him nervously. There was something in how he asked that told her he already knew, that this was what he'd been wanting from her all along.

Her hesitation grew into a long silence. She could hear the dogs, closer than ever now, feral voices raised high and keening, almost like children, crying in pain. The tattooed man's gaze bore down on her, forcing her to reply. Her hand shook as she lifted her arm to point at the longstone.

"Ah," the tattooed man said.

He smiled, but Tetchie drew no comfort from that.

"That will cost," he said.

"I... I have no money."

"Have I asked for money? Did I say one word about money?"

"You...you said it would cost...."

The tattooed man nodded. "Cost, yes, but the coin is a dearer mint than gold or silver."

What could be dearer? Tetchie wondered.

"I speak of blood," the tattooed man said before she could ask. "Your blood."

His hand shot out and grasped her before she could flee.

Blood, Tetchie thought. She cursed the blood that made her move so slow.

"Don't be frightened," the tattooed man said. "I mean you no harm. It needs but a pinprick—one drop, perhaps three, and not for me. For the stone. To call him back."

His fingers loosened on her arm and she quickly moved away from him. Her gaze shifted from the stone to him, back and forth, until she felt dizzy.

"Mortal blood is the most precious blood of all," the tattooed man told her.

Tetchie nodded. Didn't she know? Without her trow blood, she'd be just like anyone else. No one would want to hurt her just because of who she was, of how she looked, of what she represented. They saw only midnight fears; all she wanted was to be liked.

"I can teach you tricks," the tattooed man went on. "I can show you how to be anything you want."

As he spoke, his features shifted until it seemed that there was a feral dog's head set upon that tattooed torso. Its fur was the same pale hue as the man's hair had been, and it still had his eyes, but it was undeniably a beast. The man was gone, leaving this strange hybrid creature in his place.

Tetchie's eyes went wide in awe. Her short, fat legs trembled until she didn't think they could hold her upright anymore.

"Anything at all," the tattooed man said as the dog's head was replaced by his own features once more.

For a long moment, Tetchie could only stare at him. Her blood seemed to sing as it ran through her veins. To be anything at all. To be normal.... But then the exhilaration that filled her trickled away. It was too good to be true, so it couldn't be true.

"Why?" she asked. "Why do you want to help me?"

"I take pleasure in helping others," he replied.

He smiled. His eyes smiled. There was such a kindly air about him that Tetchie almost forgot what he'd said about the wild dogs, about sending them down into Burndale to hunt down her tormentors. But she did remember and the memory made her uneasy.

The tattooed man seemed too much the chameleon for her to trust. He could teach her how to be anything she wanted to be. Was that why he could appear to be anything she wanted *him* to be?

"You hesitate," he said. "Why?"

Tetchie could only shrug.

"It's your chance to right the wrong played on you at your birth."

Tetchie's attention focused on the howling of the wild dogs as he spoke. To right the wrong....

Their teeth and claws will wreak the vengeance you crave.

But it didn't have to be that way. She meant no one ill. She just wanted to fit in, not hurt anyone. So, if the choice was hers, she could simply choose not to hurt people, couldn't she? The tattooed man couldn't *make* her hurt people.

"What...what do I have to do?" she asked.

The tattooed man pulled a long silver needle from where it had been stuck in the front of his trousers.

"Give me your thumb," he said.

Gaedrian scented trow as soon as he left Burndale behind him. It wasn't a strong scent, more a promise than an actuality at first, but the farther he got from the town, the more pronounced it grew. He stopped and tested the wind, but it kept shifting, making it difficult for him to pinpoint its source. Finally he stripped his shirt, letting it fall to the ground.

He touched one of the tattoos on his chest and a pale blue light glimmered in his palm when he took his hand away. He freed the glow into the air where it turned slowly, end on shimmering end. When it had given him the source of the scent, he snapped his fingers and the light winked out.

More assured now, he set off again, destination

firmly in mind. The townsfolk, he realized, had been accurate for a change. A monster did walk the hills outside Burndale tonight.

Nervously, Tetchie stepped forward. As she got closer to him, the blue markings on his chest seemed to shift and move, rearranging themselves into a new pattern that was as indecipherable to her as the old one had been. Tetchie swallowed thickly and lifted her hand, hoping it wouldn't hurt. She closed her eyes as he brought the tip of the needle to her thumb.

"There," the tattooed man said a moment later, "it's all done."

Tetchie blinked in surprise. She hadn't felt a thing. But now that the tattooed man had let go of her hand, her thumb started to ache. She looked at the three drops of blood that lay in the tattooed man's palm like tiny crimson jewels. Her knees went weak again and this time she did fall to the ground. She felt hot and flushed, as though she were up and abroad at high noon, the sun broiling down on her, stealing her ability to move.

Slowly, slowly, she lifted her head. She wanted to see what happened when the tattooed man put her blood on the stone, but all he did was smile down at her and lick three drops with a tongue that seemed as long as a snake's, with the same kind of a twin fork at its tip.

"Yuh...nuh...."

Tetchie tried to speak—What have you done to me? she wanted to say—but the words turned into a muddle before they left her mouth. It was getting harder to think.

"When your mother was so kindly passing along all her advice to you," he said, "she should have warned you about not trusting strangers. Most folk have little use for your kind, it's true."

Tetchie thought her eyes were playing tricks on her, then realized that the tattooed man must be shifting his shape once more. His hair grew darker as she watched, his complexion deepened. No longer pale and wan, he seemed to bristle with sorcerous energy now.

"But then," the tattooed man went on, "they don't have the knowledge I do. I thank you for your vitality, halfling. There's nothing so potent as mortal blood stirred in a stew of faerie. A pity you won't live long enough to put the knowledge to use."

He gave her a mocking salute, fingers tipped against his brow, then away, before turning his back to her. The night swallowed him.

Tetchie fought to get to her own feet, but she just wore herself out until she could no longer even lift her head from the ground. Tears of frustration welled in her eyes. What had he done to her? She'd seen it for herself, he'd taken no more than three drops of her blood. But then why did she feel as though he'd taken it all?

She stared up at the night sky, the stars blurring in her gaze, spinning, spinning, until finally she just let them take her away.

*　　*　　*

She wasn't sure what had brought her back, but when she opened her eyes, it was to find that the tattooed man had returned. He crouched over her, concern for her swimming in his dark eyes. His skin had regained its almost colorless complexion; his hair was bone white once more. She mustered what little strength she had to work up a gob of saliva and spat in his face.

The tattooed man didn't move. She watched the saliva dribble down his cheek until it fell from the tip of his chin to the ground beside her.

"Poor child," he said. "What has he done to you?"

The voice was wrong, Tetchie realized. He'd changed his voice now. The low grumble of stones grinding against each other deep underhill had been replaced by a soft melodious tonality that was comforting on the ear.

He touched the fingers of one hand to a tattoo high on his shoulder, waking a blue glow that flickered on his fingertips. She flinched when he touched her brow with the hand, but the contact of blue fingers against her skin brought an immediate easing to the weight of her pain. When he sat back on his haunches, she found she had the strength to lift herself up from the ground. Her gaze spun for a moment, then settled down. The new perspective helped stem the helplessness she'd been feeling.

"I wish I could do more for you," the tattooed man said.

Tetchie merely glared at him, thinking, Haven't you done enough?

The tattooed man gave her a mild look, head cocked slightly as though listening to her thoughts.

"He calls himself Nallorn on this side of the Gates," he said finally, "but you would call him Nightmare, did you meet him in the land of his origin, beyond the Gates of Sleep. He thrives on pain and torment. We have been enemies for a very long time."

Tetchie blinked in confusion. "But... you..."

The tattooed man nodded. "I know. We look the same. We are brothers, child. I am the elder. My name is Dream; on this side of the Gates I answer to the name Gaedrian."

"He... your brother... he took something from me."

"He stole your mortal ability to dream," Gaedrian told her. "Tricked you into giving it freely so that it would retain its potency."

Tetchie shook her head. "I don't understand. Why would he come to me? I'm no one. I don't have any powers or magics that anyone could want."

"Not that you can use yourself, perhaps, but the mix of trow and mortal blood creates a potent brew. Each drop of such blood is a talisman in the hands of one who understands its properties."

"Is he stronger than you?" Tetchie asked.

"Not in the land beyond the Gates of Sleep. There I am the elder. The Realms of Dream are mine and all who sleep are under my rule when they come through the Gates." He paused, dark eyes thoughtful, before adding, "In this world, we are more evenly matched."

"Nightmares come from him?" Tetchie asked.

Gaedrian nodded. "It isn't possible for a ruler to see all the parts of his kingdom at once. Nallorn is the father of lies. He creeps into sleeping minds when my attention is distracted elsewhere and makes a horror of healing dreams."

He stood up then, towering over her.

"I must go," he said. "I must stop him before he grows too strong."

Tetchie could see the doubt in his eyes and understood then that though he knew his brother to be stronger than him, he would not admit to it, would not turn from what he saw as his duty. She tried to stand, but her strength still hadn't returned.

"Take me with you," she said. "Let me help you."

"You don't know what you ask."

"But I want to help."

Gaedrian smiled. "Bravely spoken, but this is war and no place for a child."

Tetchie searched for the perfect argument to convince him, but couldn't find it. He said nothing, but she knew as surely as if he'd spoken why he didn't want her to come. She would merely slow him down. She had no skills, only her night sight and the slowness of her limbs. Neither would be of help.

During the lull in their conversation when that

understanding came to her, she heard the howling once more.

"The dogs," she said.

"There are no wild dogs," Gaedrian told her. "That is only the sound of the wind as it crosses the empty reaches of his soul." He laid a hand on her head, tousled her hair. "I'm sorry for the hurt that's come to you with this night's work. If the fates are kind to me, I will try to make amends."

Before Tetchie could respond, he strode off, westward. She tried to follow, but could barely crawl after him. By the time she reached the crest of the hill, the longstone rearing above her, she saw Gaedrian's long legs carrying him up the side of the next hill. In the distance, blue lightning played, close to the ground.

Nallorn, she thought.

He was waiting for Gaedrian. Nallorn meant to kill the dreamlord and then he would rule the land beyond the Gates of Sleep. There would be no more dreams, only nightmares. People would fear sleep, for it would no longer be a haven. Nallorn would twist its healing peace into pain and despair.

And it was all her fault. She'd been thinking only of herself. She'd wanted to talk to her father, to be normal. She hadn't known who Nallorn was at the time, but ignorance was no excuse.

"It doesn't matter what others think of you," her mother had told her once, "but what you think of yourself. Be a good person and no matter how other people will talk of you, what they say can only be a lie."

They called her a monster and feared her. She saw now that it wasn't a lie.

She turned to the longstone that had been her father before the sun had snared him and turned him to stone. Why couldn't that have happened to her before all of this began; why couldn't she have been turned to stone the first time the sun touched her? Then Nallorn could never have played on her vanity and her need, would never have tricked her. If she'd been stone...

Her gaze narrowed. She ran a hand along the rough surface of the standing stone and Nallorn's voice spoke in her memory.

I speak of blood.

It needs but a pinprick—one drop, perhaps three, and not for me. For the stone. To call him back.

To call him back.

Nallorn had proved there was magic in her blood. If he hadn't lied, if... *Could* she call her father back? And if he did return, would he listen to her? It was night, the time when a trow was strongest. Surely when she explained, her father would use that strength to help Gaedrian?

A babble of townsfolks' voices clamored up through her memory.

A trow'll drink your blood as sure as look at you.

Saw one I did, sitting up by the boneyard, and wasn't he chewing on a thighbone he'd dug up?

The creatures have no heart.

No soul.

They'll feed on their own, if there's not other meat to be found.

No, Tetchie told herself. Those were the lies her mother had warned her against. If her mother had loved the trow, then he couldn't have been evil.

Her thumb still ached where Nallorn had pierced it with his long silver pin, but the tiny wound had closed. Tetchie bit at it until the salty taste of blood touched her tongue. Then she squeezed her thumb, smearing the few drops of blood that welled up against the rough surface of the stone.

She had no expectations, only hope. She felt immediately weak, just as she had when Nallorn had taken the three small drops of blood from her. The world began to spin for the second time that night, and she started to fall once more, only this time she fell into the stone. The hard surface seemed to have turned to the consistency of mud and it swallowed her whole.

When consciousness finally returned, Tetchie found herself lying with her face pressed against hard-packed dirt. She lifted her head, squinting in the poor light. The longstone was gone, along with the world she knew. For as far as she could see, there was only a desolate wasteland, illuminated by a sickly twilight for which she could discover no source. It was still the landscape she knew, the hills and valleys had the same contours as those that lay west of Burndale, but it was all changed. Nothing seemed to grow here anymore;

nothing lived at all in this place, except for her, and she had her doubts about that as well.

If this was a dead land, a lifeless reflection of the world she knew, then might she not have died to reach it?

Oddly enough, the idea didn't upset her. It was as though, having seen so much that was strange already tonight, nothing more could surprise her.

When she turned to where the old gnarlwood had been in her world, a dead tree stump stood. It was no more than three times her height, the area about it littered with dead branches. The main body of the tree had fallen away from where Tetchie knelt, lying down the slope.

She rose carefully to her feet, but the dizziness and weakness she'd felt earlier had both fled. In the dirt at her feet, where the longstone would have stood in her world, there was a black pictograph etched deeply into the soil. It reminded her of the tattoos that she'd seen on the chests of the dreamlord and his brother, as though it has been plucked from the skin of one of them, enlarged and cast down on the ground. Goose bumps traveled up her arms.

She remembered what Gaedrian had told her about the land he ruled, how the men and women of her world could enter it only after passing through the Gates of Sleep. She'd been so weak when she offered her blood to the longstone, her eyelids growing so heavy....

Was this all just a dream, then? And if so, what was its source? Did it come from Gaedrian, or from his brother Nallorn at whose bidding nightmares were born?

She went down on one knee to look more closely at the pictograph. It looked a bit like a man with a tangle of rope around his feet and lines standing out from his head as though his hair stood on end. She reached out with one cautious finger and touched the tangle of lines at the foot of the rough figure. The dirt was damp there. She rubbed her finger against her thumb. The dampness was oily to the touch.

Scarcely aware of what she was doing, she reached down again and traced the symbol, the slick oiliness letting her finger slide easily along the edged grooves in the dirt. When she came to the end, the pictograph began to glow. She stood quickly, backing away.

What had she *done?*

The blue glow rose into the air, holding to the shape that lay in the dirt. A faint rhythmic thrumming rose from all around her, as though the ground were shifting, but she felt no vibration underfoot. There was just the sound, low and ominous.

A branch cracked behind her and she turned to the ruin of the gnarlwood. A tall shape stood outlined against the sky. She started to call out to it, but her throat closed up on her. And then she was aware of the circle of eyes that watched her from all sides of the hilltop, pale eyes that flickered with the reflection of the glowing pictograph that hung in the air where the longstone stood in her world. They were set low to the ground; feral eyes.

She remembered the howling of the wild dogs in her own world.

There are no wild dogs, Gaedrian had told her. *That is only the sound of the wind as it crosses the empty reaches of his soul.*

As the eyes began to draw closer, she could make out the triangular-shaped heads of the creatures they belonged to, the high-backed bodies with which they slunk forward.

Oh, why had she believed Gaedrian? She knew him no better than Nallorn. Who was to say that *either* of them was to be trusted?

One of the dogs rose up to its full height and stalked forward on still legs. The low growl that arose in his chest echoed the rumble of sound that her foolishness with the glowing pictograph had called up. She started to back away from the dog, but now another, and a third stepped forward and there was no place to which she could retreat. She turned her gaze to the silent figure that stood in among the fallen branches of the gnarlwood.

"Puh—please," she managed. "I ... I meant no harm."

The figure made no response, but the dogs growled at the sound of her voice. The nearest pulled its lips back in a snarl.

This was it, Tetchie thought. If she wasn't dead already in this land of the dead, then she soon would be.

But then the figure by the tree moved forward. It

had a slow shuffling step. Branches broke underfoot as it closed the distance between them.

The dogs backed away from Tetchie and began to whine uneasily.

"Be gone," the figure said.

Its voice was low and craggy, stone against stone, like that of the first tattooed man. Nallorn, the dreamlord's brother who turned dreams into nightmares. It was a counterpoint to the deep thrumming that seemed to come from the hill under Tetchie's feet.

The dogs fled at the sound of the man's voice. Tetchie's knees knocked against each other as he moved closer still. She could see the rough chiseled shape of his features now, the shock of tangled hair, stiff as dried gorse, the wide bulk of his shoulders and torso, the corded muscle upon muscle that made up arms and legs. His eyes were sunk deep under protruding brows. He was like the first rough shaping that a sculptor might create when beginning a new work, face and musculature merely outlined rather than clearly defined as it would be when the sculpture was complete.

Except this sculpture wasn't stone, nor clay, nor marble. It was flesh and blood. And though he was no taller than a normal man, he seemed like a giant to Tetchie, towering over her as though the side of a mountain had pulled loose to walk the hills.

"Why did you call me?" he asked.

"C-call?" Tetchie replied. "But I ... I didn't...."

Her voice trailed off. She gazed on him with sudden hope and understanding.

"Father?" she asked in a small voice.

The giant regarded her in a long silence. Then slowly he bent down to one knee so that his head was on a level with hers.

"You," he said in a voice grown with wonder. "You are Hanna's daughter?"

Tetchie nodded nervously.

"*My* daughter?"

Tetchie's nervousness fled. She no longer saw a fearsome trow out of legend, but her mother's lover. The gentleness and warmth that had called her mother from Burndale to where he waited for her on the moors washed over her. He opened his arms and she went to him, sighing as he embraced her.

"My name's Tetchie," she said into his shoulder.

"Tetchie," he repeated, making a low rumbling song of her name. "I never knew I had a daughter."

"I came every night to your stone," she said, "hoping you'd return."

Her father pulled back a little and gave her a serious look.

"I can't ever go back," he said.

"But—"

He shook his head. "Dead is dead, Tetchie. I can't return."

"But this is a horrible place to have to live."

He smiled, craggy features shifting like a mountainside suddenly rearranging its terrain.

"I don't live here," he said. "I live...I can't explain how it is. There are no words to describe the difference."

"Is Mama there?"

"Hanna...died?"

Tetchie nodded. "Years ago, but I still miss her."

"I will...look for her," the trow said. "I will give her your love." He rose then, looming over her again. "But I must go now, Tetchie. This is unhallowed land, the perilous border that lies between life and death. Bide here too long—living or dead—and you remain here forever."

"But—"

Tetchie had wanted to ask him to take her with him to look for her mother, to tell him that living meant only pain and sorrow for her, but then she realized she was only thinking of herself again. She still wasn't sure that she trusted Gaedrian, but if he had been telling her the truth, then she had to try to help him. Her own life was a nightmare; she wouldn't wish for all people to share such a life.

"I need your help," she said and told him then of Gaedrian and Nallorn, the war that was being fought between Dream and Nightmare that Nallorn could not be allowed to win.

Her father shook his head sadly. "I can't help you, Tetchie. It's not physically possible for me to return."

"But if Gaedrian loses..."

"That would be an evil thing," her father agreed.

"There must be *something* we can do."

He was silent for long moments then.

"What is it?" Tetchie asked. "What don't you want to tell me?"

"I can do nothing," her father said, "but you..." Again he hesitated.

"What?" Tetchie asked. "What is it that I can do?"

"I can give you of my strength," her father said. "You'll be able to help your dreamlord then. But it will cost you. You will be more trow than ever, and remain so."

More trow? Tetchie thought. She looked at her father, felt the calm that seemed to wash in peaceful waves from his very presence. The townsfolk might think that a curse, but she no longer did.

"I'd be proud to be more like you," she said.

"You will have to give up all pretense of humanity," her father warned her. "When the sun rises, you must be barrowed underhill or she'll make you stone."

"I already only come out at night," she said.

Her father's gaze searched hers and then he sighed.

"Yours has not been an easy life," he said.

Tetchie didn't want to talk about herself anymore.

"Tell me what to do," she said.

"You must take some of my blood," her father told her.

Blood again. Tetchie had seen and heard enough about it to last her a lifetime tonight.

"But how can you do that?" she asked. "You're just a spirit...."

Her father touched her arm. "Given flesh in this half world by your call. Have you a knife?"

When Tetchie shook her head, he lifted his thumb to his mouth and bit down on it. Dark liquid welled up at the cut as he held his hand out to her.

"It will burn," he said.

Tetchie nodded nervously. Closing her eyes, she opened her mouth. Her father brought his thumb down across her tongue. His blood tasted like fire, burning its way down her throat. She shuddered with the searing pain of it, eyes tearing so that even when she opened them, she was still blind.

She felt her father's hand on her head. He smoothed the tangle of her hair and then kissed her.

"Be well, my child," he said. "We will look for you, your mother and I, when your time to join us has come and you finally cross over."

There were a hundred things Tetchie realized that she wanted to say, but vertigo overtook her and she knew that not only was he gone, but the empty world as well. She could feel grass under her, a soft breeze on her cheek. When she opened her eyes, the longstone reared up on one side of her, the gnarlwood on the other. She turned to look where she'd last seen the blue lightning flare before she'd gone into the stone.

There was no light there now.

She got to her feet, feeling invigorated rather than weak. Her night sight seemed to have sharpened, every sense was more alert. She could almost read the night simply through the pores of her skin.

The townsfolk were blind, she realized. *She* had been blind. They had all missed so much of what the world had to offer. But the townsfolk craved a narrower world, rather than a wider one, and she...she had a task yet to perform.

She set off to where the lightning had been flickering.

The grass was all burned away, the ground itself scorched on the hilltop that was her destination. She saw a figure lying in the dirt and hesitated, unsure as to who it was. Gaedrian or his brother? She moved cautiously forward until finally she knelt by the still figure. His eyes opened and looked upon her with a weak gaze.

"I was not strong enough," Gaedrian said, his voice still sweet and ringing, but much subdued.

"Where did he go?" Tetchie asked.

"To claim his own: the Land of Dream."

Tetchie regarded him for a long moment, then lifted her thumb to her mouth. It was time for blood again—but this would be the last time. Gaedrian tried to protest, but she pushed aside his hands and let the drops fall into his mouth: one, two, three. Gaedrian swallowed. His eyes went wide with an almost comical astonishment.

"Where...how...?"

"I found my father," Tetchie said. "This is the heritage he left me."

Senses all more finely attuned, to be sure, but when she lifted an arm to show Gaedrian, the skin was darker, grayer than before and tough as bark. And she would never see the day again.

"You should not have—" Gaedrian began, but Tetchie cut him off.

"Is it enough?" she asked. "Can you stop him now?"

Gaedrian sat up. He rolled his shoulders, flexed his hands and arms, his legs.

"More than enough," he said. "I feel a hundred years younger."

Knowing him for what he was, Tetchie didn't think he was exaggerating. Who knew how old the dreamlord was? He would have been born with the first dream.

He cupped her face with his hands and kissed her on the brow.

"I will try to make amends for what my brother has done to you this night," he said. "The whole world owes you for the rescue of its dreams."

"I don't want any reward," Tetchie said.

"We'll talk of that when I return for you," Gaedrian said.

If you can find me, Tetchie thought, but she merely nodded in reply.

Gaedrian stood. One hand plucked at a tattoo just to one side of his breastbone and tossed the ensuing blue light into the air. It grew into a shimmering portal. Giving her one more grateful look, he stepped through. The portal closed behind him, winking out in a flare of blue sparks, like those cast by a fire when a log's tossed on.

Tetchie looked about the scorched hilltop, then set off back to Burndale. She walked its cobblestoned streets, one lone figure, dwarfed by the buildings, more kin to their walls and foundations than to those sleeping within. She thought of her mother when she reached The Cotts Inn and stood looking at the shed around back by the stables where they had lived for all of those years.

Finally, just as the dawn was pinking the horizon, she made her way back to the hill where she'd first met the tattooed man. She ran her fingers along the bark of the gnarlwood, then stepped closer to the longstone, standing on the east side of it.

It wasn't entirely true that she could never see the day again. She *could* see it, if only once.

Tetchie was still standing there when the sun rose and snared her and then there were two standing stones on the hilltop keeping company to the old gnarlwood tree, one tall and one much smaller. But Tetchie herself was gone to follow her parents, a lithe spirit of a child finally, her gracelessness left behind in stone.

Hobbits

Maya Kaathryn Bohnhoff

Maya Kaathryn Bohnhoff's "Hobbits" first appeared in *Analog*, a venue not usually associated with the weefolk. Maya's story is definitely an unconventional twist on this motif.

After the long drought months, the four days of nonstop rain were especially welcome. Now, mist snuggled around the little frame house like a cotton-gauze blanket of faery silver.

Light from a first-floor window stained the gauze with smudges of gold. There was a scene painted in the window—a scene enacted in a million nurseries, in a thousand childhood tales: a mother bent low over the bed of her child, singing songs, listening to prayers, fielding the endless stream of last-minute questions and revelations that seem to pour out of a child's restless mind just at bedtime.

"Will it rain all night?" the little boy asked, eyeing the misty darkness outside.

"I don't know, honey," the mother replied. "It just might."

"Why?"

"Why what?"

"Why will it rain all night?"

The mother rolled her eyes and laughed. "It will rain all night if the clouds are full enough of moisture and decide to drop it all on us."

"Why do they want to drop it all on us?"

She had backed herself into a corner on that one. "They don't really *want* to do anything. They just get heavy with water and when the water is too heavy for them to hold, it falls out of the clouds. OK?"

He considered that. "OK...Mommy?"

"Yes, Evan."

"Will there be lightning and thunder and bad dreams like last night?"

His mother made a sympathetic face as she gathered up several stuffed animals and arranged them in the requisite order at his side. "Did you have a bad dream last night, honey?"

"Uh-huh." He nodded, brown eyes solemn and wide. "I dreamed there was this jet with monsters in it and it crashed-ed in our woods."

"Oh? Do you think we should be afraid?"

He made a face. "Naw. It was just a bad dream. I don't care about bad dreams, 'cause I'm a big guy.... Besides, they were just little monsters."

"Oh. OK. Well, you give me one last kiss and get to sleep. And no bad dreams tonight." She put her arms around him and kissed his ear, loving the feel of those little arms around her neck.

He kissed her cheek, then drew back and gave

her Eskimo kisses. "Will you tell Daddy not to watch those movies tonight? They're kind of scary."

"Will do, schmoo," she said, and tucked him in. She checked the night-light and moved to the door. As always, her hand was on the light switch when he said, "Oh, Mommy?"

"Yes, baby."

"I love you, Mommy."

She smiled. "I love you too, baby. G'night."

"Night."

She turned off the lights.

Out on the rain-soaked hillside in front of the house, the gold light winked out, leaving the mist a sodden gray. Color abandoned the tree trunks, and their leaves and needles melted, silver, into the gauzy mist. Where there had been a patch of light quilted onto the glistening bed of leaves and pine needles that formed the floor of a pocket glade, there was now a pool of darkness.

In the middle of that glade, a sopping pile of leaves stirred softly, shedding its deciduous scales. The shape revealed was not so unnatural-looking in the dark of a woody hillside; a twist of root, a jag or rock, a shattered stump it might be...except for the eyes.

The eyes glowed dull amber through matted leaves and blinked at the place where the nursery scene had played.

"*You* are giving your son nightmares," she accused, pointing a finger at his nose.

He looked up over the wire rims of his glasses. "I?"

She nodded. "That thing you were watching the other night—what was it?—'Horror at—'"

"Terror," he corrected. "'Terror at 37,000 Feet' ...and how could that have given him nightmares? He didn't see it."

"He *heard* it. And evidently the sound track suggested, to that fertile little five-year-old mind, a jet-load of monsters." She crooked her fingers into claws and snatched at his nose.

He caught her wrist and pulled her into his lap, crumpling the magazine he'd been reading. "I doubt there'll be any permanent damage. But, just to be safe, maybe we should can the horror and have a little romance, instead."

"Much healthier," she agreed and kissed him, reaching up to turn off the table lamp. Behind them, in the dark, the front door rattled and something scutched across the oak surface.

"Rats!" he said and swung her to her feet. "I forgot all about Troll." He turned the light back on and made his way to the door. The scratching and rattling increased, accompanied by a demanding wail. "All right, already!" He swung the door open, admitting a feline blur of alternating gray and black, then closed and locked it. They went straight to bed, Troll went straight to his food dish.

A small boy's days are full of adventure: exploring basement caverns, conquering hillsides and tree stumps, unearthing treasures buried for millennia under rocks and fallen branches. Today, the sky was an overturned silver bowl and the mist hung, suspended from it in trailing wisps and cottony tufts.

Evan was out for the first time in days and making the most of his freedom. Already he had captured six roly-polies and clutched a jar that was filling up with detenanted snail shells, pebbles, wood chips, and bits of mossy bark. Stick in hand, he examined the front patio, poking and prodding at the crevasses between the bricks. More roly-polies were forthcoming.

Bored with that, he moved up onto the gentle slope in the lea of the wood and began turning over rocks and poking wild clumps of leaves (dwarves and trolls) into submission. A particularly interesting clump caught his eye. He immediately imagined a treasure beneath the layer of moldy leaves—a rusty crown, a giant roly-poly, a frog. He approached with the stealth of a big-game photographer, stick poised. He poked the clump.

It moved—very slightly, but enough to convince a five-year-old that he had made a great find. He poked again and the pool of arboreal debris collapsed downward, leaving a tantalizing hole.

"Wow!" Little boy eyes sparkled. This was the sort of stuff his mom and dad read to him about. This had to be a Hobbit hole or something very much like it. He hunkered down on his knees, ready to dig the sodden fall of leaves away from the cave-in.

"Evan! Ev, honey!"

Concentration broken, Evan turned his head toward the house. His mother leaned out the front door, looking for him. He dropped his stick and stood. "Here, Mommy!"

She saw him in the pocket glen and smiled, waved. "Lunch, honey," she said.

He glanced back at the Hobbit hole.

"*Now*, sweetie."

"OK." He went resignedly, dragging his feet a little through the leaves, loathe to have to suspend his exploration. At the door, he turned to give the tiny cave one last, longing look.

Something fluttered for a moment there, a leaf in the slight breeze, but Evan knew he'd seen the Hobbit wave.

It began raining again during lunch and, mothers being who they are, Evan did not get back to visit the Hobbit hole. He watched it briefly from his bedroom window. The view was good, but the hole merely sat there and refused to be entertaining. He got bored with it and played with his train set, and when his mother took a break from her writing, he had her read to him about Hobbits.

It sat, still, in the slough of decaying vegetation and watched the window. Waves of exhilaration coursed through it. The small creature was staring at it again through the transparent doorway, its face framed in one of the little square panels. Well, not at it, precisely, for it couldn't be seen, hiding, waiting in the leaves. It could feel the small creature's interest, knew how close it had come earlier that day...only to fail. Frustration shook the little frame huddled in Evan's Hobbit hole. To come so close and to fail.

It sensed in the overhanging clouds and the movement of air masses that there might not be another opportunity like that one for some time. If the rain continued to fall, the small creature would remain locked away inside the domicile. It would have to find a way to reach inside the walls of the structure, for *these* creatures were the most interesting it had seen since the Landing. They didn't live in the open as other denizens of this place did, and they manipulated their environment like the Great Ones. They communicated in complex audio patterns and they had curiosity. **Specimens exhibiting complex communications capabilities are especially worthy of study, as this may indicate advanced intelligence.**

It shivered with anticipation and considered how the shell of the domicile was to be breached.

"There's a Hobbit hole in our front yard, Mommy," Evan told her eagerly.

She handed him a stuffed bunny and glanced sideways at his father, who, having completed his part in the bedtime ceremony and delivered the required hugs and kisses, was on his way back to the family room.

He grinned at her. "Hobbits are definitely up your alley, hon," he said. "See you tomorrow, Ev."

Ev waved absently while his mother stuck her tongue out at her husband's retreating back.

"Mommy!" he giggled. "That's not nice!"

She looked hangdog, pouting her lower lip. "Am I in trouble?"

He gave her a mock-scolding glare, then threw his arms around her neck, nearly toppling her over. "Nope! But, Mommy, I found a Hobbit hole in the yard!"

She made her eyes wide. "Really? Where?"

"There." He wriggled around in her arms and pointed, his finger smudging the glass. "Right outside my window on the hill. See?"

She squinted. In the fading gray light all she could see was a small depression in the center of the near circular glade—a puddle of black amid less-black. "Are you sure that's a Hobbit hole? Maybe that's Rabbit's House."

"Yeah, and that's his front door, huh? Just like in Winnie the Pooh. Do you think I'd get stuck if I tried to go inside?"

"You just might."

He pouted at her. "I was almost going to find out today when you called me for lunch. Then it rained and you wouldn't let me go back out. I left my roly-polies and my shells 'n stuff out there."

"Oh. Sorry about that, kiddo."

"You could go out and get them," he suggested sweetly.

She could never resist those eyes. They were the mirror image of her own and just now they were coy and pleading.

"Oh, all right!" She surrendered and planted a

kiss on his nose. "Now, go to sleep so I can get out there before it's completely dark."

She got up and moved to the door, raised her hand to the light switch.

"It's on the edge of the patio," he said.

She paused. "What is?"

"The bowl with the roly-polies!" *Gee,* Mom! his tone said. How could you *forget?*

"Oh," she said. "A *bowl* full of roly-polies. How delicious!"

She could almost hear his nose wrinkle as she flicked off the light. "You don't *eat* them!" he objected, then, "You don't think *Troll* would eat them?"

"Somehow, I doubt that. Don't worry. I'll get your roly-polies and add them to your collection."

"And my other stuff? In the jar?"

"And your other stuff in the jar. Now, good night."

"Night, Mom."

By the time she got outside it really was dark. She took a small flashlight, just in case Evan's stuff turned out to be out of range of the front porch light. It wasn't. Quite. Glancing over down the patio, she could just see the sheen of the jar on the stone lip that formed one side of "Hobbit Glade."

Smiling, she made her way over to it. She had to turn on her flashlight to check the catch in the bowl. The roly-polies were intact, lying curled like tiny armadilloes in the bottom. She picked up the treasures carefully and started to turn around. The flash beam swept the glade and caught something in its beam—amber beads in a twisted black setting.

Reflexively, she turned the light back. The amber beads stared at her from among the leafy cover of Evan's Hobbit hole, then winked out all together.

"Oh-ho!" she murmured, squinting at the sunken bowl. "Hobbits, indeed. I hope we don't have to call an exterminator."

A tapping noise behind her made her jump and spin. In the soft glow of his night-light, she could see Evan at his bedside window. He waved. She held up his treasury, then mouthed, "Back to bed, Fred." He grinned and disappeared, popping out of sight like a gopher down a hole. She cast one last glance at the glade, then went inside.

She deposited Evan's roly-polies in the terrarium where he kept his micropets, then peeled off her sweater and went into the family room.

"Karen, did you see this?" Her husband emerged from the recesses of his favorite chair, waving the evening paper.

"When would I have had a chance to see that? You've had your clutches on it since you brought it home."

He thrust the front page at her. "Do you believe they've put this tripe on the front page?"

She stared at it, struggling for comprehension. "UFO Landing Site in Pine?" asked the headline. Beneath it, a banner added, "Farmers Claim Missing Livestock as Evidence."

"What?" She blinked, then grabbed the paper. "Oh, this is great!"

"You *would* think so. Personally, I think it's absurd."

She perched on the arm of his chair. "Well, of course it's absurd. But just think of the possibilities."

"What—of little green men or big silver robots coming to carry away our livestock? Abduct our children and senior citizens?"

"No. I was just thinking, you know, what if they were accused of it and they were innocent?"

"Innocent by virtue of nonexistence? That's an interesting angle."

Karen made a rude noise and turned her attention back to the paper. She read a bit, grimaced, then shuddered. Finally, handed the paper back. "Not my genre," she said.

"Ah-ha!" He pounced on her squeamishness. "What's the matter, Karen? Can't handle it when the cute little aliens turn out not to be so cute?"

"They haven't turned out to be anything yet— least of all aliens."

"Oh, come on. I know you. You're still expecting to meet Klaatu or E.T."

"I don't believe there are aliens in Pine stealing baby animals and—and dissecting them."

"Now, now. What kind of attitude is that for a science fiction writer? There could be aliens. And they could be *bad* aliens. Twisted, evil."

"That's nonsense. If they've developed the technology necessary to achieve space travel, they must also have attained the spiritual capacity necessary to survive long enough to develop it."

"Oh, but what if not? What if this is a—uh—a slave race of some alien intelligence—"

"*Slave* race?"

"Or robots. Will you buy robots?"

"Honestly, Matt, I hate it when you play Devil's Advocate." She caught the pleading expression in his eyes and sighed. "OK, OK. For the sake of argument, Mr. D.A., yes, I suppose there could be robots."

"Right, and let's say, maniacal descendants of previously intelligent, well-balanced researchers. Now, suppose these minions of a Greater Intelligence go awry and land here and begin looking at the local fauna as specimens...or even snack food."

"Oh, *please!*"

"What's to keep that from happening? Who says those UFO abductees aren't telling the literal truth? The Prime Directive is a human concept thought up by one of your crowd, it isn't a Universal Law."

"Yes it is," she returned. "Cosmic Law of Non-Interference: One race of sentient beings shall not interfere with the course of another's evolution or abuse its resources."

"Oh, really? Well, even if there was such a law, you couldn't expect everybody to abide by it. It's unenforceable. Some nasty old overlord could send a passel of underlings here to carry away our first born." Karen was shaking her head. "Why not?"

"Because it's a Natural Law."

"Oh, sure. And who's going to enforce this Natural Law?"

"God," she said simply, and got up to head for the kitchen.

He followed her. "I hate it when you play Divine

Authority," he complained. "What about Hitler? Doesn't Hitler put a monkey wrench in your Cosmic Natural Law, Ms. D.A.?"

"That's entirely different." She poured herself a cup of coffee and glopped in powdered creamer. "*We* produced Hitler. Humanity did. We're responsible for the forces that go into producing Hitlers."

"So then, if Hitler had been born on Alpha Centauri, he wouldn't be allowed to terrorize humans on Earth."

"Something like that."

"And if he tries?"

"God stops him." She went back to the family room with Matt trailing her.

"Oh, I get it. Bring on the thunderbolts, right? No, wait—too old-fashioned—how about laser beams?"

Karen glanced at him wryly as she curled up in her fireside rocker to edit a manuscript. "I said it was a *natural* law, Matthew, not a parlor trick."

"Then how's the law going to be enforced?"

"Do I look like God?" she asked rhetorically, then proceeded to ignore him.

It cowered in the hole beneath the leaves, awed by the Thing that had come out of the house—the Thing with the Light. Painful. The Light hurt.

It now thought about how it must get inside. It had crawled to the porch the night before when all light within had been extinguished. It had gone to the door and waited on the pad before it, but the door did not open. A security system must be in force, it reasoned although its finely-tuned audio sensors hadn't detected one. It must use its native talents then. When all lights inside had gone out, it began to dig.

It was a little after midnight when the first clots of stone began to fall to the basement floor. There was little noise and that might have been the rustle of a pigeon's wings or the drip of water from an aging pipe. In a few minutes the rain of rubble stopped and fluorescent amber eyes peered out of a hole the size of a man's head.

The dark within and below was welcome and easily fathomed. It oozed through the hole bonelessly and dropped to the floor, reorienting once there. Up now, it reasoned, into the levels above. Up to where They lived, the huge, towering ones and the desired small one. Its digits twitched, blunt alloy talons whispering with excitement; its olfactory sensors were alert, filtering the overwhelming array of alien odors. They told it nothing—the variety was too great, too strange.

Almost hungry with anticipation, it began to search the dank place for an upward way. There was an odd sense of familiarity here, and it wondered why, when they had this living place below, the giant beings lived above where there was so much light. Their eyes must be wonderfully strange to allow it. And that strangeness made them desired. **Specimens from vastly different environments should prove of special interest.**

Near the center of the big, dark, square room, it found the sloping frame that ran to the upper regions. There was a portal at the top of the frame; a portal big enough for the giant ones. It hissed at the thought of them, its lips drawing back from a circle of tiny, inward-curving needles—gleaming, metallic. Stuff of light-terrors, they were, untouchable. Only the little ones could be taken. Only the young ones could be used. **A specimen must not exceed the ability of one unit to subdue it preparatory to study.**

Ungainly, galumphing, unused to this kind of motion, it mounted the staircase. It was slow, but nearly silent. At the top of the climb, it reoriented itself again and began the journey through the sleeping house, across the hall, through the family room, toward the room it determined must hold the thing desired.

In the portal, odors assailed it—too varied, swirling, confusing. Light speared its eyes—light from a single point low on the wall. Turning its head away from the light, it sought and located the field of warmth generated by the small creature's body.

The little boy, sleeping and dreaming of Hobbits and Moles at tea-parties, turned over onto his back and murmured, "I'd like ice cream, please."

It felt a thrill as the soft sound breathed into its aural membranes. Just up there, just on that lumpy platform, somewhere amid the tortured shapes of bedding and stuffed toys, was the Prize.

It caught the edge of the bed and drew itself up; saw, as through a haze, the white shape of the boy. It perched there near his feet, trembling, cringing a little in the glare from the night-light, and positioned its augmented teeth, starting the flow of paralyzer into the cartilage behind the needles.

The thing that reared out of the jumbled shapes on the bed was a creature from the most horrible nursery-light terror—blacker than the blackest cave, furred and hideously formed. And the eyes! They glowed red as life's water in the piercing spray of light. The horrible mouth opened on impossibly long fangs and shrieked.

It froze for a moment only, caught in terror's paralysis, then tried to leap away as the small creature sat up and added its voice to the din.

"Mommy! Daddy! There's a rat in my room! Mommy!"

But the moment was too long, the hideous enemy too quick.

Karen and Matt reached the family room as a striped blur arced through it and disappeared under a coffee table. Evan appeared in the hallway.

"Mommy! It's a big ol' rat! Troll's got a rat!"

"Oh, God," moaned Karen. "Let him out, honey. Quick!"

Galvanized by the horrible sounds coming from under the table, Matt obeyed, racing to the front door to open it. "C'mon, Troll. Outside!"

Karen rounded the table. "Psst!" she hissed. "Go on, Troll. Outside!" She clapped her hands.

The cat moved like tiger-striped lightning, its catch clutched in strong feral jaws. He flew across the family room, a furry shot, his victim's gangling unratlike limbs, a blur.

Matt slammed the door after him and went to comfort his son, already sobbing into the arms of his mother.

"It's all right, Ev, honey. It's gone now. Troll took it away."

The little boy's sobs turned to snuffles and finally ceased. Ev drew back from his parents a bit, then wiped his eyes and blinked. "I wonder if he'll leave any *bones*."

Out on the rain-soaked hillside in front of the house, a gold light winked on, turning the mist to glory. In the center of the patch of light, unnoticed by the family framed by the bedroom window, Troll finished his hero's meal, licked whiskered lips, and began to clean himself and purr. There was, between his paws, a tiny pile of metal needles and curving platelets—the stuff of Dwarves's chain-mail shirts and gauntlet gloves. But he was a fastidious cat and left no bones at all.

The Stoor's Map

John Dalmas

John Dalmas has made a name for himself as a
master of military science fiction. I remember him
once saying that he used to read *The Lord of the
Rings* to his children as a bedtime story. In "The
Stoor's Map" he creates a world of his own to
rival Tolkien's Middle-earth.

Rory Hoy heaved on the stout oak pry pole with
all the hard strength of his forty-four pounds, and felt
the stone pallet's edge lift a bit. Liam Maqsween got a
deeper purchase with his own then, and in a moment
the granite block slid off both pallet and cart, thudding heavily to the ground. Liam straightened and
wiped sweat from his forehead with the big red ker-
chief that normally hung like a flag from his pocket.
Then both men hopped down from the low cart.

"Well, lad," said Liam, "that's it for the day. Come
in and I'll pay you." They went into the low shed, one
end of which served as his office, and from a chest
beside his writing table he took a purse, loosening the
drawstring and peering inside. Plucking out a silver

half crown, he pressed it into the younger man's thick hand.

"Thank thee, sir."

Liam nodded. "Thank you for the help," he said, completing the formula. Then added, "I've got odds and ends to tend to in the smithy in the morning—small tasks that won't need help. Meet me at the quarry after lunch."

"Noon at the quarry. I'll be there, Mr. Maqsween."

Rory stuffed the half crown in his pocket and left the office. That last block had taken a while to cut and drag. Then add the loading and hauling...And his mother didn't stand for coming late to the table; he'd best take his supper at the inn. That was an advantage in being the innkeeper's son; he could eat there without charge, since he paid full board at home.

The graveled road, the only road, wound through Meadowvale, curling around low stone houses that had been built not in rows but wherever the builders had built them, starting four hundred years earlier when Meadowvale was newly settled. The inn was near the village center, at one end of the common, where spreading elms awaited picnickers, and where, on fall evenings, young tomtaihn, kin to hobbits, stood in the dusk, rakes in hand around burning leaf piles, talking in the fragrant smoke.

Hoy's Inn was more a tavern than an inn, for Meadowvale, well within the Great Forest, was small and saw few travelers. In olden times, the founders of Meadowvale had lived in or around the town of Oak Hill, thirty leagues away. Until some four hundred years back, when the big people arrived—soldiers of King Gnaup of Saxmark, and his count, and the count's sheriff—and said the land belonged now to the king.

Around Oak Hill, the countryside was rolling farmland, with patches of woods on the steeper slopes and along the streams, and Oak Hill itself had been— no doubt still was—a town, not a village. A sizable river, the Abhainn Hobb, flowed past it from the south, and a highway passed through it from southwest to northeast, with a bridge over the Hobb. There'd been both barge traffic and wagon traffic, and folk traveling through on ponyback. Thus there'd been a need in Oak Hill for a sizable inn, with rooms and beds large enough for stoors. (The rare big people who'd come by, however, had slept in the stable, in the hay; the rooms hadn't been *that* big.) The Oak Hill innkeepers, the Hoy family, had been both well-to-do and influential; Hoys had been sheriff, even mayor. Here in Meadowvale though, they were no more than most other families. Which grated on the Hoys, even after four hundred years.

Just now, Rory Hoy wasn't thinking about that, though. He was thinking about roast beef, parsnips, and buttered beets, or maybe sweet yellow peas, with wheat bread and butter, a wedge of good Mirrorudh cheese, and perhaps a mug of his father's ale, if the old tomteen wasn't watching closely. (Nob Hoy didn't approve of youngsters drinking, especially on the house, and the tomtaihn regarded twenty-five-year-olds as youngsters.)

Rory went in through the kitchen—the front way was for paying guests—though he'd eat in the pot room, the common room, with the customers.

"Rory!"

The sharp voice was his father's. "Yessir?"

"Doney's off on an errand for me, and there's a customer waiting to be served; a stoor. See to it!"

"Yessir." It wasn't fair, Rory thought; he'd worked hard all day. But he put a good face on, and went into the pot room.

The stoor was hulking and angular, ill-fitted to the bench and table. Meadowvale could go months without seeing one, and the villagers had mixed feelings about them. Stoors were wanderers, not settled reliable folk, though surely they had homes somewhere, with mothers and fathers. Mostly they traveled singly, which in itself made them strange to the social, even gregarous tomtaihn. They traded, bought, and sold. Bargains could be had from them, or what seemed like bargains—things you couldn't otherwise get, at a price you were content with, or at least willing to pay. But people had been fleeced by them, too, and it was rumored that some were spies for King Hreolf.

"Sir," Rory said, "may I serve you?"

The stoor's black eyes were level with Rory's own, though the stoor was seated and the bench low. He was far smaller than big people, but he'd probably stand an ell in height, Rory thought, about half again his own thirty-one inches. The face was lean and knobby—cheekbones, brows, and jaw—flagged with great flaring eyebrows like wings, and topped by a thatch of stiff, curly hair. The hands were knobby too, with tufts of wiry hair on the fingers.

The stoor looked the tomteen over and spoke in a thick stoor brogue. "Tha's weerin' a smith's leather apron," he said, ignoring the young tomteen's question.

"Yessir. A quarryman's apron, actually. May I serve you?"

"Tha's just koom fra work, then?"

"Yessir. To eat my supper. My father's the host here, and the potboy is off on errands, so he told me to serve you. What would you like?" He recited the fare to the man, then, and the stoor ordered, seeming not to consider cost, though his clothes were rough and worn. When Rory brought his food, the stoor motioned to the bench across from him.

"Tha hasn't eaten. Happen tha'd sup wi' me."

The temptation was strong. Rory'd never talked with a stoor before, had scarcely seen one close up. In fact, he hadn't talked to a stranger of any sort more than three or four times in his life, and those had been tomtaihn from other villages. And if the stoor *was* a spy for King Hreolf, surely there was nothing he could tell him that would harm Meadowvale.

So though his father might well berate him for it afterward, he brought his own meal to the table, and they talked. The stoor, instead of pumping Rory, told him of places the young tomteen had never heard of. He favored the Great Forest and the districts adjacent though, he said. The stoors too had the protection of the Forest Soul, like the other halfling folk. Otherwise he'd not travel here, where trolls could be met with.

When he'd finished eating, he took his purse from his pack and shook out some coins, to sort the cost with knobby fingers. Several of the coins seemed to be gold! The young tomteen's eyes widened. "Sir," he said, almost in a whisper, "are those—gold pieces?"

The winglike eyebrows rose while the stoor's voice lowered. "Aye. Would tha keer to be toochin' one of 'em?"

"If I might. I've never seen one before." Rory picked one up. The currency used in Meadowvale was mostly old and worn smooth, minted long ago at Oak Hill in the days of tomtaidh dominion there, though other coins, mostly Saxi, were also seen, having entered the Meadowvale economy through trade with travelers. This one looked—not fresh minted perhaps, but not worn. The marks on it he thought might be dwarf runes. "Do you know where it came from?" he asked.

The stoor looked around before answering, as if to be sure that no one else heard. "Oh, aye! Tha mought say, in a manner of speakin'. Near enough ah'd gaw for more, if ah—Though 'tis a dangerous place, s'truth. 'Twere a long time agaw, an ah'd plenty of time, ah tawd maself. But there were always another place to see, an' ah were never one to set great store on wealth. Long as ah'm eatin'." He gestured as if pointing out his own worn clothes, then shrugged. "An naw that ah'm so near the place, ah dawn't be yoong an' venturesome naw more."

The stoor didn't look so old to Rory, maybe fifty. Stoor bodies must wear out more quickly than tomtaidh bodies, he decided. "There's more gold then?" he asked. "Near here?"

"Hoo! More? A whole cask more!" He motioned with his hands as if to indicate size, a chest more than two feet long, and half as wide and high. "Thaw not all gold; some o' it's jewels—rubies and emeralds and pearls. Ah only tewk a handful. Ah were afoot—hadn't naw pony—an' . . . 'Twas near the Dank Land, tha sees, wi' trawlls an' bears abawt, an' wargs an' worse. An' the Forest Soul dawn't tooch there." The stoor's brow knitted, as if in troubled thought. "The Dank Land's got its awn soul, dark . . ." He shrugged. "Though naw doot a bold lad with a good pony, if he didn't linger . . ." Another shrug. "But ah'm nae yoong naw. Mah awd knays dawn't let me climb brants naw more, nor clamber through rocks and windfalls.

"As for bein' near—It's naw farther, or not mooch, than a long day's pony ride. Even given that the way's through trackless forest and rough hills." He waved toward the west, then suddenly thrust his face at the young tomteen, his voice a whisper. "Why? Were tha thinkin' of gawin' there?"

Rory didn't flinch. "If you'd draw me a map," he murmured. "I'd pay."

The black eyes examined him thoughtfully. "Can I troost thee?"

Rory nodded vigorously, though unsure where trust entered in, or where it might lead.

"What would tha pay for sooch a map?"

Rory knew exactly how much money he had, including the half crown in his pocket, and being a Hoy, named a sum that left room for dickering. "Twenty-five crowns."

The stoor shook his head. "'Tis worth far more than that."

"Thirty then."

The stoor examined him thoughtfully. "Ah'd take naw less than a hoondred."

Rory felt his hopes fall like the granite block had when pried from the cart.

"Ah'll tell thee what. Tha'rt an honest-lewkin' lad, an' ah have little doot tha's a man o' thy word. So ah'll take the risk. Besides, ah'm gettin' naw yoonger. An' if a hoondred crowns is more than tha has naw—why later, with the treasure cask in thy cellar, payin' a hoondred will seem like nawthin' to thee." The stoor looked around again, then murmured: "Fifty crowns naw, an' a hoondred more when ah next koom through Meadowvale. Which ah'll make a point of doin' within the year."

"Thirty-eight," the young tomteen said desperately. "It's all I have." Then he remembered the coin in his pocket. "Thirty-eight and a half. And the other hundred for sure, when I've got the treasure."

The stoor seemed to brood on it a long minute. Then, "Bring me a paper," he said. "Naw, a parchment. Paper's naw good for sunthin' 'portant as this."

Parchment? Where could he lay hands on a parchment? ... "Wait here a minute, sir," said Rory, "I'll be right back." He left the room then, deliberately not hurrying. Once outside though, he speeded to a trot. His home was less than forty yards away, and as he walked through the front door, no one was in the living room. He could hear his mother in the kitchen, rattling pans. What he sought was on the wall, a parchment perhaps a dozen inches on a side, with a motto inked on it:

HE WHO WOULD HAVE
MUST FIRST LABOR
THEN HOLD

and coins in watercolors. A great-grandmother had made it. With a tough thumbnail, the young tomteen pried the tacks from the corners, then went quietly to his room, where he kept his money, and left with it.

It could be days before anyone missed the parchment, he told himself. It had been there forever; people rarely looked at it anymore. And by the time it was missed, he'd be rich. Then no one would mind, not even his mother.

Sween Maqsween, his missus Aleen, and Megh, their only daughter, were in the sitting room. The supper things had been put away, and Megh, like her mother, sat embroidering. Megh was good at needle-work, as at most things she did.

The figure her needle was shaping was a young tomteen, well formed and with the rare, coppery red hair that made all the lasses of Meadowvale cluck and coo at the sight of Rory Hoy, the handsomest lad in the valley.

There was a knock at the door, and as the only offspring present, Megh got to her feet and answered. At twenty-six inches in height and twenty-eight pounds, to get off a chair was no effort at all, surely not for someone just nineteen years old.

It was Rory Hoy she opened to. Pleased, she asked him in.

Among the tomtaihn, a young person, child or grown, doesn't enter the home of a peer and begin a conversation until respects have been paid to any parent present. Thus when he stepped in, Rory bowed deeply.

"Good evening, Mister Maqsween, Missus Maqsween. I trust the Forest Soul is being good to you."

"Come in, young Hoy," the old tomteen grunted. "The Forest Soul is as good to us as we deserve, no more, no less." The formula complete, he raised an eyebrow. "I suppose it's Megh you've come to see."

"Begging your pardon, sir, ma'am, it is indeed."

"Well, then," the old man said, and gestured to two chairs in a corner by the family bookshelf.

"Begging your pardon, sir, but I'd hoped to speak in greater privacy than this."

Both eyebrows rose this time. "Did you now? Are you thinking we'd eavesdrop, the missus and me?"

"Sir," Rory answered, "I have no doubt you'd never strain to listen, but the room is small, and it would be hard not to hear."

"Hmh!" Rory could feel the old tomteen's eyes sharpen. "And what might it be you'd not want us to hear?"

He dug in his heels. Politely. "Sir, ma'am, you were young and unwed once. What was it you said to one another then?"

Aleen Maqsween hid a smile, while old Sween's eyebrows, instead of rising again, drew down in a knot. "You're overbold, young Hoy."

"Yessir. I'm sorry, sir."

"And you, Meghwan, do you wish to step outside with this young scoundrel?"

She blushed. "Yes, Father."

The frown relaxed and died. "So." He reached to his smoking stand, then turned to his daughter while he packed his pipe with pipeweed. "Meghwan, you may go out and sit with this young man in the arbor for the time it takes me to smoke two bowls. But by the time I knock the dottle from my pipe, you're to be back inside."

She brightened. "Thank you, Da. We'll be perfectly nice."

"Hmh!" Old Sween watched them move to the door. "And Meghwan!"

"Yes, Da?"

"*No kissing!*"

Megh Maqsween blushed. "Da! Of course not!" The young people stepped outside then, closing the door behind them.

Aleen Maqsween laughed quietly, gently, when they'd gone, and mimicked her daughter. "'Da! Of course not!'" She laughed again. "You're hard on the lad, Maqsween."

"Indeed. He'd not know what to think if I wasn't. And after all, he's only twenty-five. He's five more years, or four and a half, before he's of marrying age." Maqsween grunted again. "It's too bad he got interested in the girl so young." He reached, and squeezed his wife's hand gently. "It's not easy, being in love with the prettiest girl in the valley, and having to wait. I know. But it's my duty to see that he does."

Megh let Rory hold her hand while they walked to the arbor. A humpbacked moon rode high, the moonlight shining on her straw-blond hair. There'd not been a tomteen with hair like hers, in Meadowvale, since Maev the Lovely, some hundred years since, and Maev lacked the sweet disposition of Megh Maqsween. Also Megh was lovelier, Rory was sure, a fairy child grown to womanhood. He longed to cup her face and kiss it tenderly. He had once, and it had troubled her.

Now, at the arbor, she sat down on the single seat, leaving him to sit alone on the double seat opposite. "What was it thou came to tell me, Rory?" she asked.

And her eyes were blue, in Meadowvale a rarity almost as great as her blond hair, though her grandmother had blue eyes before her.

"Rory?"

"Oh! Yes. I—I'm going to be rich, Megheen."

"Rich?"

He reached inside his shirt, took out the parchment, and held it so the moonlight shone on it for her. "Look!"

She peered, straining. "He who would have..." she began.

"Oh! Sorry," he said, and turned it over. "This side."

"It...Is it a map?"

"A treasure map."

"Treasure map? Where did you get it?"

"From a stoor, a stoor at the inn. He sold it to me."

"And it's real? How do you know?"

The question jarred Rory, jarred words out of him. "He was wealthy. Oh, not that he dressed wealthy, but his purse...I waited on him, and when it was time to pay, he opened his purse and poured part of it out on the table. So full of gold pieces it was, he had to sort through them to find coppers to pay with! Old coins, with dwarf runes on them! And pearls, emeralds, rubies! My eyes were out to here!" He gestured.

"And he sold you the map?"

"He did!"

"For how much?"

"All the money I had—thirty-eight crowns. Thirty-eight and a half, but he left me the half crown. Plus another hundred I'm to pay him when he next comes by. He trusts me. And a hundred crowns will seem like nothing to me then, I'll be so wealthy."

"But—Why would he sell you the map? He could go there himself and get the treasure."

"You'd have to see him to understand. He's old, old and lame. And the treasure's hard to get to, in a cave in the Cliffy Mountains. On the side toward the Dank Land!"

Her eyes were large in the moonlight, large and shadowed dark. "Oh, Megheen!" he whispered, "my love, you're so beautiful! And I love you so much! I can't stand to wait another four years. With the treasure, I'll be rich enough, no one will complain if we marry young. We'll give a wedding party that they'll talk about forever!"

He looked longingly at her.

"And I love you, Rory Hoy. Enough that, wait or not, rich or not, you're the one I'll marry."

He slid off the seat onto his knees before her. Her hands had been folded in her lap, and he took them in his own, kissing them passionately. Gently she removed them. "Da will be smoking that second pipe by now."

Rory Hoy got slowly to his feet. Surely not the second pipe already. But she was right: it wouldn't do to stay out here kissing her like that in the night. It would tear him up inside.

She stood too, and hand in hand they walked back to the house, saying nothing.

When he left the Maqsweens', despondency settled on Rory Hoy, and a feeling of unworthiness. He saw himself now as gullible, a fool, and he'd lied to Megh—been less than truthful. Even the night was darker; clouds covered the moon now. It would rain tonight, he guessed. He hoped it would be over by morning.

It was pitch-dark when he awoke, as he'd intended when he'd laid down. He went to his window and, looking out, saw stars. The moon was down, and being late in the second quarter, this meant dawn was near.

It was time.

He'd packed everything he needed, before ever he'd snuffed his candle. Now he had only to pull on his clothes, buckle his belt, grab his pack, and leave. He'd left his window open to the night; even mosquitoes don't bite halflings where the Forest Soul rules. Now he climbed out and trotted softly to the pony barn.

Not only the grass was wet, but the dirt as well. It had rained while he slept, as he'd thought it would.

In the barn he'd prepared too. The pack saddle and straps he'd set on the floor, just inside the door. He went to Blacky, the pony he'd chosen, led him outside, and strapped the pack saddle to his back. The pony nickered softly, and Rory hushed him. His mother was a light sleeper (though not as light as he thought), and it wouldn't do to waken her.

As he led it toward the road, he saw a rider approaching, a large, dark figure on a large, dark pony with a pack pony trailing. The stoor, he thought, and held back, not wanting to meet him. An emptiness filled him as he watched the stoor ride by; it seemed to him the man had tricked him, that there was no treasure, that he'd given his life savings for—a piece of sky.

He pushed the thought away. It was done now. The stoor had cheated him or he hadn't. If he hadn't, there was a treasure out there, waiting. A treasure that could make the Hoys rich again, important again, that would make his father respect him at last. A treasure that would let him marry Megh Maqsween without waiting all those years.

The stoor and his animals passed on down the road, and Rory Hoy started off, jaw set. He stopped at the inn, tying his pony to a pear tree in back. Lantern light shone through the back windows; his cousin Doney would be inside, firing up the big cookstove and the ovens for the morning's baking.

Doney was surprised to see him, and even more to see the short sword at his side. As Rory packed food for three days, he explained to Doney that he had business to attend to. Doney, who was seventeen, stared wide-eyed; it sounded very mysterious.

The first hint of dawnlight was showing in the east when Rory left. He paused at the Maqsween smithy, and on the anvil left a note to Liam, prepared the evening before, weighting it with a chisel.

Visibility was improving notably when he reached

the upper end of the meadow from which Meadowvale took its name. According to the rough map the stoor had drawn for him, he needed to follow the Mirrorudh west to its source in the Cliffy Mountains. There'd be a pass above the headwaters, of course, and on the other side, the headwaters of another stream, one that flowed into the Dank Land. Where that stream flowed out of the mountains, there should be a talus slide at the foot of a steep, a "brant" the stoor had called it, and near it a cave. The cave. According to the map.

The young tomteen ground his teeth. The treasure he'd believed in without questioning, the evening before, he greatly doubted now. Disbelieved. And was sure the Megh had disbelieved when he'd told her. But he'd carry through with his plan; it was the only way he could truly and finally know.

At age thirty, a young man was sent out of his father's home, unless of course the old man was dead or disabled and he the inheriting son. And while old Sween Maqsween had had a foot crushed by a granite block that slipped from a sling, he could hobble well enough to take care of a man's duties about the house and garden.

Thus Liam Maqsween lived in a bachelor house at the upper end of the valley, against the very edge of the forest, not a furlong from where Rory Hoy had passed in the first faint light of dawn. At Oak Hill, their ancestors had followed the old custom of living in hillside burrows, and this bachelor house, with its thick rock walls, was dug into the side of a low hummock, looking like a stony extension of it. On the hummock stood a huge golden birch with curling yellow bark that seemed almost to grow from the mossy, sod-covered slate roof.

An old widow came in each evening to cook a proper meal; the others were each bachelor's own responsibility. The sun was up, and Liam Maqsween had eaten bacon and eggs, with bread toasted in the oven and spread with butter and marmalade. Now he sat outside in the sunshine, which felt good in the morning cool, smoking his pipe and drinking a cup of shade-mint tea before going to the smithy. It had rained in the night, laying the dust and sweetening the air.

While he drank, his young cousin Tom came trotting up. "Liam," said the lad, "I've just come from your da's. Megh's gone! Disappeared!" Tom's job it was to climb the ladder into Sween Maqsween's hayloft each morning and throw down hay for the cow and ponies. While he was doing it, old Sween had stumped out to the barn and told him, asking him to bring the message. The old man was upset, as well he might be.

Liam thanked him, quickly finished his tea, and hurried off to his parents' house. Megh had left on her pony before they'd wakened, they told him, taking only her cloak and raincape, a loaf of bread, and some cheese.

"And have you no idea where she might have gone?" Liam asked.

"I've a suspicion," his father said. "Rory Hoy was here last evening and asked to speak to her alone. I agreed, and they went to the arbor to talk. She was back sooner than I could smoke a pipe, but long enough to set some plan in motion, something they'd thought out before. I think they've run off," he finished glumly.

Liam went out and saddled a pony, thinking as he did. He didn't believe she'd do that, or that Rory would ask her to. But then, he didn't know what else to think. He'd ride by the Hoys and ask for Rory, then decide what next to do.

Margo Hoy was no help to him. She didn't know where her son was, she said. He'd gone before breakfast. If Liam found him, he was to tell him his mother was upset with him. It scarcely needed telling; Margo Hoy was usually upset with someone, most often her son. Liam promised and left.

So. Rory and Megh had both disappeared. It seemed that his father suspected rightly. But where would they have gone? Five leagues north was Troutrudh, the largest of the three tomtaidh villages in the forest. Four leagues south was Mulberry, smaller than Meadowvale. If a lad was to run off, he'd need to find work, and Troutrudh was the likeliest for that. But...Liam shook his head. It didn't add up. Rory had at least some idea what it cost to keep a home and wife. What would there be for him in Troutrudh, or anywhere else? His whole family lived in Meadowvale, and all his friends.

Muttering a coarse word beneath his mustache,

Liam touched the pony's ribs with his heels and rode home. If he was going to ride to Troutrudh, he'd want his raincape, and happen his cloak to sleep in, if it came to that.

On his way, he stopped at the smithy. He'd forged an ax head for a customer, earlier that week. He'd lay it out on the bench, with a note, so the purchaser could pick it up, should he stop by. On the anvil he found the note that Rory had left him. "Dear Mister Maqsween—I'm sorry I won't be able to meet you at the quarry after lunch. Something has come up. I hope to be back in a few days. I'll tell you about it then. Respectfully, Rory Hoy."

Somehow it made the hair bristle on Liam's neck. He stared hard at the note, as if to see what lay behind it, but saw nothing that wasn't written. On an impulse he went outside and scanned the moist ground for tracks. And found hoofprints, shod, left since last night's rain. They had to be Rory's.

He jogged his pony home, where he got not only his raincape and cloak, but his short sword and bow. Then he took the sporting arrows from his quiver and replaced them with the broad-headed arrows that each male tomteen kept to defend the village, should it ever be necessary. As he did, he wondered why. He'd never shoot Rory or strike him with the sword.

He took them anyway, then rode back to the smithy and followed the tracks. Near the forest's edge they came to the Mirrorudh, where he found a second set, of a smaller pony. Megh's, he had no doubt. So they'd connived. He shook his head.

They'd ridden into the forest, along the stream. Her pony followed; here and there it's hoof marks lay atop the larger. In the forest though, in places, the tracks separated, as if Megh was picking a different way around the occasional patches of blowdown. Then they'd rejoin. Almost as if they hadn't ridden together— as if they were going to the same place separately, with the Mirrorudh their guide.

None of it made sense. There was nothing for them in the forest—no way to live, to shelter and feed themselves. Yet if they were looking for privacy—if that was all—they needn't have gone more than a furlong into the woods. Nor would they have run off in a way to make themselves missed and invite pursuit.

Liam shook his head as if to shake off confusion. He thought of simply following the stream himself—it would be faster than watching for hoofprints—but if he did and they left it, he'd lose them. Best keep on as he was. They'd surely stop to rest along the way; he'd catch them then.

As a boy with other boys, Rory had explored up the Mirrorudh as much as a mile, a long distance for short tomtaidh legs, particularly in pathless wilderness. Now he'd gone well beyond that, dismounting at times to lead his pony through sapling patches or awkward terrain. For the low rolling hills of home had given way to higher, rougher hills, and pack saddles weren't made for comfortable riding.

Here the Mirrorudh had cut a ravine, and he'd

had to leave it, riding and walking along a bordering ridge, sometimes on the crest, sometimes picking his way along the side. It was noon, give or take a bit, and broken ground had shunted him into a notch, shaggy with firs. Now, close before his pony, a rivulet rattled over a pebbled bed toward the Mirrorudh, itself audible a distance to his right.

He paused to wipe sweat, and wondered if these were the Cliffy Mountains yet, or if there was worse to come.

Meanwhile it seemed a good place to eat. He led the pony to the rivulet, then, on hands and knees, lowered his face to the water, just upcurrent of his thirsty mount. Thirst slaked, he refilled his leather flask and moved to take his rucksack from the pack saddle.

A jay began to shriek on the slope behind him, the same jay, he guessed, that had called alarms at his own passing, minutes earlier. *What's roused it now?* he wondered. *Bear? Wolf? Troll?* The possibilities interested but didn't worry him. The Forest Soul had laid her protection over halflings. Within her domain, only creatures with souls of their own—men and other halflings—could harm him. Even his pony was immune when he was with it.

He stood with a hand on the reins, hoping to spy something interesting. In his whole life, all he'd ever seen of wolf and bear was tracks and dung, though once he'd thought he'd seen a troll at twilight, peering from the forest's edge.

The jay continued for a noisy minute, and having

done its duty, it stopped. Then Rory heard shod hooves clatter on rock outcrop, and curiosity became concern. Quickly he led the pony behind a thicket of sapling firs, and peered out. Shortly he saw movement, glimpsed first a dun hide, then a bobbing pony head. Then the entire pony came into view, with its rider.

Rory stared. "Megh!" he called softly, and led his own pony out where she could see.

"Rory!' Her expression was of relief, gladness.

He met her at the rivulet, took her hand, and helped her down. "What are you doing here?"

"I—It seemed to me that—you might not come back. If you were disappointed. If the stoor had lied to you. But if I was with you, you would." She paused, then spoke more softly. "And I don't want to lose you."

"Ah, Megheen!" He longed to take her in his arms, but held back. It would be risky, and unfair to both of them.

Her eyes met his, soberly. "Have you eaten yet?" she asked.

He shook his head.

"Neither have I."

"Well then—"

They ate by the rivulet, side by side on a rock, while their ponies, one dun, one black, grazed a patch of larkspurs on the bank. When they'd finished, they looked again at the map. With her there, somehow hope took root in Rory's heart. Maybe there was a treasure; maybe they'd return rich to Meadowvale.

Then they got on their ponies again and rode west.

In midafternoon they reached a bowllike cove, the birthplace of the Mirrorudh, the spring that gave it being. The climb to the divide above, though not rough or long, was steep; the two tomtaihn hiked it to spare their ponies. The crest was mostly stone, its trees sparse. From it they could look back over miles of high hills that diminished eastward. Westward they dropped more sharply, to the Dank Lands that stretched flat to the horizon, partly wooded, partly open fen, bathed in sunlight but somehow murky.

The two young tomtaihn stood for a minute. "Best we go on," Rory said at last and, meshing his fingers for a step, boosted Megh atop her pony. Then he climbed onto his own, and they set off downhill. The creek below, according to his map, would take them to the cave and wealth. Or not, as the case might be.

They'd gone scarcely a furlong when a fly bit Rory's temple. He'd never been bitten before.

The troll had little tolerance for daylight, and in summer, when nights were short, he grew restless toward sundown.

On this particular day he'd sheltered in a hole where a pine had been uprooted by wind and hung up in the tops of others. Between the uptilted root disk and the lip of the hole, there'd been just room for him to crawl in. He'd slept there most of the day.

Then hunger had wakened him, strong hunger; he hadn't eaten for two days, and trolls are notorious for their appetites.

Now he lay peering out, eyes squinted nearly shut against what to him was blinding glare, though the late sunlight was soft, mellow. A movement caught his eyes, and through the blur he saw two animals moving down the creek, each big enough to feed him for a day. They'd pass him seventy or eighty yards away. Their scent on the breeze was complex and unfamiliar, though perhaps long ago... His mouth began to water, and he strained to see more clearly. One of them had two necks, one at the front where it belonged, the second rising from the middle of its back. The other—The other seemed to be following something that walked upright.

He shook his shaggy head. Before long the sun would set. When the dusk was thick enough, he'd come out and follow them, follow and kill them, for he trailed by scent.

They were passing in front of him when the spider came, one of the great spiders that even he took care to avoid.

Rory saw it before Megh did, saw it charge from ambush across the foot of a talus slope, charge so fast, so shockingly fast, he had no time to draw his sword. He didn't see Megh's dun rear back, didn't see her fall, and her scream didn't register. Then the spider was on him, clawed front limbs grasping, palps clutching, and in a moment beyond horror he saw the two great jaws gape, each with its curved fang, then mercifully passed out. The fangs sank into his shoulders, and from them venom flowed.

Because he'd gone limp, the fangs withdrew more quickly than they might have. Then the spinnerets secreted thread almost as thick as wrapping cord, and sticky, the spider wrapping them 'round and 'round him till the tomteen was nearly mummified. But the mummy was porous. It was no part of the spider's intention that he suffocate.

When he was wrapped, it went to Megh Maqsween, who lay in an unconscious heap where she'd landed. It bit her briefly and wrapped her too. Then, with its palps, it picked Rory up and carried him to its lair. When he was deposited, it returned for Megh.

It crushed neither of them against its hard sharp shoulder plates. It didn't intend to eat them itself.

Liam Maqsween had traveled without a break, eating in the saddle and walking from time to time to rest his pony. He too had been bitten by flies and mosquitoes after crossing the divide; he'd left the domain of the Forest Soul.

He knew he wasn't far behind the others now. Twice, where they'd crossed the small creek, the water that had dripped from their horses hadn't entirely dried yet on the rocks.

Here and there along the creek were narrow stretches of meadow, and as he entered one of them from a stand of pines, he saw two ponies plodding uphill toward him. He recognized the dun at once, his sister's. The other wore a pack saddle, like a sawbuck on its back. They slowed down when they saw him, then stopped, waiting. He kicked his own pony to a trot, hurrying to them, and they stayed for him. He stopped when he reached them, examining.

Nothing all day had made much sense: his sister's departure, Rory's note, the nature of their early trail, or their coming to this country of fearful reputation. Now here were their ponies, riderless, with lathered sweat drying on them. Megh's still wore saddlebags.

And the sun was low; in an hour, dusk would begin. Liam Maqsween shivered. Sliding from his saddle, he gathered their reins and remounted. At first the other ponies were reluctant to follow, but he was firm, and after a moment they fell in behind him.

In a quarter hour he came out of forest into open grassy meadow, flanked on one side by thick pines and on the other by a talus slope, a fan of loose rocks, with boulders heaped and jumbled in places at its foot. The hair bristled on his neck; it seemed to him he was watched. Rory and Megh had been thrown from their ponies. Must have been. And being no expert rider—no one in Meadowvale was—he stopped. He transferred his quiver to his back, unholstered his bow and slung it from his right shoulder, then dismounted, to lead the animals by the reins, gripping his short sword with his left hand. The way led downward, the slope tapering, easing. A hundred yards more brought him to Megh's cloak, lying on the ground. She'd have removed it in the heat of day, perhaps laying it loose across the pony's withers. This must be where she'd been thrown.

Again his neck hairs crawled, and he stopped to scan about him. He saw nothing, but felt danger, and detoured to his left, to put more distance between him and the forest edge. He'd passed the foot of the talus slope before he saw the two cave mouths, the smaller nearby. Tunnel mouths more likely, for they were square.

Then he saw movement in the larger. Something extended from it, and he dropped the reins. Behind him the ponies stamped, snorting nervously; Liam edged upslope toward the smaller opening.

The spider came out then, looked at him, and for just a moment Liam froze. Behind him the ponies stampeded; he didn't notice; his attention was riveted on the spider. Even at eighty yards it looked huge, taller than the ponies, and the spread of its legs was several times its height. Then it charged, and the spell was broken. Running faster than he'd have thought possible, Liam sprinted toward the smaller hole, and when it seemed he'd be too late, stopped abruptly. Bristly legs swept to clutch him, and he swung his sword with all the strength of his rock-hard body. It struck, severing the leg at a joint, and at the same instant he ducked low. The other leg missed, and somehow Liam found himself in the tunnel entrance, scrabbling for safety on all fours. Two spans inside he stopped, panting, eyes stinging with sweat. Half a minute earlier there'd been none.

He was aware of a dry, high-pitched chittering

close outside. There was no room to swing freely—
there was little more than room to stand—but he
struck at it with his short sword as best he could, and
cut it deeply behind the claws. The limb withdrew,
and the chittering shrilled almost beyond Liam's frequency perception, setting his teeth on edge. Then it
stopped, and silken threads the size of stout string
began to lash the opening. Liam took quick steps
backward, afraid of being snared. After a moment
though, he realized that the spider was simply closing
the opening with a tough silken mesh.

He sat back onto the floor and examined his
surroundings in the light that shone through the
newly woven door. Clearly the tunnel had been roughly
squared, its walls and ceiling showing chisel marks.
The floor had been sanded, and now was littered with
small bones; some predator had denned there, might
still den there, might be behind him now. He rolled to
his knees and peered back into the dimness, seeing
nothing. Who, he wondered, had carved it, and
when?

Crouching, sword in hand, he began to explore.
Gradually the tunnel curved, darkening, and in some
seventy or eighty yards met a larger tunnel, high
enough for a big person to walk upright. He stood at
the junction, evaluating. Was it big enough for the
spider? In height perhaps, but clearly not in width,
which he judged at four arm spans. To his left, deeper
in the mountain, he thought he heard water splashing
on stone. To his right he could see the daylit square of
the large entrance, distant enough that where he

stood, the tunnel was almost as dark as moonless night. Slowly, softly, sword tightly gripped, Liam moved toward the light.

He'd gone most of the way when he heard a sound, faint and dry, as if something had scuffed against rock. Holding his breath, he stopped. The sound did not repeat. There was more light here, but he saw nothing to account for the sound, and moved forward again, even more cautiously, hardly breathing. Suddenly the spider was in front of him, blocking the light, its row of eyes, like big black beads, staring at him from scant ells away. Its bristly palps groped, and with a cry he jumped back.

He crouched panting, heart thudding. The groping palps couldn't reach him, and striding forward, he struck at one with all his strength, felt the sword bite. The spider jumped back, chittering wildly, the move jerking the sword from Liam's hand. The tomteen pounced after it, snatched it up, and scampered well back in the tunnel.

The spider had jumped to his right, out of view. Clearly there was a larger room, an entryway of some sort, between him and the entrance. Its lair, he decided, the place it took its victims, its food. Megh and Rory might well be there, or their bodies, what was left of them.

Liam knew more about spiders than was comfortable just then. The forest tomtaihn, normally unthreatened by other life forms, and being small themselves, close to nature, and typically unhurried, tended to watch things like spiders and insects—study them if you will. Especially during childhood and adolescence. He knew, for example, that spiders, after biting their prey, commonly crush them before sucking the juices from them. Sometimes though, the crushing and feeding are postponed, while at least sometimes the prey still lived after being bitten.

Megh and Rory might be alive in the entryway, though no doubt well wrapped with silk.

So despite the frenzied, high-pitched chittering, Liam edged toward the room again, keeping close to the right wall, his short sword in his left hand. From just short of the tunnel mouth, he could see much of the entryway's left half. It was square, about twelve yards long and twelve wide, and perhaps twice as high as the tunnel he was in. High enough for the dwarves or orcs of old, or big men if it came to that, to stand with long spears upright, ready to sally forth. There was even a ledge along the wall, for them to sit on while waiting.

On the sand-covered floor, among bones and other debris, were six silk-wrapped objects. Five were oblong, of various sizes. The other was larger and round, its diameter possibly twice Liam's height; an egg sac, he decided, and felt hope. The silk-wrapped food might well be alive, alive and fresh, awaiting the hatch.

Then the mother would crush the bundled victims as food for her hatchlings. He'd have to act before then.

The chittering had died. Quietly Liam moved back down the tunnel to the smaller branch he'd come from, and up it to its entrance. Cautiously he touched the silk that covered it. It was less sticky than he'd feared. Seemingly the stickiness dried in time, and was lost. With his sword he cut till the door covering was free, then pulled it inside and folded it against a wall. Warily he looked out. The sun had nearly set, and daylight had begun to dim, the beginning of dusk. He stepped outside, picked up a stone the size of his fist, and threw it as far as he could, downhill. It struck audibly on bare rock and bounced, and as he'd hoped, the spider came half out the other entrance, looking not toward him, but in the direction of the sound.

Slowly he stepped back into the opening, watching. The spider moved farther, a step at a time, then rushed downhill a few steps and paused. A thought occurred to Liam, a plan. He backed inside, then hurried down the narrow tunnel as fast as he dared in the darkness, into the larger tunnel, and up it to the entryway.

The spider was still outside. Quickly he went to the bundle he suspected was Megh, and dragged it into the tunnel, then returned for the one he hoped was Rory. One at a time he dragged them to the side tunnel, and up it to near its opening.

It was time to learn the worst. He started with the smallest bundle, using his pocket knife to saw the tough threads, not sticky at all now, only tacky. Once cut, the casing peeled off readily. Inside was Megh, her face slack, her limbs limp. Liam wet his cheek, held it to her open mouth, and felt faint cooling. She breathed, barely.

Then he freed Rory. The lad's short sword was still in its scabbard, and his rucksack on his back. Liam removed them and laid them aside.

For a few minutes he massaged and pummeled first Megh, then Rory, hoping to stimulate circulation, but his mind was on other things. Assuming he could revive them, how could they escape? Was the spider active at night? Many small ones were. He'd injured it twice, but not seriously. Could he somehow cripple or kill it?

He stopped his massaging to peer out the entrance. He couldn't see the spider. Was it hunting? Had it returned to her lair? *Or was it crouching in ambush on the steep slope just above his door?* A typical spider could cling to a wall or cross a ceiling, but not one weighing hundreds of pounds, even with eight feet to grip with... It would be a matter of steepness and surface.

His eyes found a pebble just outside the opening. He snatched it up and jumped back, then hurried again through the tunnels. The entryway was darker than before. He threw the pebble in, against the wall. There was no response, so sword ready, he followed it.

One of the other food bundles was small enough for him to drag readily. He pulled it from the room, and through the tunnels to where Megh and Rory lay. There he freed it, a wildcat as large as Megh, or larger; so far, so good.

Again he looked out, then jumped out and back. Nothing had pounced. Grabbing the wildcat by the tail, he pulled it just outside the opening and arranged it in a pose of natural sleep. The sun was down now. Would the spider see it? Would she be fooled?

He went back inside, laid his unsheathed sword on a piece of casing, and massaged the comatose tomtaihn, first one, then the other, positioning himself so he could see the wildcat as he worked. Shortly Rory responded, muttering incoherently for a moment. When he stilled again, his breathing was more nearly the normal breathing of sleep, and Liam gave his full attention to Megh.

It was full twilight when suddenly the spider was there. Liam saw her crouch over the wildcat, grasp it awkwardly with wounded palps, and thrust her two fangs into the body. Moving quickly but smoothly, Liam took his sword and was out the opening, striking hard at the spider's head. He felt the blade bite through thick chiton armor. The creature didn't try at once to grab him. Instead she jumped backward a dozen feet, chittering wildly, gathering herself as Liam scurried back inside.

Had he damaged it critically? Enough that it might die, or...? Again it began weaving threads of silk across the opening, this time not stopping so soon, and his shelter grew almost pitch-dark. He crouched in the blackness, massaging his sister till at last she too muttered something briefly and lapsed into sleep.

That accomplished, Liam took a swallow of water from the leather flask on his belt, lay down beside his sword, and slept himself.

But only briefly. He awoke, galvanized by a snuffling outside the tunnel, and rolled to a crouch. His hand found his sword. Something pushed on the door mesh, then abruptly it burst inward as a hand thrust through, huge and hairy. With a spasm of energy, Liam hacked at it. Its hardness startled him; the blade cut, but not as deeply as he'd hoped.

The hand jerked back to a roar of pain and rage, and Liam grabbed first Megh, then Rory, pulling them farther into the tunnel. The huge hand thrust in again, six feet or more, groped and withdrew empty. Liam shook like an aspen leaf. *A troll,* he thought. *It's a troll.*

There was silence for a long three or four minutes, then he heard something grunting, coming nearer, until it was just outside. Abruptly there was a loud thud, and the moonlight was gone, except for a little that came in at one side. The troll had brought a boulder, and blocked the opening with it.

Liam felt chagrin; he'd lost an option, his exit. On the other hand it had been a dangerous option, with a troll snooping around. He lay back down, but this time sleep failed to come. He thought of the egg sac. When would it hatch? And what? A hundred young the size of his head? Likelier, he thought, a dozen the size of Megh. And in his experience, the young were simply small copies of the mother. Suppose they hatched tonight? Would they come down the tunnel hunting?

He sat up, found the door mesh where he'd set it aside, and with his pocket knife cut off a fistful of strands. Then he groped for Rory's rucksack; perhaps there'd be a match pot. There was, and striking a match, he held its yellow flame to the strands, which lit, burning more strongly than he'd hoped, too rapidly for good torches. It lasted long enough, though, for him to cut several more, should they be needed.

That done, he lay down again, and this time slept.

He awoke to Rory's hand on his shoulder. His first thought, as he shook off an evil dream and sat up, was that the Dank Land had its own vile soul.

Enough light got in past the boulder to see by, dimly; day had come. The younger tomteen's face was drawn as if he had a bad case of grippe. He spoke in a near whisper.

"Liam! What happened?"

Despite Rory's whispering, Liam touched finger to lips, then answered as quietly. "What do you remember?"

The young man's eyes went out of focus. "A—spider. Huge! Taller than the ponies! It was on me almost before I knew it."

Liam gestured at the intact shells that had been Rory's cocoon. "It stung you and wrapped you up in that. Then took you to its lair. Both of you; you and Megh."

There was accusation in his voice. Then Rory told him what had happened: the stoor, the map, everything. "How did you rescue us?" he finished.

It was Liam's turn to recite, all of it including the troll, the boulder, and the egg sac. "And now," he finished, "it's time to do away with her. And her eggs. Then we can go home."

While Liam described his plan, he took the lid from the match pot and handed matches to Rory, who put one in each pocket. Then, working in the thin light, he tied patches of silk to several of his broad-headed arrows. Meanwhile Megh awoke, and Rory talked to her briefly in an undertone. "All right," Liam murmured when he'd finished his work, "let's do it."

"Right," said Rory. He'd already buckled on his scabbard, and had his short sword in hand. Liam looked at Megh, who nodded, and the two male tomtaihn moved off quietly down the tunnel. At the junction, Liam took two arrows from his quiver and held them, with his bow, in his right hand. Then they moved up the larger tunnel even more quietly. Liam didn't know if spiders slept, but if they could catch her sleeping, they might drive several arrows into her before she could leave.

She was awake. Almost unbreathing, they peered at her. She was palpating the egg sac, and Liam could see it move. It reminded him of young kittens playing in a bag. The arrow he nocked had a swatch of silk tied below the head. His left hand held the arrow at his ear; the right held the bow, slightly bent. "Now!" he hissed. Rory struck a match against the rock wall, once, then again before it flared. The spider had turned, the row of beady eyes fixed on them. Rory touched flame to silk; it caught, and in the manner of his people, Liam straightened his bow arm, thrusting the bow forward, and let go the arrow. It drove into the egg sac, the swatch of burning silk sticking to the outside, and instantly it began to burn.

Almost as quickly the spider rushed at them, her already damaged forelimbs reaching futilely. Liam nocked and loosed the other arrow, driving it almost to the feathers between breastplate and head. She rose tall and curved her abdomen, pointing her spinnerets forward between her legs, and began to spew silk wildly, loops of it snaking into the tunnel, sending the two tomtaihn stumbling backward out of the way. Before Liam could shoot again, the opening was half-obscured, but he sent another arrow through it, and another, hearing them sock into flesh. His head hurt fiercely, and he realized it was from the chittering, which had risen above hearing. Together they turned and ran, missing the side tunnel the first time. Before they got back to Megh, both of them had stopped to retch, their already empty stomachs spasming.

They dozed briefly, then returned to the junction of the two tunnels. The chittering still went on, dropping to audibility, then rising above it, so they retreated again. Next they tried to move the boulder, to no avail. *Of all the times not to have hammer and chisel,* Liam thought. Surely, though, the spider couldn't keep it up indefinitely. Either she'd die or go out to hunt, perhaps after laying more eggs if she was able.

After a bit they slept again, again with evil dreams, and awoke to hunger. The younger tomtaihn were hungriest, and weak from the venom. Liam and Rory went to the junction, this time with all the torch material they could carry, then deeper down the large tunnel, lighting their short-lived torches one by one. They found the water Liam had heard the first day, drank and filled their leather flasks. The last quick torch burned out, and they walked back in darkness.

The curtain the spider had woven was thick enough that little light glowed through. Gathering his resolve, Liam struck it with his sword, and at once the chittering began again. Once more they fled. Back in their side tunnel they paused.

"She didn't sound as strong as before," Rory said.

Liam considered. "I think you're right," he said. "She must be weakening. Maybe tomorrow she'll be dead, or the day after. We've got water, and we can do without food a few days."

So they went back to Megh, and all three lay about dozing. Liam woke again to Rory's touch. "Liam! I've been back down the tunnel, to the entryway. I tried the curtain and heard nothing, so I cut a hole to see through. She's down, Liam, she's down! I saw a leg move, but it was weak!"

Liam rolled to his feet, reaching for belt and

sword, then slung his quiver and strung his bow. Together they went down the tunnel, this time with
Megh following.

At the silk curtain, Liam peered through the
hole. It was as Rory'd said. Together they began to
chop on the thick mesh, clearing the way entirely,
dragging the segments aside. There was a smell of
charred protein, the young in the egg sac. Meanwhile
the spider didn't move. When the doorway was clear,
Liam stepped forward and drove a broad-headed
arrow into the thorax, just in front of the waist. It
drove through the chiton and disappeared, feathers
and all. He sent another, and another, and they
became aware of a different smell, vile gases issuing
from the arrow holes.

"She's dead," Liam said. "She must be." But still
he didn't move to strike her with his sword; there
might be a final spasm of life left in her. Turning, he
looked at the egg sac. Rory was already staring, but
not at the charred remains of spiders half his size. On
the ledge behind them was a casket, half an ell long, a
foot wide, and higher than its width. He kicked dead
spiders aside and opened it; when he spoke, it was
with awe.

"Liam! It's real!"

Liam strode to it. It was nearly full of gold and
jewels. "Well!" he said. He could think of nothing
more. Megh had come in, and stood peering between
them without enthusiasm, saying nothing at all.

"We'll need the ponies," Liam said. Before they
left, though, he went to the spider after all and drew

the arrow from between her head and breastplate, putting it in his quiver. While he did this, Rory put a handful of coins into each front pocket. They hurried out then, into the sunshine, hunger forgotten. Fingers in their mouths, they whistled, loud and shrill, then stood waiting, intent for the sound of hooves.

"They could be halfway home by now," Rory said.

"Let's see if we can find tracks," Liam replied. "I'd think my Tam would hang around, if he could. If the troll didn't take him."

The troll. Rory looked about, despite the sunshine. They went to the creek and started up it, going half a mile or more, then stopped. Ahead, three ravens were flapping up, and the tomtaihn went to see what had drawn them. The bones of a pony lay strewn about, with patches of hide and black hair. The pack saddle lay smashed.

"I can make another saddle," Rory said. He picked up the pack saddle straps, folded them, and stuffed them in his rucksack. "I'll use saplings and spider cord."

Liam nodded. "If we can find a pony to wear it."

He'd hardly said it before they heard hooves. Megh's little dun came galloping out of the woods ahead, slowed when it saw them, and trotted the rest of the way, stopping beside its mistress.

"Well then, Megh," Liam said, "are you willing that she carry the chest?" He turned to Rory. "We'll have to dump part of it out. It's too heavy as it is."

"Liam." It was Megh who spoke. "I'm not sure I am. Willing, that is."

Her brother stared, brows raised, but she was looking at Rory Hoy now. "What would you do with it?" she said. "The treasure, I mean."

Rory stammered, confused. "Why—I'd—I'd take some of it to—to Abhaihnseth, and hire a builder to build a grand home for us beside the rudh. And you could buy the furnishings. And some of it..." He stopped. "Between the two of us, we'd find things to use it for. Buy old Connorleigh's farm; he's getting old for all that work and has no children. The money would keep him well the rest of his life."

"You'd make the village famous then? For its wealth?"

He stared, beginning to see her point.

"What's kept Meadowvale safe these years?" she asked. "Since our grandsires settled it, four hundred years ago. And what would happen when it became known that there was wealth there?"

Rory looked at Liam for help. The rock cutter looked back thoughtfully. "How much gold could you carry in your pockets, Rory?" he asked.

"I suppose—a hundred pounds' worth in each, or a hundred fifty. Five hundred pounds, more or less."

"More than I'll ever own," Liam said.

Rory shook his head. "Not so! I'll share! Without your help I'd be spider food, right now."

Liam shook his head. "For a bit there, the sight of all that treasure went to my head. But Megh's right: for us, wealth is dangerous. Even deadly. And I live well, Rory, without riches. I'll live even better when Caithlain A'Duill comes of age, three months hence."

Rory stared sullenly at his furry feet. "My family was wealthy once," he said, then turned defiantly to Liam. "Wealthy and important."

"A different time, Rory, a different world. Before the big folk came. And old Connorleigh would sell for two hundred pounds, or so I've heard."

"And a hundred crowns for the stoor, when he comes," Megh put in. "That comes to twelve pounds more." She frowned. "Even four hundred pounds would cause talk, if people knew."

Liam took it from there. "You can say the stoor told you about a map to a pot of coins he'd heard of. Hidden in a hollow tree on the South Fork of the Mirror, near where it crosses the Mulberry Road. He less than half believed in it, so he sold it to you. You told Megh of it, and she told me, and the three of us went to look. Found it, too, we did, though it took us a while. The map was rough, and there are lots of hollow trees. It was a clay pot, with two hundred twelve pounds all told. Enough to buy old Connorleigh out. You can give me ten, to help make the story convincing. Anything more than two hundred twelve you can hide, and use later."

Rory Hoy looked first at Liam, then Megh, seeing not friends now but antagonists. The treasure was his to decide on. They'd played their part, to be sure, but he'd led them, paid his life savings for the map. And wealth would buy more than a mansion and goods, it would buy the respect of his father, his...

Howling broke his thoughts and galvanized all three of the tomtaihn. They turned downstream to see. A pack of wolves was running toward them. Beside the tomtaihn stood a pine, not large, its dead lower branches within reach. "Climb!" roared Liam, and grabbing Megh, boosted her, then he and Rory followed, using branch stubs like ladder rungs, breaking some of them in the scramble. They didn't stop till they were among green branches, a safe height up.

The wolves stopped in a ring around the base, seven of them. The leader was bigger than any wolf ought to be, Liam thought.

"Who are you, and what do you want?" Liam called down.

The leader grinned, tongue lolling. "You killed one of my master's sentries here, and the other cannot abide the daylight. So we were sent."

Each of the tomtaihn heard the unspoken words. "Well then," said Liam, who sat lowest. He took the bow from his shoulder, nocked an arrow, and shot at him. An awkward shot, from a branch, but not awkward enough to explain the result. The shot seemed straight, then turned aside. The other wolves moved about restlessly, but the leader still grinned.

"Your arrows cannot harm me, halfling. I have my master's essence."

"Well then!" Liam drew again, but this time sent

the arrow at the nearest other wolf. It struck between ribs, and with a yelp the animal went down. The others scattered, all but the leader, to circle at a little distance.

Now the grin was gone. "No loss, halfling, no loss."

"Maybe not. But you cannot reach us, any more than my arrows can reach you."

"I need not. At dusk the other sentry will come, and pluck you like cherries, or shake you out, or break off the tree if he'd rather."

Liam glowered, then spoke, not to the wolf. "Rory, take the bow," he said, "and the quiver. The soul of the Dank Land didn't send seven of them by accident, and now they're only six. And I'm left-handed."

Staring, Rory took bow and quiver as Liam had ordered. Seven was the perfect number; there was power in it. And stories had it that the left hand had strength against magic. "What are you going to do?" he asked.

"It's one thing for sorcery to stop a flying arrow. It's something else to stop a blow delivered by a living arm. Be ready to shoot any of the others that try to enter in." With that, the tomtaidh rock cutter drew his short sword and jumped from the tree.

The move was so unexpected, the lead wolf jumped back, and Liam set upon him, hacking. The first stroke took an ear off, and a cheek, and dug into a shoulder, but the next missed as the animal jumped aside. The others moved in then, but warily, and from his perch, Rory downed another. They drew back.

"You took me by surprise, halfling." The leader's thoughts seemed to hiss like a snake. "You will not surprise me again." Then it drove at Liam. His blade seemed to land, as if the creature lacked the power to stop it, but this time did not cut, striking like a cudgel. Again the others drew in, again one took an arrow deeply, and again the survivors retreated, far enough that from his branch, Rory had no shot at them.

Now the leader circled the sturdy tomteen. No trace of a sneer remained on its damaged face. Its right eye was swelling where the last blow had struck.

"Hold the bow," Rory told Megh. She took it, and he clambered quickly to a lower branch, then took the bow back. The lead wolf moved in again, slashing, shed a blow off its shoulder and tore Liam's sleeve half off before he beat it back. Another wolf rushed. An arrow took it in the neck, and after spinning, snapping at the shaft, it fled. But bright blood ran from Liam's right arm now, dripping on the ground.

Again the leader circled, and again drove in. This time though, instead of slashing, it held on, and with a terrible snarling swung the tomteen like a doll and dashed him to the ground. Another darted in, and Rory's arrow missed. It grabbed Liam by a leg before a second arrow took it in the flank. It yelped, grabbed again, and again Rory shot, felling it.

"The bow! Take it!" he shouted, then moved the quiver from his shoulder to a branch stub and jumped even before he drew his short sword. The sixth wolf had also moved in; now it sidled away, and Rory attacked the leader from behind, taking it by surprise as it shook Liam, his blade slamming its hindquarters—but not biting!

It dropped the mauled, unmoving tomteen and turned. "You are dead, halfling," it thought to Rory. The other wolf, paler than the rest, circled to get behind him.

As a girl, Megh Maqsween had often shot with her brother at the archery butts. Sisters sometimes did. Now she nocked the last arrow, not heeding its corroded head. From where she sat she had no shot at the pale wolf, so she drew down on the leader and let fly.

The arrow struck, but not deeply. It hit the shoulder, then sliced along ribs and flank, leaving an ugly bloody streak, but no major wound. The leader started, stared upward a long moment in surprise, then staggered, fell, got half up and fell again. The final wolf, the pale one, turned away and trotted off.

Rory stared up at Megh, then in amazement at the pack leader. Then he moved to Liam and dropped to his knees. "Liam! Liam! Oh, Liam!" The rock cutter's arm and shoulder were deeply lacerated, and blood soaked his torn breeches. Quickly, Rory pulled the breeches off him. The leg bites too were deep, but the flesh was not greatly torn.

"Megh!" Rory cried. "He'll live! Get the dun, if you can. We'll tie him on. Quickly, lass, before something else comes!"

She tossed down the bow and empty quiver and climbed down. While she whistled for her pony, Rory gathered arrows and put them in the quiver, noting the corrosion on one. *The one from the spider,* he thought, *and poison.* Then he gave bow and quiver to his sweetheart, hoisted the thick-bodied Liam onto his back, and started hiking up the pass, Megh following. They hiked for three or four furlongs before the pony reappeared. Then, with a struggle, they got Liam across its back and tied him on with the straps Rory had salvaged. That done, they hiked again, driving hard, sweat blurring their eyes, their legs burning with fatigue. They'd not have dreamed they could go uphill so far so fast. At least the forest was sparse here, with fewer blowdowns to bypass.

They went a mile, another, in little more than an hour. And always with a sense of pursuit. At last, on an overlook, they paused. Ahead, it was as far again to the divide. Behind—Behind something was coming, a pack of somethings, seven great wild hogs, led by a boar far bigger than the pony. "Megh!" said Rory, "get on the pony and ride!"

She stared at him.

"Now!" he barked, and, grabbing her, half slung her up behind Liam. *"Now ride!"* He slapped the pony with the flat of his short sword, and it jumped forward, almost unseating the girl, who pale as milk, held on to the body of her brother as the pony went uphill at a hard-driving run.

Rory turned then, sheathed his sword and strung his bow. *I'll use the poison arrow first,* he told himself. *On the boar. He'll have the essence of the Dank Land's Soul, no doubt. If I kill him, the others may take me, but they'll likely go no farther.*

Again the hogs came into view, their thick hair dark. No pony could keep pace with them; he doubted that other swine could, unpossessed. *O Forest Soul!* he thought, *help me if you can!* Then he nocked the corroded arrow.

They thundered on, disappeared again among some trees, then reappeared scarcely a hundred feet away, the hair along their spines a bristling ridge.

And stopped abruptly, actually skidding in the dirt. The towering boar stared at Rory, red-eyed, then looked past him, upward toward the divide, and Rory could hear his thought. "He is mine, this little one! And the others are mine! This is my domain!"

The answer was not in words, but Rory felt the message. *Not this time, evil one. Call back your swine. Your master died long ago; two others of these halflings destroyed him. You have no source to renew your weakening strength now. Your days are numbered.*

The great boar snorted, pawed the ground, and, instead of turning back, charged at Rory. His arrow met it, glanced from its thick skull, furrowing the scalp, stopping in the shoulder hump. Then it was on him—and yet it wasn't, for it seemed somehow to pass through him without impact. Rory fell, not knocked down but overwhelmed. Then the boar wheeled, as if to try again, stopped, and fell over.

At once the other swine turned and thundered off downhill.

They were waiting with the pony, on the divide. Liam was lying conscious on the ground, his wounds bandaged with strips cut from shirt and breeches. When Megh saw Rory laboring up the trail, she ran to him, throwing herself into his arms.

"I was so afraid for you, darling!" she said.

"And I," he answered. They walked to Liam, arms around each other's waists. "How are you feeling, Mr. Maqsween?"

Liam grunted. "I'll live, *Mr.* Hoy." He paused. "If you're ready to go on, I think I can ride without being hogtied."

"I'm ready, Mr. Maqsween."

Liam chuckled. "Good. And on the way down, you can tell me what happened. I'll see what I can do with Da when we get back to Meadowvale. He'll be upset with you, but I've a strong influence on him. And the business is mine now."

They brought the dun and boosted him on.

When the wave of pain had settled and the grimace left his face, Liam looked down at Rory. "I know you took two fistfuls from the chest. That should be enough to pay down on Connorleigh's and buy a good keg of ale for the wedding. And still pay the Stoor his hundred crowns."

He chuckled then, and they started down toward the Mirrorudh.

The Origin of the Hob

Judith Moffett

Judith Moffett won the John W. Campbell Award as Best New Writer of 1987. In her story "The Hob" (from which this is excerpted), Judith provided an extraterrestrial explanation to the halfling mythos.

Jenny Shepherd, as she tramped along, watched the roke roll toward her with almost as little concern. Years ago, on her very first walking tour of Yorkshire, Jenny—underequipped and uncertain of her route— had lost her way in a thick, dripping fog long and late enough to realize exactly how much danger she might have been in. But the footpath across Great and Little Hograh Moors was plain, though wetter than it might have been, a virtual gully cut through the slight snow and marked with cairns, and having crossed it more than once before Jenny knew exactly where she was. Getting to the hostel would not be too difficult even in the dark, and anyway, she was equipped today to deal with any sort of weather.

In order to cross a small stone bridge the path led steeply down into a streambed. Impulsively Jenny decided to take a break there, sheltered somewhat from the wind's incessant keening, before the roke should swallow her up. She shrugged off her backpack, leaned it upright against the bridge, and pulled out one insulating pad of blue foam to sit on and another to use as a backrest, a thermos, a small packet of trail gorp, half a sandwich in a Baggie, a space blanket, and a voluminous green nylon poncho. She was dressed already in coated nylon rain pants over pile pants over soft woolen long johns, plus several thick sweaters and a parka, but the poncho would help keep out the wet and wind and add a layer of insulation.

Jenny shook out the space blanket and wrapped herself up in it, shiny side inward. Then she sat, awkward in so much bulkiness, and adjusted the foam rectangles behind and beneath her until they felt right. The thermos was still half full of tea; she unscrewed the lid and drank from it directly, replacing the lid after each swig to keep the cold out. There were ham and cheese in the sandwich and unsalted peanuts, raisins, and chunks of plain chocolate in the gorp.

Swathed in her space blanket, propped against the stone buttress of the bridge, Jenny munched and guzzled, one glove off and one glove on, in a glow of the well-being that ensues upon vigorous exercise in the cold, pleasurable fatigue, solitude, simple creature comforts, and the smug relish of being on top of a situation that would be too tough for plenty of other people (her own younger self, for one). The little beck poured noisily beneath the bridge's span and down toward the dale and the trees below; the wind blew, but not on Jenny. She sat there tucked into the landscape, in a daze of pure contentment.

The appearance overhead of the first wispy tendrils of mist merely deepened her sense of comfort, and she sat on, knowing it would very soon be time to pack up and go but reluctant to bring the charm of the moment to a close.

A sheep began to come down the streambed above where Jenny sat, a blackface ewe, one of the mountain breeds—Swaledale, would it be? or Herdwick? No, Herdwicks were a Lake District breed. With idle interest she watched it scramble down jerkily, at home here, not hurrying and doubtless as cozy in its poncho of dirty fleece as Jenny herself was in her Patagonia pile. She watched it lurch toward her, knocking the stones in its descent—and abruptly found herself thinking of the albino deer in the park at home in Pennsylvania: how when glimpsed it had seemed half deer, half goat, with a deer's tail that lifted and waved as it walked or leapt away and a prick-eared full-face profile exactly like the other deers'; yet it had moved awkwardly on stubby legs and was the wrong color, grayish white with mottling on the back.

This sheep reminded her somehow of the albino deer, an almost-but-not-quite-right sort of sheep. Jenny had seen a lot of sheep, walking the English uplands. Something about this one was definitely funny. Were its legs too *thick*? Did it move oddly? With the fog swirling more densely every second it was hard to say just *what* the thing looked like. She strained forward, trying to see.

For an instant the mist thinned between them, and she perceived with a shock that the sheep was *carrying something in its mouth*.

At Jenny's startled movement the ewe swung its dead flat eyes upon her—froze—whirled and plunged back up the way it had come. As it wheeled it emitted a choked high wheeze, perhaps sheeplike, and dropped its bundle.

Jenny pushed herself to her feet, dis-cocooned herself from the space blanket, and clambered up the steep streambed. The object the sheep had dropped had rolled into the freezing water; she thrust in her ungloved right hand—gritting her teeth—and pulled it out. The thing was a dead grouse with a broken neck.

Now Jenny Shepherd, despite her name, was extremely ignorant of the personal habits of sheep. But they were grazing animals, not carnivores—even a baby knew that. Maybe the sheep had found the dead grouse and picked it up. Sheep might very well do that sort of thing—pick up carrion and walk around with it—for all Jenny knew. But she shivered, heaved the grouse back into the water, and stuck her numb wet hand inside her coat. Maybe sheep *did* do that sort of thing; but she had the distinct impression that something creepy had happened, and her mood was spoiled.

Nervously now she looked at her watch. Better get a move on. She slipped and slid down to the bridge and repacked her pack in haste. There were four or five miles of open moor yet to be crossed before she would strike a road, and the fog was going to slow her down some. Before heaving the pack back on Jenny unzipped one of its outside pockets and took out a flashlight.

Elphi crashed across the open moor, beside himself. How *could* he have been so careless? Failing to spot the walker was bad enough, yet if he had kept his head all would have been well; nobody can swear to what they see in a fog with twilight coming on. But dropping the grouse, that was unpardonable. For a hundred and fifty years the success of the concealment had depended on unfaltering vigilance and presence of mind, and he had demonstrated neither. That he had just woken up from the winter's sleep, that his mind was burdened with trouble and grief, that walkers on the moors were scarcer than sunshine at this month and hour—none of it excused his incredible clumsiness. Now he had not one big problem to deal with, but two.

The old fellow groaned and swung his head from side to side, but there was no help for what he had to do. He circled back along the way he'd come so as to intersect the footpath half a mile or so east of the bridge. The absence of boot tracks in the snow there had to mean that the walker was heading in this direction, toward Westerdale, and would presently pass by.

He settled himself in the heather to wait; and minutes later, when the dark shape bulked out of the roke, he stepped upright into the path and blocked it. Feeling desperately strange, for he had not spoken openly to a human being in nearly two centuries, Elphi said hoarsely: "Stop reet theear, lad, an' don't tha treea ti run," and when a loud, startled *Oh!* burst from the walker, "Ah'll deea thee nae ho't, but thoo mun cum wiv me noo." His Yorkshire dialect was as thick as clotted cream.

The walker in its flapping garment stood rigid in the path before him. "What—I don't—I can't understand what you're *saying*!"

A woman! And an American! Elphi knew an American accent when he heard one, from the wireless, but he had *never* spoken with an American in all his life—nor with *any* sort of woman, come to that. What would an American woman be *doing* up here at this time of year, all on her own? But he pulled his wits together and replied carefully, "Ah said, ye'll have to cum wiv me. Don't be frighted, an' don't try to run off. No harm will cum ti ye."

The woman, panting and obviously badly frightened despite his words, croaked, "What in God's name *are* you?"

Elphi imagined the small, naked, elderly, hair-covered figure he presented, with his large hands and feet and bulging, knobby features, the whole wrapped up in a dirty sheepskin, and said hastily, "Ah'll tell ye that, aye, but nut noo. We's got a fair piece of ground ti kivver."

Abruptly the walker unfroze. She made some frantic movements beneath her huge garment and a bulky pack dropped out onto the ground, so that she instantly appeared both much smaller and much more maneuverable. Elphi made himself ready to give chase, but instead of fleeing she asked, "Have you got a gun?"

"A *gun* saidst 'ee?" It was Elphi's turn to be startled. "Neea, but iv thoos's na—if ye won't gang on yer own feet Ah'll bring thee along masen. Myself, that's to say. But Ah'd ruther not, 'twould be hard on us both. Will ye cum then?"

"This is *crazy! No,* dammit!" The woman eyed Elphi blocking the trail, then glanced down at her pack, visibly figuring the relative odds of getting past him with or without it. Suddenly, dragging the pack by one shoulder strap, she was advancing upon him. "Get out of the way!"

At this Elphi groaned and swung his head. "Mistress, tha mun cum, and theear's an end," he exclaimed desperately, and darting forward he gripped her wrist in his large, knobbly, sheepskin-padded hand. "Noo treea if tha can break loose."

But the woman refused to struggle, and in the end Elphi had no choice but to yank her off her feet and along the sloppy footpath for a hundred yards or so, ignoring the noises she made. He left her sitting in the path rubbing her wrist and went back for the pack, which he shouldered himself. Then, without any more talk, they set off together into the fog.

By the time they arrived at the abandoned jet mine that served the hobs for a winter den, Jenny's tidy mind had long since shut itself down. Fairly soon she had stopped being afraid of Elphi, but the effort of grappling with the disorienting strangeness of events was more than her brain could manage. She was hurt and exhausted, and more than exhausted. Already, when Elphi in his damp fleece had reared up before her in the fog and blocked her way, she had had a long day. These additional hours of bushwhacking blindly through the tough, mist-soaked heather in the dark had drained her of all purpose and thought beyond that of surviving the march.

Toward the end, as it grew harder and harder for her to lift her peat-clogged boots clear of the heather, she had kept tripping and falling down. Whenever that happened her odd, dangerous little captor would help her up quite gently, evidently with just a tiny fraction of his superhuman strength.

Earlier she had remembered seeing circus posters in the Middlesbrough station while changing from her London train; maybe, she'd thought, the little man was a clown or a "circus freak" who had run off into the hills. But that hadn't seemed very probable; and later, when another grouse had exploded under their feet like a feathered grenade and the dwarf had pounced upon it in a flash and broken its neck—a predator that efficient—she'd given up the circus idea for a more terrifying one: maybe he was an escaped inmate of a mental hospital. Yet Elphi himself, in spite of everything, was somehow unterrifying.

But Jenny had stopped consciously noticing and deciding things about him quite a long while before they got where they were going; and when she finally heard him say "We's heear, lass," and saw him bend to ease back the stone at the entrance to the den, her knees gave way and she flopped down sideways into the vegetation.

She awoke to the muted sound of a radio.

Jenny lay on a hard surface, wrapped snugly in a sheepskin robe, smelly and heavy but marvelously warm. For some moments she basked in the comforting warmth, soothed by the normalness of the radio's voice; but quite soon she came fully awake and knew—with a sharp jolt of adrenaline—what had happened and where she must be now.

She lay in what appeared to be a small cave, feebly lit by a stubby white "emergency" candle—one of her own, in fact. The enclosure was stuffy but not terribly so, and the candle burned steadily where it stood on a rough bench or table, set in what looked to be (and was) an aluminum pie plate of the sort snack pies are sold in. The radio was nowhere in sight.

Someone had undressed her; she was wearing her sheet sleeping bag for a nightie and nothing else.

Tensely Jenny turned her head and struggled to take mental possession of the situation. The cave was lined with bunks like the one in which she lay, and in each of these she could just make out...forms. Seven of them, all evidently deep in sleep (or cold storage?) and, so far as she could tell, all creatures like the one that had kidnapped her. As she stared Jenny began to breathe in gasps again, and the fear that had faded during the march returned in full strength. *What was this place? What was going to happen to her? What the hell was it all about?*

The first explanation that occurred to her was also the most menacing: that she had lost her own mind, that her unfinished therapeutic business had finally caught up with her. If the little man had not escaped from an institution, then maybe she was on her way to one. In fact, Jenny's record of mental stability, while not without an average number of weak points, contained no hint of anything like hallucinations or drug-related episodes. But in the absence of a more obvious explanation her confidence on this score was just shaky enough to give weight and substance to such thoughts.

To escape them (and the panic they engendered) Jenny applied herself desperately to solving some problems both practical and pressing. It was cold in the cave; she could see her breath. Her bladder was bursting. A ladder against one wall disappeared into a hole in the ceiling, and as the cave appeared to have no other entryway she supposed the ladder must lead to the outside world, where for several reasons she now urgently wished to be. She threw off the robe and wriggled out of the sleeping bag—catching her breath at the pain from dozens of sore muscles and bruises—and crippled across the stone floor barefoot; but the hole was black as night and airless, not open, at the top. Jenny was a prisoner, naked and in need.

Well then, find something—a bucket, a pan, anything! Poking about, in the nick of time she spotted her backpack in the shadows on the far wall. In it was a pail of soft plastic meant for carrying water, which Jenny frantically grubbed out and relieved herself into. Half full, the pail held its shape and could be stood, faintly steaming, against the wall. Shuddering violently, she then snatched bundles of clothes and food out of the pack and rushed back into bed. In point of fact there wasn't all that much in the way of extra clothing: one pair of woolen boot socks, clean underwear, slippers, a cotton turtleneck, and a spare sweater. No pants, no shoes, no outerwear; she wouldn't get far over the open moor without any of those. Still, she gratefully pulled on what she found and felt immensely better; nothing restores a sense of confidence in one's mental health, and some sense of control over one's situation, like dealing effectively with a few basic needs. Thank God her kidnapper had brought the pack along!

Next Jenny got up again and climbed to the top of the ladder; but the entrance was closed by a stone far too heavy to move.

The radio sat in a sort of doorless cupboard, a tiny transistor in a dimpled red plastic case. BOOTS THE CHEMIST was stamped on the front in gold, and a wire ran from the extended tip of its antenna along one side of the ladder, up the hole. Jenny brought it back into bed with her, taking care not to disconnect the wire.

She was undoing the twisty on her plastic bag of food when there came a scraping, thumping noise from above and a shaft of daylight shot down the hole. Then it was dark again, and legs—whitish hair-covered legs—and the back of a gray fleece came into view. Frozen where she sat, Jenny waited, heart thumping.

The figure that turned to face her at the bottom of the ladder looked by candlelight exactly like a very old, very small gnome of a man, covered with hair—crown, beard, body, and all—save for his large hands and feet in pads of fleece. But this was a superficial impression. The arms were longer and the legs shorter than they should have been; and Jenny remembered how this dwarf had ranged before her on four limbs in the fog, looking as much like a sheep in a backpack as he now looked like a man. She thought again of the albino deer.

They contemplated one another. Gradually, outlandish as he looked, Jenny's fear drained away again and her pulse rate dropped back to normal. Then the dwarf seemed to smile. "It's a bright morning, the roke's burned off completely," he said in what was almost BBC English with only the faintest trace of Yorkshire left in the vowels.

Jenny said, calmly enough, "Look: I don't understand any of this. First of all I want to know if you're going to let me go."

She got an impression of beaming and nodding. "Oh, yes indeed!"

"When?"

"This afternoon. Your clothes should be dry in time; I've put them out in the sun. It's a rare bit of luck, our getting a sunny morning." He unfastened the sheepskin as he spoke and hung it from a peg next to a clump of others, then slipped off his moccasins and mitts and put them on the shelf where the radio had stood. Except for his hair he wore nothing.

Abruptly Jenny's mind skittered away, resisting this strangeness. She shut her eyes, unafraid of the hairy creature but overwhelmed by the situation in which he was the central figure. "Won't you please explain to me what's going on? Who are you? Who are *they*? What is this place? Why did you make me come here? Just—what's going *on*?" Her voice went up steeply, near to breaking.

"Yes, I'll tell you all about it now, and when you've heard me out I hope you'll understand what happened yesterday—why it was necessary." He dragged a stool from under the table and perched on it, then quickly hopped up again. "Now, have you enough to eat? I'm afraid we've nothing at all to offer a guest at this time of year, apart from the grouse—but we can't make any sort of fire in this clear weather and I very much doubt you'd enjoy eating her raw. I brought her back last night in case anyone else was awake and hungry, which they're unfortunately not...but let me see: I've been through your pack quite thoroughly, I'm afraid, and I noticed some packets of dehydrated soup and tea and so forth; now suppose we were to light several more of these excellent candles and bunch them together, couldn't we boil a little pot of water over the flames? I expect you're feeling the cold." As he spoke the old fellow bustled about—rummaged in the pack for pot and candles, filled the pot half full of water from Jenny's canteen, lit the candles from the one already burning, and arranged supports for the pot to rest on while the water heated. He moved with a speed and economy that were so remarkable as to be almost funny, a cartoon figure whisking about the cave. "There now! You munch a few biscuits while we wait, and I'll do my best to begin to clear up the mystery."

Jenny had sat mesmerized while her abductor rattled on, all the time dashing to and fro. Now she took out tea, sugar, dried milk, two envelopes of Knorr's oxtail soup, and a packet of flat objects called Garibaldis here in England but raisin biscuits in America (and squashed-fly biscuits by the children in *Swallows and Amazons*). She was famished, and gradually grew calm as the old fellow contrived to sound more and more like an Oxbridge don providing a student with fussy hospitality in his rooms in college. She had not forgotten the sensation of being dragged as by a freight train along the footpath, but was willing to set the memory aside. "What became of your accent? Last night I could barely understand you—or aren't you the same one that brought me in?"

"Oh, aye, that was me. As I said, none of the others is awake." He glanced rather uneasily at the

row of shadowy cots. "Though it's getting to be high
time they were. Actually, what's happened is that most
of the time you were sleeping, I've been swotting up
on my Standard English. I used the wireless, you see.
Better switch it off now, actually, if you don't mind,"
he added. "Our supply of batteries is very, ah, irregu-
lar, and where should *we* be now if there hadn't been
any left last night, eh?" Silently Jenny clicked off the
red radio and handed it to him, and he tucked it
carefully back into its cubby. Then he reseated himself upon the stool, looking expectant.

Jenny swallowed half a biscuit and objected, "How
can you totally change your accent and your whole
style of speaking in one night, just by listening to the
radio? It's not possible."

"Not for you, of course not, no, no. But we're
good at languages, you see. Very, very good; it's the
one thing in us that our masters valued most."

At this Jenny's wits reeled again, and she closed
her eyes and gulped hard against nausea, certain that
unless some handle on all this weirdness were not
provided *right away* she might start screaming helplessly
and not be able to stop. She *could not* go on chatting
with this Santa's elf for another second. Jenny Shepherd was a person who was never comfortable unless
she felt she understood things; to understand is, to
some extent, to have control over. "Please," she pleaded, "just tell me who and what you are and what's
happening here. Please."

At once the old fellow jumped up again. "If I
may—" he murmured apologetically and peered again

into the treasure trove of Jenny's backpack. "I couldn't help but notice that you're carrying a little book I've seen before—yes, here it is." He brought the book back to the table and the light: the Dalesman paperback guide to the Cleveland Way. Swiftly finding the page he wanted he passed the book over to Jenny, who got up eagerly from the bed, holding the robe around her, to read by candle-light:

The Cleveland area is extremely rich in folklore which goes back to Scandinavian sources and often very much further. Perhaps the hobs, those strange hairy little men who did great deeds—sometimes mischievous, sometimes helpful—were in some way a memory of those ancient folk who lingered on in parts of the moors almost into historic times. In the years between 1814 and 1823 George Calvert gathered together stories still remembered by old people. He lists twenty-three "Hobmen that were commonly held to live hereabout," including the famous Farndale Hob, Hodge Hob of Bransdale, Hob of Tarn Hole, Dale Town Hob of Hawnby, and Hob of Hasty Bank. Even his list misses out others which are remembered, such as Hob Hole Hob of Runswick who was supposed to cure the whooping cough. Calvert also gives a list of witches. . . .

But this was no help, it made things worse! "You're telling me you're a *hob*?" she blurted, aghast. What nightmarish fantasy was this? "Hob...as in hobbit?" However dearly Jenny might love Tolkien's master-piece, the idea of having spent the night down a hobbit-hole—in the company of seven dwarves!—was a completely unacceptable idea. In the real world hobbits and dwarves must be strictly metaphorical, and Jenny preferred to live in the real world all the time.

The odd creature continued to watch her. "Hob as in hobbit? Oh, very likely. Hob as in hobgoblin, most assuredly—but as to whether *we* are hobs, the answer is yes and no." He took the book from her and laid it on the table. "Sit down, my dear, and bundle up again; and shall I pour out?" for the water had begun to sizzle against the sides of the little pot.

"What did you mean, yes *and* no?" Jenny asked a bit later, sitting in bed with a steaming Sierra cup of soup balanced in her lap and a plastic mug of tea in her hands, and thinking: This better be good.

"First, may I pour myself a cup? It's a long story," he said, "and it's best to begin at the beginning. My name is Elphi, by the way.

"At least the dale folk called me Elphi until I scarcely remembered my true name, and it was the same with all of us—we took the names they gave us and learnt to speak their language so well that we spoke no other even among ourselves.

"This is the whole truth, though you need not believe it. My friends and myself were in service aboard an exploration vessel from another star. Hear me out," for Jenny had made an impatient movement, "I said you need not believe what I tell you. The ship called here, at Earth, chiefly for supplies but also for information. Here, of course, we knew already that only one form of life had achieved mastery over nature. Often that is the case, but on my world there were two, and one subordinate to the other. Our lords the Gafr were physically larger than we and technologically gifted as we were not, and also they did not hibernate; that gave them an advantage, though their lives were shorter (and that gave *us* one). We think the Gafr had been with us, and over us, from the first, when we both were still more animal than thinking thing. Our development, you see, went hand in hand with theirs, but their gift was mastery and ours was service—always, from our prehistory.

"And from our prehistory our lives were intertwined with theirs, for we were of great use to one another. As I've said, we Hefn are very good with languages, at speaking and writing them—and also we are stronger for our size than they, and quicker in every way, though I would have to say less clever. I've often thought that if the Neanderthal people had lived on into modern times their relations with *you* might have developed in a similar way ... but the Gafr are far less savage than you and never viewed us as competitors, so perhaps I'm wrong. We are very much less closely related than you and the Neanderthal people."

"How come you know so much about the Neanderthalers?" Jenny interrupted to ask.

"From the wireless, my dear! The wireless keeps us up-to-date. We would be at a sad disadvantage without it, don't you agree?

"So the Gafr—"

"How would you spell that?"

"*G, a, f, r*. One *f*, not two, and no *e*. The Gafr designed the starships and we built them and went to work aboard them. It was our life, to be their servants and dependents. You should understand that they never were cruel. Neither we nor they could imagine an existence without the other, after so many eons of relying upon one another.

"Except that aboard my ship, for no reason I can now explain, a few of us became dissatisfied and demanded that we be given responsibilities of our own. Well, you know, it was as if one day the sheepdogs hereabouts were to complain to the farmers that from now on they wanted flocks of their own to manage, with the dipping and tupping and shearing and lambing and all the rest. Our lords were as dumbfounded as these farmers would be—a talking dog, you see. When we couldn't be reasoned or scolded out of our notion and it began to interfere with the smooth functioning of the ship, the Gafr decided to put us off here for a while to think things over. They were to come back for us as soon as we'd had time to find out what running our own affairs without them would be like. That was a little more than three hundred and fifty years ago."

Jenny's mouth fell open; she had been following intently. "Three hundred and fifty of *your* years, you mean?"

"No, of yours. We live a *long* time. To human eyes we appeared to be very old men when still quite young, but now we are old indeed—and look it too, I fear.

"Well, they put fifteen of us off here, in Yorkshire, and some dozen others in Scandinavia somewhere. I often wonder if any of that group has managed to keep alive, or whether the ship came back for them but not for us—but there's no knowing.

"It was early autumn; we supposed they meant to fetch us off before winter, for they knew the coming of hard winter would put us to sleep. They left us well supplied and went away, and we all had plenty of time to find life without the Gafr as difficult—psychologically, I suppose you might say—as they could possibly have wished. Oh, yes! We waited, very chastened, for the ship to return. But the deep snows came and finally we had to go to earth, and when we awoke the following spring we were forced to face the likelihood that we were stranded here.

"A few found they could not accept a life in this alien place without the Gafr to direct their thoughts and actions; they died in the first year. But the rest of us, though nearly as despairing, preferred life to death—and we said to one another that the ship might yet return.

"When we awoke from our first winter's sleep, the year was 1624. In those days the high moors were much as you see them now, but almost inaccessible to the world beyond them. The villages were linked by a few muddy cart tracks and stone pannier trods across the tops. No one came up here but people who had business here, or people crossing from one dale into another: farmers, poachers, panniermen, Quakers later on...the farmers would come up by turf road from their own holdings to gather bracken for stock bedding, and to cut turf and peat for fuel, and ling—that's what they call the heather hereabouts, you know—for kindling and thatching. They burned off the old ling to improve the grazing, and took away the burned stems for kindling. And they came after bilberries in late summer, and to bring hay to their sheep on the commons in winter, as some still do. But nobody came from outside, passing through from one distant place to another, and the local people were an ignorant, superstitious lot as the world judges such things, shut away up here. They would sit about the hearth of an evening, whole families together, and retell the old tales. And we would hang about the eaves, listening.

"All that first spring we spied out the dales farms, learnt the language, and figured our chances. Some of us wanted to go to the dalesmen with our story and ask to be taken into service, for it would have comforted us to serve a good master again. But others—I was one—said such a course was as dangerous as it was useless, for we would not have been believed and the Church would have had us hunted down for devil's spawn.

"Yet we all yearned and hungered so after direction and companionship that we skulked about the farms despite the risk, watching how the men and milkmaids worked. We picked up the knack of it easily enough, of milking and churning and threshing and stacking—the language of farm labor as you might say!—and by and by we began to lend a hand, at night, when the house was sleeping—serving *in secret,* you see. We asked ourselves, would the farmers call us devil's spawn for *that?* and thought it a fair gamble. We'd thresh out the corn, and then we'd fill our pouches with barley and drink the cat's cream off the doorstep for our pay.

"At least we thought it was the cat's cream. But one night at harvesttime, one of us—Hart Hall it was—heard the farmer tell his wife, 'Mind tha leaves t'bate o' cream for t' hob. He deeas mair i' yah neet than a' t'men deea iv a day.' That's how we learnt that the people were in no doubt about who'd been helping them.

"We could scarcely believe our luck. Of course we'd heard talk of witches and fairies, very superstitious they were in those days, and now and again one would tell a tale of little men called hobmen, part elf, part goblin as it seemed, sometimes kind and sometimes tricksy. They'd put out a bowl of cream for the hob, for if they forgot, the hob would make trouble for them, and if they remembered he would use them kindly."

"That was a common practice in rural Scandinavia too—to set out a bowl of porridge for the *tomte,*" Jenny put in.

"Aye? Well, well...no doubt the cats and foxes got the cream, before *we* came! Well, we put together every scrap we could manage to overhear about the hobmen, and the more we heard the more our way seemed plain. By great good fortune we looked the part. We *are* manlike, more or less, though we go as

readily upon four feet as two and stood a good deal
smaller than the ordinary human even in those days
when men were not so tall as now, and that meant no
great harm would come of it should we happen to be
seen. That was important. There hadn't been so many
rumors of hobbish helpfulness in the dales for a very
long time, and as curiosity grew we were spied upon
in our turn—but I'm getting ahead of my tale.

"By the time a few years had passed we'd settled
ourselves all through these dales. Certain farmsteads
and local spots were spoken of as being 'haunted bi
t'hob'; well, one way and another we found out where
they were, and one of us would go and live there and
carry on according to tradition. Not all of us did that,
now—some just found a farm they liked and moved
in. But for instance it was believed that a certain hob,
that lived in a cave at Runswick up on the coast, could
cure what they called t'kink-cough, so one of us went on
up there to be Hob Hole Hob, and when the mothers
would bring their sick children and call to him to cure
them, he'd do what he could."

"What *could* he do, though?"

"Not a great deal, but more than nothing. He
could make them more comfortable, and unless a
child was very ill he could make it more likely to
recover."

"How? Herbs and potions?"

"No, not at all—merely the power of suggestion.
But quite effective, oh, aye.

"There was a tradition too of a hob in Farndale
that was the troublesome sort, and as it seemed wisest

not to neglect that mischievous side of our ledger altogether, once in a while we would send somebody over there to let out the calves and spill the milk and put a cart on the barn roof, and generally make a nuisance of himself. It kept the old beliefs alive, you see. It wouldn't have done for people to start thinking the hobs had all got good as gold, we had the sense to see that. The dalesfolk used to say, 'Gin t'hobman takes ti yan, ya'r yal reet i' t'lang run, but deea he tak agin' 'ee 'tis anither story!' We wanted them to go right on saying that.

"But we did take to them—aye, we did indeed, though the Gafr and the dalesmen were so unalike. The Yorkshire farmer of those times, for all his faults, was what they call the salt of the earth. They made us good masters, and we served them well for nigh on two hundred years."

Jenny wriggled and leaned toward Elphi, raptly attending. "Did any of you ever *talk* with humans, face-to-face? Did you ever have any human friends, that you finally told the truth to?"

"No, my dear. We had no friends among humans in the sense you mean, though we befriended a few in particular. Nor did we often speak with humans. We thought it vital to protect and preserve their sense of us as magical and strange—supernatural, in fact. But now and again it would happen.

"I'll tell you of one such occasion. For many and many a year my home was at Hob Garth near Great Fryup Dale, where a family called Stonehouse had the holding. There was a Thomas Stonehouse once, that lived there and kept sheep.

"Now, the time I'm speaking of would have been about 1760 or thereabouts, when Tommy was beginning to get on a bit in years. Somehow he fell out with a neighbor of his called Matthew Bland, an evil-tempered fellow he was, and one night I saw Bland creep along and break the hedge, and drive out Tommy's ewes. Tommy was out all the next day in the wet, trying to round them up, but without much luck, for he only found five out of the forty, and so I says to myself: here's a job for Hob. The next morning all forty sheep were back in the field and the hedge patched up with new posts and rails.

"Well! but that wasn't all: when I knew Tommy to be laid up with a cold, and so above suspicion himself, I nipped along and let Bland's cattle loose. A perfectly hobbish piece of work that was! Old Bland, he was a full fortnight rounding them up. Of course, at the time the mischief was done Tommy had been in his bed with chills and a fever, and everybody knew it; but Bland came and broke the new fence anyway and let the sheep out again—he was that furious, he had to do something.

"As Tommy was still too ill to manage, his neighbors turned out to hunt the sheep for him. But the lot of 'em had wandered up onto the tops in a roke like the one we had yesterday evening, and none could be found at all. All the same, that night Hob rounded them up and drove them home, and repaired the fence again. Bear in mind, my dear, that such feats as the farmers deemed prodigious were simple enough for us, for we have excellent sight in the dark, and great strength in the low gravity here, and are quick on our feet, whether four or two.

"Now, four of Tommy's ewes had fallen into a quarry in the roke and broken their necks, and never came home again. When he was well enough he walked out to the field to see what was left of the flock and cut some hay for it—this was early spring, I remember, just about this time. We'd awakened sooner than usual that year, which was a bit of luck for Tommy. I saw him heading up there, and followed. And when I knew him to be grieving over the four lost ewes I accosted him in the road and said not to fret anymore, that the sheep would be accounted for and then some at lambing time—for I knew that most were carrying twins, and I meant to help with the lambing as well, to see that as many as possible would live.

"He took me then for an old man, a bit barmy though kindly intentioned. But later, when things turned out the way I'd said, it was generally talked of—how there was no use Matthew Bland trying to play tricks on Tommy Stonehouse, for the hobman had befriended him, and when t'hobman taks ti yan . . . aye, it was a bit of luck for Tommy that we woke early that spring.

"But to speak directly to a farmer so, that was rare. More often the farmer took the initiative upon himself, or his wife or children or servants did, by slipping out to spy upon us at work, or by coming to beg a cure. There was talk of a hob that haunted a cave in the Mulgrave Woods, for instance. People would put their heads in and shout, "Hobthrush Hob! Where is thoo?" and the hob was actually meant to reply—and the dear knows how *this* tradition began— 'Ah's tying on mah lef' fuit shoe. An' Ah'll be wiv thee—noo!' Well, we didn't go as far as that, but once in a while one of us might slip up there for a bit so's to be able to shout back if anyone called into the cave. Most often it was children.

"Mostly, people weren't frightened of t'hob. But as I've said, we thought it as well to keep the magic bright. There was one old chap, name of Gray, with a farm over in Bransdale; he married himself a new wife who couldn't or wouldn't remember to put out the jug of cream at bedtime as the old wife had always done. Well, Hodge Hob, that had helped that family for generations, he pulled out of there and never went back. And another time a family called Oughtred, that farmed over near Upleatham, lost *their* hob because he died. That was Hob Hill Hob, that missed his step and broke his neck in a mine shaft, the first of us all to go out since the very beginning. Well, Kempswithen overheard the Oughtreds discussing it— whyever had the hob gone away?—and they agreed it must have been because one of the workmen had hung his coat on the winnowing machine and forgot it, and the hobman had thought it was left there for *him*—for everyone knew you mustn't offer clothes to fairies and such or they'll take offense.

"Well! We'd been thinking another of us might go and live at Hob Hill Farm, but after that we changed

our minds. And when a new milkmaid over at Hart
Hall spied on Hart Hall Hob and saw him flailing away
at the corn one night without a stitch on, and made
him a shirt to wear, and left it in the barn, we knew
he'd have to leave there too, and he did. One curious
thing: the family at Hart Hall couldn't decide whether
the hob had been offended because he'd been given
the shirt at all, or because it had been cut from coarse
cloth instead of fine linen! We know, because they
fretted about it for months, and sacked the girl.

"At all events we'd make the point now and then
that you mustn't offend the hob or interfere with him
or get too close and crowd him, and so we made out
pretty well. Still hoping for rescue, you know, but
content enough on the whole. We were living all
through the dales, north and south, the eleven of us
who were left alive—at Runswick, Great Fryup,
Commondale, Kempswithen, Hasty Bank, Scugdale,
Farndale, Hawnby, Broxa...Woof Howe...and we'd
visit a few in-between places that were said to be
haunted by t'hob, like the Mulgrave Cave and Obtrush
Rook above Farndale. It was all right.

"But after a longish time things began to change.

"This would be perhaps a hundred and fifty
years ago, give or take a couple of decades. Well, I
don't know just how it was, but bit by bit the people
hereabouts began to be less believing somehow, less
sure their grandfathers had really seen the fairies
dance on Fairy Cross Plain, or that Obtrush Rook was
really and truly haunted by the hobman. And by and
by we began to feel that playing hob i' t'hill had ceased

to be altogether safe. Even in these dales there were people now that wanted explanations for things, and that weren't above poking their noses into our affairs.

"And so, little by little we began to withdraw from the farms. For even though we were no longer afraid of being taken for Satan's imps and hunted down, concealment had been our way of getting by for such a very long time that we preferred to go on the same way. But for the first time in many a long year we often found ourselves thinking of the ship again and wishing for its return. Yet I fear the ship was lost, and I'll tell you why I think so.

"The Gafr discovered a way of looking back in time, a time window they can set up in a place, through which they can see everything that ever happened in that place, all the way back to the beginning. And whoever they see through the window can see them too, my dear. That's the point. It's costly, but not so costly to look into the recent past that they wouldn't have used the window had they ever come back. So ever since we were left here, we'd taken it in turns each day, except in winter, to pass the spot where we'd been 'put ashore,' so that one of us would be sure to see the open window and receive the message."

"'Unavoidably delayed—hang on till three hundred seventieth year of exile'?"

"No, not a telegram—a familiar face, speaking to us from the future. A face in a window.

"But the message never came, and gradually we drew back out of the dales to the high moortops, moved into the winter dens we'd been using right along, and set ourselves to learning how to live up here entirely—to catch grouse and hares, and find eggs and berries, instead of helping ourselves to the farmers' stores. Oh, we were good hunters and we loved these moors already, but still it was a hard and painful time, almost a second exile. I remember how I once milked a ewe—thinking to get some cream—only to find that it was the jug set out for me by the farmer's wife that I wanted and missed, for that was a symbol of my service to a master that respected what I did for him; but a worse time was coming.

"There were mines on the moors since there were people in the land at all, but not so very long after we had pulled back up out of the dales altogether, iron-stone began to be mined in Rosedale on a larger scale than ever before, and they built a railroad to carry the ore right 'round the heads of Rosedale and Farndale and down to Battersby Junction. I daresay you know the right of way now as a footpath, my dear, for part of it lies along the route of the Lyke Wake Walk. But in the middle of the last century men came pouring onto the high moors to build the railroad. Some even lived up here, in shacks, while the work was ongoing. And more men poured across the moors from the villages all 'round about, to work in the Rosedale pits, and then there was no peace at all for us, and no safety.

"That was when we first were forced to go about by day in sheepskin.

"It was Kempswithen's idea, he was a clever one!

The skins weren't too difficult to get hold of, for sheep die of many natural causes, and also they are easily killed, though we never culled more than a single sheep from anyone's flock, and then always an old ewe or a lame one, of little value. It went against the grain to rob the farmers at all, but without some means of getting about by daylight we could not have managed. The ruse worked well, for nearly all the railroad workers and miners came here from outside the dales and were unobservant about the ways of sheep, and we were careful.

"But the noise and smoke and peacelessness drove us away from our old haunts and onto the bleakest part of the high moors where the fewest tracks crossed. We went out there and dug ourselves in.

"It was a dreary time. And the mines had scarcely been worked out and the railroad dismantled when the Second War began, and there were soldiers training on Rudland Rigg above Farndale, driving their tanks over Obtrusch Rook till they had knocked it to bits, and over Fylingdales Moor, where we'd gone to escape the miners and the trains."

"Fylingdales, where the Early Warning System is now?"

"Aye, that's the place. During the war a few planes made it up this far, and some of the villages were hit. We slept through a good deal of that, luckily— we'd found this den by then, you see, an old jet working that a fox had opened. But it was uneasy sleep, it did us little good. Most particularly, it was not good for us to be of no use to any master—that began to do us active harm, and we were getting old. Two of us died before the war ended, another not long after. And still the ship did not return."

Something had been nagging at Jenny. "Couldn't you have reproduced yourselves after you came up here? You know—formed a viable community of hobs in hiding. Kept your spirits up."

"No, my dear. Not in this world. It wasn't possible, we knew it from the first, you see."

"Why wasn't it possible?" But Elphi firmly shook his head; this was plainly a subject he did not wish to pursue. Perhaps it was too painful. "Well, so now there are only eight of you?"

"Seven," said Elphi. "When I woke yesterday Woof Howe was dead. I'd been wondering what in the world to do with him when I so stupidly allowed you to see me."

Jenny threw the shadowed bunks a startled glance, wondering which contained a corpse. But something else disturbed her more. "You surely can't mean to say that in the past hundred and fifty years not one of you has ever been caught off guard until yesterday!"

Elphi gave the impression of smiling, though he did not really smile. "Oh, no, my dear. One or another of us has been caught napping a dozen times or more, especially in the days since the Rosedale mines were opened. Quite a few folks have sat just where you're sitting and listened, as you've been listening, to much the same tale I've been telling *you*. Dear me, yes! Once we rescued eight people from a train stalled in a late spring snowstorm, and we've revived more

than one walker in the last stages of hypothermia—
that's besides the ones who took us by surprise."

His ancient face peered up at her through scrag-
gly white hair, and Jenny's apprehension grew. "And
none of them ever told? It's hard to believe."

"My dear, none of them has ever remembered a
thing about it afterward! Would we take such trouble
to keep ourselves hidden, only to tell the whole story
to any stranger that happens by? No indeed. It passes
the time and entertains our guests, but they always
forget. As will you, I promise—but you'll be safe as
houses. Your only problem will be accounting for the
lost day."

Jenny had eaten every scrap of her emergency
food and peed the plastic pail nearly full, and now she
huddled under her sheepskin robe by the light of a
single fresh candle, waiting for Elphi to come back.
He had refused to let her climb up to empty her own
slops and fetch back her own laundry. "I'm sorry, my
dear, but there's no roke today—that's the difficulty.
If ever you saw this place again you would remember
it—and besides, you know, it's no hardship for me to
do you a service." So she waited, a prisoner beneath
the heavy doorway stone, desperately trying to think
of a way to prevent Elphi from stealing back her
memories of him.

Promising not to tell anybody, ever, had had no
effect. ("They all promise, you know, but how can we
afford the risk? Put yourself in my place.") She cudg-
eled her wits: what could she offer him in exchange

for being allowed to remember all this? Nothing came. The things the hobs needed—a different social order on Earth, the return of the Gafr ship, the Yorkshire of three centuries ago—were all beyond her power to grant.

Jenny found she believed Elphi's tale entirely: that he had come to Earth from another world, that he would not harm her in any way, that he could wipe the experience of himself from her mind—as effortlessly as she might wipe a chalkboard with a wet rag—by "the power of suggestion," just as Hob Hole Hob had "cured" the whooping cough by the power of suggestion. Somewhere in the course of the telling both skepticism and terror had been neutralized by a conviction that the little creature was speaking the unvarnished truth. She had welcomed this conviction. It was preferable to the fear that she had gone stark raving mad; but above and beyond all that, she did believe him.

And all at once she had an idea that just might work. At least it seemed worth trying; she darted across the stone floor and scrabbled frantically in a pocket of her pack. There was just enough time. With only seconds to spare, she burrowed back beneath the sheepskin robe where Elphi had left her.

The old hob backed down the ladder with her pail flopping from one hand and her bundle of clothes clutched in the opposite arm, and this time he left the top of the shaft open to the light and cold and the wuthering of the wind. He had tied his sheepskin on again. "Time to suit up now, I think—we want to set you back in the path at the same place and time of day." He scanned the row of sleepers anxiously and seemed to sigh.

Jenny's pile pants and wool socks were nearly dry, her sweaters, long johns, and boots only dampish. She threw off the sheepskins and began to pull on the many layers of clothing one by one. "I was wondering," she said as she dressed, "I wanted to ask you, how could the hobs just *leave* a farm where they'd been in secret service for maybe a hundred years?"

Elphi's peculiar flat eyes peered at her mildly. "Our bond was to the serving, you see. There were always other farms where extra hands were needed. What grieved us was to leave the dales entirely."

No bond to the people they served, then; no friendship, just as he had said. But all the same…"Why couldn't you come out of hiding now? People all over the world would give anything to know you exist!"

Elphi seemed both amused and sad. "No, my dear. Put it out of your mind. First, because we must wait here so long as any of us is left alive, in case the ship should come. Second, because we love these moors and would not leave them. Third, because here on Earth we have always served in secret, and have got too old to care to change our ways. Fourth, because if people knew about us we would never again be given a moment's peace. Surely you know that's so."

He was right about the last part anyway; people would never leave them alone, even if the other objections could be answered. Jenny herself didn't want to leave Elphi alone. It was no use.

As she went to mount the ladder the old hob moved to grasp her arm. "I'm afraid I must ask you to wear this," he said apologetically. "You'll be able to see, but not well. Well enough to walk. Not well enough to recognize this place again." And reaching up he slipped a thing like a deathcap over her head and fastened it loosely but firmly around her neck. "The last person to wear this was a shopkeeper from Bristol. Like you, he saw more than he should have seen and was our guest for a little while one summer afternoon."

"When was that? Recently?"

"Between the wars, my dear."

Jenny stood, docile, and let him do as he liked with her. As he stepped away, "Which was the hob that died?" she asked through the loose weave of the cap.

There was a silence. "Woof Howe Hob."

"What *will* you do with him?"

Another silence, longer this time. "I don't quite know ... I'd hoped some of the rest would wake up, but the smell ... it's beginning to trouble me too much to wait. I don't imagine you can detect it."

"Can't you just wake them up?"

"No, they must wake in their own time, more's the pity."

Jenny drew a deep breath. "Why not let *me* help you, then, since there's no one else?"

An even longer silence ensued, and she began to hope. But "You can help me *think* if you like, as we walk along," Elphi finally said, "I don't deny I should be grateful for a useful idea or two, but I must have you on the path by late this afternoon, come what may." And he prodded his captive up the ladder.

Aboveground, conversation was instantly impossible. After the den's deep silence the incessant wind seemed deafening. This time Jenny was humping the pack herself, and with the restricted sight and breathing imposed by the cap she found just walking quite difficult enough; she was too sore (and soon too winded) to argue anymore.

After a good long while Elphi said this was far enough, that the cap could come off now and they could have a few minutes' rest. There was nothing to sit on, only heather and a patch of bilberry, so Jenny took off her pack and sat on that, wishing she hadn't eaten every last bit of her supplies. It was a beautiful day, the low sun brilliant on the shaggy, snowy landscape, the sky deep and blue, the tiers of hills crisp against one another.

Elphi ran on a little way, scouting ahead. From a short distance, with just his back and head showing above the vegetation, it was astonishing how much he really did move and look like a sheep. She said as much when he came back. "Oh, aye, it's a good and proven disguise, it's saved us many a time. Mind you, the farmers are hard to fool. They know their own stock, and they know where theirs and everyone else's ought to be—the flocks are heafed on the commons and don't stray much. 'Heafed,' that means they stick to their own bit of grazing. So we've got to wear a fleece with a blue mark on the left flank if we're going

one way and a fleece with red on the shoulder if we're
going another, or we'll call attention to ourselves and
that's the last thing we want."

"Living *or* dead," said Jenny meaningfully.

"Aye." He gave her a sharp glance. "You've thought
of something?"

"Well, all these abandoned mines and quarries,
what about putting Woof Howe at the bottom of one
of those, under a heap of rubble?"

Elphi said, "There's fair interest in the old iron
workings. We decided against mines when we lost
Kempswithen."

"What did you do with *him*? You never said."

"Nothing we should care to do again." Elphi
appeared to shudder.

"Haven't I heard," said Jenny slowly, "that fire is a
great danger up here in early spring? There was a
notice at the station, saying that when the peat gets
really alight it'll burn for weeks."

"We couldn't do that!" He seemed truly shocked.
"Nay, such fires are dreadful things! Nothing at all
will grow on the burned ground for fifty years and
more."

"But they burn off the old heather, you told me
so yourself."

"Controlled burning that is, closely watched."

"Oh." They sat silent for a bit, while Jenny thought
and Elphi waited. "Well, what about this: I know a lot
of bones of prehistoric animals, cave bears and Irish
elk and so on—*big* animals—were found in a cave at
the edge of the park somewhere, but there haven't

been any finds like that on the moors because the acid in the peat completely decomposes everything. I was reading an article about it. Couldn't you bury your friend in a peat bog?"

Elphi pondered this with evident interest. "Hmm. It might be possible at that—nowadays it might. Nobody cuts the deep peat for fuel anymore, and bog's poor grazing land. Walkers don't want to muck about in a bog. About the only chaps who like a bog are the ones that come up to look at wildflowers, and it's too early for them to be about."

"Are there any bogs inside the fenced-off part of Fylingdales, the part that's closed to the public?"

Elphi groaned softly, swinging his head. "Ach, Woof Howe did hate it so, skulking in that dreary place. But still, the flowers would have pleased him."

"Weren't there some rare plants found recently inside the fence, because the sheep haven't been able to graze them down in there?"

"Now, that's true," Elphi mused. "They wouldn't disturb the place where the bog rosemary grows. I've heard them going on about the bog rosemary and the marsh andromeda, over around May Moss." He glanced at the sun. "Well, I'm obliged to you, my dear. And now we'd best be off. Time's getting on. And I want you to get out your map, and put on your rain shawl now."

"My what?"

"The green hooded thing you were wearing over your other clothes when I found you."

"Oh, the poncho." She dug this out, heaved and

hoisted the pack back on and belted it, then managed to haul the poncho on and down over pack and all, despite the whipping of the wind, and to snap the sides together. All this took time, and Elphi was fidgeting before she finished. She faced him, back to the wind. "Since I helped solve your problem, how about helping me with mine?"

"And what's that?"

"I want to remember all this, and come back and see you again."

This sent Elphi off into a great fit of moaning and headswinging. Abruptly he stopped and stood, rigidly upright. "Would you force me to lie to you? What you ask cannot be given. I've told you why."

"I *swear* I wouldn't tell anybody!" But when this set off another groaning fit, Jenny gave up. "All right. Forget it. Where is it you're taking me?"

Elphi sank to all fours, trembling a little, but when he spoke his voice sounded ordinary. "To the track across Great Hograh, where we met. Just over there, do you see? The line of cairns?" And sure enough, there on the horizon was a row of tiny cones. "You walk before me now, straight as you can, till you strike the path."

Jenny, map in hand and frustration in heart, obediently started to climb toward the ridge, lifting her boots high and clear of the snow-dusted heather. The wind was now at her back. Where a sheep track went the right way she followed it until it wandered off course, then cast about for another; and in this way she climbed at last onto the narrow path. She stopped to catch her breath and admire the view, then headed east, toward the youth hostel at Westerdale Hall, with the sun behind her.

For a couple of miles after that Jenny thought of nothing at all except the strange beauty of the scenery, her general soreness and tiredness, and the hot, bad dinner she would get in Westerdale. Then, with a slight start, she wondered when the fog had cleared and why she hadn't noticed. She pulled off the flapping poncho—dry already!—rolled it up, reached behind to stuff it under the pack flap, then retrieved her map in its clear plastic cover from between her knees and consulted it. If that slope directly across the dale was Kempswithen, then she must be about *here,* and so would strike the road into Westerdale quite soon. She would be at the hostel in, oh, maybe an hour, and have a hot bath—hot wash, anyway, the hostel probably wouldn't have such a thing as a bathtub, they hardly ever did—and the biggest dinner she could buy.